A CRIMINAL GAME

A SUSPENSE NOVEL

D.L. WOOD

SILVERGLASS PRESS

A CRIMINAL GAME
A Suspense Novel
Book One in The Criminal Collection

A Criminal Game is a work of fiction. Names, characters, places and incidents either are the product of the author's imagination or are used fictitiously. Any resemblance to actual persons, living or dead, events or locales is entirely coincidental and beyond the intent of either the author or publisher.

ISBN-13: 978-1-69607-529-9 (Print)
First edition
Silverglass Press
Huntsville, Alabama

D.L. Wood
www.dlwoodonline.com
Huntsville, Alabama

ACKNOWLEDGMENTS

Thank you to those who helped bring *A Criminal Game* about:

My early readers, for wading through what was essentially a draft;

Sarah Nuss, for her keen insights and her willingness to be honest and tell me when something could be better;

Kirsten Harbers, for putting everything aside to read through the final draft so I could meet my deadline;

Bobby Plummer, for his detailed explanations of why firearms may or may not make a sound before firing them;

Danielle Rogers, for making me laugh when I needed a reality check;

Jason Pierce, for his advice on the criminal justice process;

Jeff and Melanie Robertson, for helping out with last minute NYC video clips;

Friend and fellow author, Luana Ehrlich, for always being a source of encouragement;

My parents, Bob and Lynn Plummer, for their constant support; and,

My husband, Ron, for putting up with late nights of typing, fits over plot problems and hijacked vacation days.

I couldn't do this without all of you.

For Mike and Pam.
Two of the bravest people I've ever known.
Well done.

PROLOGUE

I can't believe this is how it ends.

Evie's heart slammed into her rib cage as her knees, weak and shaking, threatened to give way. A warm, sticky breeze kicked up the tendrils of sable hair that had long since shaken loose from her low bun. They danced around her face, oblivious to the danger on the rooftop in Queens, as the burnished rays of the early morning sun cut through the sky.

This can't be how it ends. A wave of lightheaded panic rolled through her, making her dizzy. She forced herself to keep standing. To be steady. Because she needed to be ready. She needed to run—had to run. But there was nowhere to go. So, she stayed there, her insides like ice despite the stifling, humid air, holding her frozen where she stood. Just feet away from *him.*

He raised the sleek, black gun. She should have known better. She should have realized...but, that was the point, wasn't it? She wasn't *meant* to have realized. And now she was going to suffer for it. Except, she wasn't the only one who would suffer. The physical pain of that reality stabbed her in the chest as she stared down the barrel, moments away from losing everything.

1

12 HOURS EARLIER

The number 7 westbound train rattled through Queens toward Manhattan. Evie Diaz stared out the window, the same, unchanging scenes that she witnessed daily whizzing past. The same people, the same cars, the same gaudy billboards...it was comfortingly routine. Chilled air from the ventilation system blew across her face and she sighed at its touch. August in New York City could be scorching, and after baking all day in the heat, the air inside the subway car was suffocating whenever the air conditioning failed. But today it vigorously pumped icy air into the compartment, keeping her sweat-free on the forty-minute ride from her two-bedroom apartment in Flushing to Grand Central. It was a good thing, too, because she would have plenty of opportunity to work up a sweat during the six-block walk south from Forty-Second Street to the Wexsor Hotel, where she worked as the night manager.

Unfortunately, the cool air did nothing to combat the stale

smell that time and use had seared into the space, or the zesty scent of the curry-laced takeout held in the lap of the man sitting across from her. At 7:05 p.m., the westbound car was half full, likely with many other night-shifters heading in to start their workday. Several wore uniforms—delivery, hospital, and such. Only one wore a suit. At the far end of the car, an older woman Evie presumed to be a grandmother spoke to a young girl in rapid Spanish. The girl, who looked to be about six, shook her pigtails vehemently in protest against whatever the woman was saying, a sour pout emerging on her lips.

Evie smiled, reminded of her own spirited daughter, who had done more than her fair share of pouting in her five short years. Evie turned her gaze from the little girl, replacing her with visions of her Gabriella, laughing and running away from her last week as Evie demanded she leave the penguin exhibit and follow her to the exit of the Central Park Zoo.

She'll be watching Disney Channel now, waiting for Eleanor to finish preparing her supper of...what? Probably hot dogs and mac and cheese, she thought, one of the three meals Gabby would agree to eat these days. Eleanor was a godsend, quite literally, Evie believed. The widow was a retired postal worker who lived across the hall and had befriended Evie and Mark when they moved into their apartment nearly six years ago. A year later, when their daughter Gabby arrived, Eleanor became something like a grandmother to her. When Evie had bemoaned the cost of daycare, Eleanor suggested Evie take her on as Gabby's nanny. It had worked seamlessly—this warm, wonderful woman simply crossing the hall to keep Gabby whenever Evie's shift overlapped with Mark's workday, which, to their disappointment, was most weekdays.

As a stockbroker in the downtown office of Cripps Securities in the heart of the financial district, Mark would have to leave home around six thirty in the morning to catch his train. If they were lucky, Evie would get home from her night shift about an hour before that, giving them a tiny window of time together. But if she was delayed at all, or if the trains were slow, they would miss each other coming and going. The same thing was prone to happen even more so in the evenings. She had to leave home by 6:45 p.m. to make it into Manhattan for her shift, but as a junior trader, Mark often stayed late at work and wouldn't make it home before then. Yes, they had the weekends to make up for it, but sometimes there would be several weekdays in a row when they wouldn't see each other, and those stretches were awful.

Looking toward the East River, she saw an eastbound 7 train in the distance, racing toward her westbound 7. On nights when she didn't get to see Mark before she left their apartment, she would stare out the windows of her train as it raced along, hoping for an eastbound 7 just like this one to pass her. Whenever one did, she would wonder if Mark was coming home on the other train, and whether he was reading one of his spy novels, or the *Wall Street Journal*, or catching a few minutes of sleep before taking over for Eleanor.

As she had so many times before, she shifted in her seat and waited for the trains to meet. As the opposite train rumbled by, a chill fluttered through her, and she put her hand against the window, reaching toward it. As if Mark could sense her presence there. As if there were a possibility he was in one of those cars, riding home again, instead of six feet underground in Capshaw Cemetery.

It would be three years next month since he died. Three years of leaving her daughter in Eleanor's care each night that she worked. Three years of Eleanor sleeping over till Evie arrived home at around six in the morning to slip in before Gabby woke. She felt the tears coming again. They always did when she dwelled too long on Eleanor's role in their lives and the reality rushing headlong toward them, that soon it wouldn't work that way, couldn't work that way, anymore. Soon Gabby would lose yet another person who loved her.

No. Can't go there.

The train reached the Hunters Point Avenue station where the line burrowed beneath the ground, shutting out the sun as it prepared to travel under the East River on its journey to Manhattan. After taking a deep, cleansing breath, Evie exhaled, forcing her thoughts to something else as the train rattled on toward Grand Central Station.

~

AS EVIE EMERGED from the station at Grand Central on Forty-Second Street, the haze of dusk had begun to settle over the streets of Midtown Manhattan. On this stretch, the streetlights had already flicked on, bathing the busyness in an artificial glow. Rush hour never ended in this city, and, the same as every other night, the incessant honking and bumper-to-bumper traffic of cars driving uptown, downtown, to the FDR, or one of the bridges was going strong. Every time she stepped out into the cacophony from the depths of the subway below, she marveled at how often people spoke of being "assaulted" by the noise, as if it were violent or unwelcome. To her it felt more like an embrace. Like a friend welcoming her home. It had taken seven years for this Texas girl to feel that way, but now, she could not imagine living anywhere else.

She crossed at the light and continued west for a few blocks toward Fifth Avenue. There she turned south at the corner of Forty-Second and Fifth, so that her path took her directly in front of the massive structure that was the iconic branch of the New York Public Library. She nodded a greeting at the twin lions cut from Tennessee marble that flanked the steps leading to the library's entrance. "Patience. Fortitude," she whispered, calling them by name.

Her heart winced a bit as she passed them, longing for a brief visit, but she kept her pace steady. This place had been one of their favorites. They would make a picnic of it in Bryant Park, situated directly behind the library, grabbing sandwiches or sushi or whatever, and spread out a blanket on the small patch of green in the belly of this concrete jungle. Then they would pop inside and explore the current temporary exhibits, or the permanent ones that were their favorites.

Now, sometimes when she caught the train early, she would make a detour up those steps, into the room where the institution's copy of the Gutenberg Bible was displayed, one of less than fifty left in the world. She would stand before the glass case that housed it, staring at the red and black inks that filled whatever page the book was opened to, wondering what it would be like to be able to read Latin and personally understand the precise message conveyed there.

Evie's breathing slowed as the image of the book's pages swam in her mind. Mark had brought her to the library that first week in the city after their graduation from Baylor University. They were full of promise then—graduates for six weeks, a married couple for four, moving back to the city of his youth and preparing to take on the world.

"Imagine," Mark had said as they stood in front of that case, his dark eyes riveted to the pages. "Imagine the hand that set the blocks that produced that page. Do you think he knew? Do you think he knew how this would change the world?"

He was like that. *Had been like that,* she thought, catching herself. Mark had considered everything. He had always looked for the deeper meaning. Asked the deeper questions. It was one of the reasons she had fallen for him. He had seen something deeper in this ancient book, in this piece of the past and of his faith. It had been important to him and so it had become important to her. After everything, it brought her comfort to think that the messages represented by that text had been offering hope and answers to humankind for over twenty centuries, long before a car accident had taken a boy named Mark from a girl named Evie, and that it would continue to do so long after.

Ignoring the stinging in her heart, she sped up, crossing Fortieth Street at the next light. She kept up this pace for several blocks until finally turning right at Thirty-Fifth Street, headed toward the center of the block where the rippling red-and-navy flag of the Wexsor Hotel flapped in the breeze.

The entrance of the hotel sported two revolving front doors, adorned with gleaming brass and spotless glass panels etched with the "WH" emblem. The building itself was a grand edifice that recalled the New York of another era. Originally constructed for a stately bank in the first part of the twentieth century, a veined, creamy marble covered the exterior of the first floor. To the right of the doors, a rectangular bronze marker read, "Third Bank of Manhattan, 1908." Though the bank had gone under in November of 1929, the marker remained like a tombstone.

To the left of the doors, Wilson Vickers stood at his post, vibrant and enthusiastic as always. With a huge smile splitting his deeply lined, sepia-toned face, he greeted an arriving hotel guest emerging from a limousine parked at the curb. Wilson was a six-foot-seven tower of muscle and kindness who had played as an offensive lineman for C.W. Post College on Long Island in the eighties before a knee injury destroyed a promising bid for the NFL. He was the first to befriend Evie when she started at the Wexsor five years ago and the first from work to come see her after Mark's death. As the crowd on the sidewalk in front of Evie parted, Wilson caught sight of her and winked warmly. Evie grinned back, just before her gaze fell on the hotel's complimentary on-call Lexus SUV also parked against the curb, and its ginger-haired driver.

With his brownish-red locks, fair skin, and lanky range, you would expect, if movie stereotypes held true, that the driver boasted a name like Patrick O'Callahan or something equally Irish. But instead he had been christened "Bruno Agnellini" by his parents, a name that conjured up images of a sturdy, Popeye-armed bouncer, not the lithe man in his late twenties who was now opening the Lexus's rear door for one of the Wexsor's bejeweled senior guests.

Bruno turned and caught Evie watching him. She smiled, but as usual, he offered only a cursory nod. It had been this way since he began driving for the Wexsor four months earlier. Evie had tried at first to be friendly, chat when they would pass, smile wide and whatnot, but he had only ever tipped his head or replied with the briefest of answers when not responding at all would have been inexcusably rude.

She nodded back at him, fighting a desire to roll her eyes, then grasped the handle to the modest employee's entrance to the left of the main doors and slipped inside.

2

Catcher slid into the recessed alcove behind the scaffolding lining West Fiftieth Street and waited, his nerves firing, as he scanned the block for signs of anyone still following him. A putrid scent drifted up from the black plastic bags of trash piled onto the curb, presumably from the gyro shop at his back. The stench stung his nostrils, and he began breathing through his mouth.

He had spotted them just after leaving his apartment in Hell's Kitchen—two men striding down opposite sides of the street, both wearing caps and sunglasses, one in a black T-shirt, the other in a light, army-green windbreaker. They weren't very discreet, and a few backward glances convinced Catcher that they were, in fact, following him. He was pretty sure he recognized them, too, even from a distance. Seeing them now in his mind's eye, he tensed. A windbreaker in August did not bode well. It certainly wasn't for keeping the chill off.

He rubbed the back of his neck, realizing that he wouldn't be able to go back to his place now.

How did they find me?

He was certain the roommates that shared his one-bedroom space would not have talked. During their first night there, he had told them in excruciating detail what had happened to the last guy who made the mistake of talking about Catcher's business. As neither wanted to lose the apartment or a week to a beating-induced coma, they had quickly sworn to keep quiet.

So, what had gone wrong?

The slow traffic rumbling by in the evening exodus from Manhattan provided a steady soundtrack to his surveillance. So far, there was no sign of them here. His breathing slowed, confidence growing that maybe he had successfully lost them a few blocks back by ducking down into, then quickly back out of, an underground subway stop that was crazy busy at this hour. Even so, he remained still, wanting to be sure before he moved.

The reality that they had found him still made his mind spin. As a matter of survival, he always made sure none of his business associates knew where he lived. That measure, combined with his skill at staying off the radar when he needed to, had kept him out of Saul's grasp for the last three weeks. Before that, he had managed to hold him off by spending two weeks claiming things were still too hot for them to connect. When Saul finally refused that excuse, Catcher had stalled by not showing up at the meets Saul kept arranging, blaming his failure to appear on various emergencies, risks, and sheer confusion about times and locations, until Saul had laid down an ultimatum. Catcher had gone radio silent then. He knew that was the equivalent of painting a bullseye on his own head, but he also knew that all would be forgiven once he turned up with Saul's share, plus interest. Everything would be kosher then.

"Yo, move it. You can't just stand there blocking the door," barked a gruff voice from behind him, and Catcher turned to see a heavyset man with greasy brown hair and a dirty white apron tied around his thick waist standing in the doorway to the gyro shop.

"Yeah, whatever," Catcher grunted. Taking one last look down the sidewalk, he stepped out from the scaffolding and began walking as fast as he could without running, his eyes darting back and forth sharply as he strode away.

3

"You're late," Gerald Tomassian fussed as Evie stepped into his office, one of many rooms in the back offices of the Wexsor, well hidden from the eyes of hotel guests, squirreled away in windowless spaces behind closed doors. The day manager's thinning, slicked back hair and cartoon-slim mustache perfectly underscored his fastidious personality. He needled Evie with his gaze, before turning back to the computer screen on his desk. "Nice of you to finally get here," he said.

She glanced at her watch. *7:55 p.m.* "I'm not late, Gerald. I'm five minutes early. As usual," she countered.

"*Mr. Tomassian*," he emphasized, "if you please, Ms. Diaz." The words issued crisply from between his not-quite-straight teeth, sounding not-quite British. Gerald maintained he had acquired the slightly irregular accent while growing up as an army brat on a base somewhere in the UK. That was as specific as he ever got. But Evie believed it was more likely something he had picked up from repeated listening to British baking shows than something he had developed naturally as a child. She, Wilson, and several other co-workers had a bet going over where Gerald truly hailed from. She had put her money on Long Island, and if she could ever prove it, she would be pocketing nearly three hundred dollars.

"They're expecting you upstairs," Gerald snipped, tapping away on the computer and not looking at her. "Food service arrived fifteen minutes ago."

"Then they should just be ready for me now," she answered smoothly, refusing to ruffle at his brusqueness. "I'm good, so you can take off as soon as you're done. I shouldn't be upstairs for long."

Gerald pursed his lips disapprovingly, his eyes flicking up from his computer. "Don't dawdle," he told her. "The Hanson-Dolittle wedding reception has been going on since six and lasts—"

"Yes, till midnight, I know," she said as she started to back out of his office.

"Well, there have already been a number of additional requests tonight from that group, and I don't want to get stuck here dealing with them."

"I'll be back before you know it," she promised and turned down the hall, headed for the door connecting the back offices to the lobby. As she pushed through it, she felt a smile hitch itself onto her face, and she didn't need to see Gerald to know that a superior scowl had probably fastened itself onto his.

The door opened to the employees' area behind the black marble-topped front desk that stretched across one entire wall of the Wexsor's lobby. As Evie moved past the desk into the reception area, she was struck, as always, by the lavishness that draped the room from floor to ceiling. Though not particularly large, what it lacked in dimension it more than made up for in opulence, from the four-tiered crystal chandelier suspended over the room to the Persian rugs that anchored the supple, cream leather Viraneli sofas. Intoxicating floral arrangements that were brought in fresh daily—this evening in hues of bright cornflower blue and tropical pink—were displayed on ornate, gold-painted tables tucked beneath mirrors and oil masterpieces hung on the walls, on loan from the Wexsor Art Collection housed in the flagship hotel in London. She passed it all as she headed to the elevator vestibule, the Jimmy Choo heels she had changed into after her commute clacking efficiently on the beige travertine tile.

They were her extravagance, these shoes. They were the only pair like it that she owned. She only wore them at work, changing into them and out of her running shoes at the start of each shift. Though far too expensive for a personal splurge, they were a necessity here. Because she, like the flowers and the paintings that adorned the room, was part of the decor of the Wexsor, and she, like the rest of the decor, needed to make a certain impression.

A dozen or so people occupied the lobby—chatting at the front desk, checking their phones while seated in the velvety side chairs, or nursing a drink at the polished wood tables of the bar overlooking the grand space. The elevator vestibule was deserted. Evie pressed the call button, calculating how much time it would take for the closest one, currently on the eighteenth floor, to reach her. It was a game she often played and she had gotten very good at it. She began her countdown from twenty-eight seconds. The bell pinged at two.

The doors slid open, revealing a couple in their mid-forties, or at least, a couple trying to pass themselves off as being in their mid-forties. He wore a cashmere sweater and gold watch; she had layered several strands of pearls over a wrap-around dress finished with copper platform sandals. Both had foreheads that were far too smooth for anyone beyond eight years of age.

"Mr. and Mrs. Clifton. How are we this evening?" Evie greeted, stepping aside to allow them to pass.

"Fine, thank you," Mr. Clifton replied, running a hand

through his jet black hair. Mrs. Clifton sniffed and kept walking.

Evie had always thought it was odd that not a single guest had ever asked her how she knew them by sight. She wondered how they would feel about the electronic catalog of photos the hotel kept on guests, usually consisting of stills pulled from a hidden front desk camera. This allowed staff to memorize the names and faces of important patrons, elevating the personalized service the Wexsor offered. The guests' routine acceptance of this familiarity without question baffled her, but then again, she knew people liked to feel important, and nothing accomplished that like knowing who someone was even though they didn't know you. It fed the ego. And people rarely questioned anything as long as you fed their ego.

Evie stepped onto the elevator and pressed "25." The Wexsor's twenty-fifth floor was two shy of the top and comprised solely of sizable luxury suites. The twenty-sixth floor was reserved for permanent residents, of which the hotel had eight. The twenty-seventh floor had four penthouse suites, apartment-sized units often occupied by dignitaries and celebrity guests. The US Ambassador to Australia had stayed in one the week before while visiting for a trade forum in association with the United Nations. Although all four were presently empty, last year's Oscar winner for Best Actress had booked two of the suites for all of September when she would be shooting scenes in the city for her upcoming project.

An electric tingle rippled through Evie as the car rose, taking her upstairs like it had every single Tuesday night for the last two years.

Who would be there tonight?

Possibilities trailed through Evie's brain until the elevator arrived at the twenty-fifth floor. She walked out, turning down the hallway to the right, the tingle intensifying as she strode toward the last door, mentally counting off the other suites as she went.

2510. 2508.

It wasn't ever easy to leave Gabby, but Tuesdays at least gave her something to look forward to. It had become her favorite workday precisely because of this aspect of her job.

2506. She stopped between suites 2506 and 2504 for a quick check of her reflection in the gold-filigree mirror that hung above a decorative limestone-topped table. Her dark, silky brown hair was tightly coiled in a bun at the base of her neck, hairspray deftly keeping all potential flyaways in place. Her navy pantsuit was perfectly tailored and unwrinkled, though the nameplate pinned to her jacket *was* skewed a degree or two. She straightened it, then rubbed lightly beneath one eye, wiping away a few flakes of mascara that her eyelashes had discarded onto her olive skin.

Evie wrinkled her nose as she inspected the faint vertical line that had begun carving itself into the space between her eyebrows, likely the end product of too much worrying during recent years.

Would Violet and Noelle, her college roommates, notice it when they came to visit next month?

The girls were throwing her a weekend birthday bash in the Big Apple—Violet had threatened to make T-shirts—to celebrate Evie's last days in her twenties before she turned thirty in September. Evie couldn't help but let a small smile slip as she thought about her friends' upcoming stay. It had been too long since they had all been together nearly two years ago on that trip to Virginia Beach on the anniversary of Mark's death. She always felt lighter, less burdened, after spending time with them, as if their presence banished another bit of the lingering darkness. Her heart warmed thinking about the three of them hitting the town. It couldn't come soon enough.

Turning away from the mirror, she pressed on down the hall.

2502. She pulled out her keycard.

2500. It was the last suite, positioned at the far end of the hallway. Evie pressed her card to the reader on the door, and when the light flashed green, she turned the brass handle and pushed.

4

Suite 2500 was reserved each Tuesday night for the same guest. As Evie did on every one of those nights, she stepped inside the foyer to the sight of a large casino-grade poker table set up on the far left of the suite's enormous sitting room. To the right of the poker table, two plush sofas faced each other. The coffee-and-gold striped upholstery popped against the cream carpet and damask light-blocking curtains that were drawn in front of the expanse of windows that took up an entire wall. Set with its back to those shielded windows and centered between the couches was a fully stocked portable bar, currently being organized by the bartender.

The oval poker table had room for up to eight players around three sides, with the fourth side boasting a small cutout for the dealer. At present, an attendant was busy evenly spacing six leather chairs around it. The grass-green of the table's surface stood in stark contrast to the more neutral palette of the room.

Evie stifled a grimace as she took note of the man seated on one of the couches, currently tapping away on his phone. He was massive, strapping enough to be a professional bodybuilder, but dressed in a suit sharp enough to have come straight from Bergdorf Goodman. He was the private security man hired for the suite by the game's host, and in all the time Evie had been doing this, he had never spoken so much as a word to her. She knew him only as "Thompson" and, taking her cue from him, ignored him. He did the same, continuing to tap on his phone. The truth was he made her nervous—a living reminder that what went down in this room every Tuesday, though legal, was not risk free or without its shadier side. And that sometimes gave her pause, made her wonder if she should be involved in it at all. It wasn't like she had a choice. As night manager, it was her responsibility to liaise with the game host, to ensure that all was well and deal with any overarching issues. It didn't hurt that the tips he slipped her every Wednesday morning on his way out were really good. She and Gabby needed the extra cash.

She pivoted away from the couches, turning toward the dark-haired bartender and his glistening countertop. "Hey, Ben."

"Evening, Ms. Diaz," he replied, his hands deftly polishing a cut crystal glass.

"How's it looking?" she asked, walking closer and studying the array of bottles displayed on the bar. *Belvedere. Tanqueray. Glenlivet.* "Anything need replenishing?"

Ben shook his head. "Already taken care of."

"Good."

"Ms. Diaz?"

The female voice sounded from her left. Twisting in that direction, Evie saw Dana, the suite's butler, sweep toward her from the larger of two bedrooms that flanked either side of the sitting room. By her estimation the woman was barely shy of six feet tall, towering over Evie's five feet seven inches.

"Dana?"

"We had a problem with the food tonight," she said, her

neck flushing pink against the collar of her starched white button-down. "The tuna rolls were off."

"Where are they?" Evie asked, moving toward the linen-draped buffet table prepared on the side of the sitting room opposite the windows. She scanned the bright silver service pieces for the offending fare.

"No, I took care of it. They're bringing up shrimp skewers instead."

"Okay. Just no—"

"Crab. I know. He hates it."

Evie nodded and smiled. Dana was good at her job. She had been the butler for the game for the last year. Suite butlers, bartenders, and such were highly transient, and it was unusual for someone to stay in a position like that for as long as a year, but then, the tips were fantastic. They highly discouraged turnover.

"Hello?" A deep, friendly voice came from the foyer. Evie recognized it immediately.

Speak of the devil.

"Mr. Jamison," she said warmly, stepping over to him. "Everything is all set for tonight."

Evie guessed that James Jamison was in his late forties, though she had never actually asked. He wore a navy sports coat and light blue shirt with tan gabardine trousers. There was something piercing about his nearly black eyes, like he always knew exactly what was going on at any given moment. He kept his dark brown hair close shaven, detracting from the beginnings of its recession. He was trim, but not muscled, as if all his working out went into simply keeping the weight off.

"Perfect," Jamison said, swinging off his finely tailored jacket and handing it to Dana, who had conveniently appeared at his arm just in time to take it. "They should be arriving soon."

For two years, James Jamison had been running this elite,

high-stakes Texas Hold'em poker game at the Wexsor, starting at nine o'clock in the evening. Typically the games would close down between three and four in the morning, though on rare occasions they continued into the mid-morning of the next day.

The players that attended this game came ready to win or lose more money in one evening than Evie would probably see in a lifetime. No one outside the room knew the precise amounts that changed hands, and the only staff members permitted in the room during the game were the bartender, the butler, and Evie. They had all been sworn to secrecy. Evie had herself witnessed one hand worth over one million dollars, and once Dana had hinted that a Lake Tahoe deed had been tossed into the pot.

Evie had been the hotel contact for the game since its inception. Jamison had made it known that he appreciated the way she handled the needs of the room, and also seemed to have taken to her on a personal level. As a result, she oversaw all the arrangements from food to drink to setup to any one-off needs the players might have. Not only were the tips she received from Jamison and the players fantastic—this year she was saving them to take a Disney cruise with Gabby and Eleanor over Christmas—but the up-close contact with celebrities was hands down the most engaging part of her job. This special status that she enjoyed, along with its perks, was likely the reason Gerald Tomassian was perpetually cross with her on Tuesdays.

It wasn't that Gerald didn't get other opportunities to interact with celebrities. At a hotel like the Wexsor, all of the upper management employees had to handle requests from its more famous guests at some point. But usually this contact was limited to five minutes here or there, providing information or hand-delivering something and, quite often, involved communicating with the celebrity's assistant more than with the celebrity themselves.

But here, in this suite, Evie met and spoke with famous individuals at length, having real conversations as they played for hours. Evie usually stayed less than fifteen minutes at a time—she did have other responsibilities in the hotel—but over the course of the night she would make routine visits to make sure that all was well. And during those times when the hotel was dead, which it ordinarily was at three thirty in the morning, she might push her luck, staying until she was called away by some other pressing issue.

Jamison never seemed to mind her presence. In fact, his hefty tips suggested he encouraged it. In part, she thought it was because it allowed him to utilize her as a kind of alternate host to himself. Someone to keep the players happy. Yes, she was there for business reasons, but the players definitely seemed to enjoy her company.

She had been told that she was easy to talk to. And, according to some, not awful to look at either, which also probably helped. Over the years she had met a trifecta of Tony-, Oscar-, and Emmy Award-winning actors and actresses. A few Grammy winners. Authors, politicians, and even one member of royalty from a country that used to govern the very city they were in. Some of the players weren't famous. They were simply people with more money than they could ever spend, seeking creative ways to blow it.

Many played only one time and never came back. Some would hit the game whenever they were in town. Then there were the regulars, many of whom she was on a first-name basis with. One guitarist from a pop band that had hit the Top 40 three times that year had invited her and Gabby to his house in the Hamptons for his daughter's seventh birthday last month. The party was so Disney-fied, with a dozen live characters and a child-sized Cinderella castle constructed on the grounds, that Gabby thought they had gone to Disney World five months early.

In general the players liked her and, for the most part, she liked them. There were exceptions, though. Players that, like Jamison's security man, unnerved her, giving off a distinctly sketchy vibe. These players rarely spoke to her other than to ask for something, and she was not on a first-name basis with any of them. Nor did she want to be. Unlike the majority of the players, who Evie believed were completely above board, she suspected that these other few were probably so far below the board that they couldn't even touch it anymore.

As for Jamison, she wasn't sure which camp he fell into.

Whenever she did have questions, she was smart enough not to ask them. That might be interpreted as nosiness, which would almost certainly result in her expulsion as liaison. Instead she fed off whatever tidbits the others first provided, though, usually, that was in the realm of benign chit-chat rather than facts that offered her a truer picture of anyone there. Jamison was incredibly tight-lipped about himself, and in two years she hadn't learned anything that definitively put him in or out of the sketchy group. She had Googled him, of course, but came up with nothing helpful. That outcome, combined with the fact that she thought his name sounded like it had been pulled from a comic book, strongly suggested there was more to him than met the eye.

"The safe is coming right behind me," he announced, walking over to Ben to collect his usual Vodka Collins, which the bartender had just finished pouring into a tall glass.

Evie nodded, moving to the door to be ready to open it when the inevitable knock came. Each game night, about an hour before play was to start, a safe was delivered on a hand truck by men in nondescript gray uniforms. It arrived covered in a bottomless cardboard box, a clever disguise, deterring any criminal curiosity. For the duration of the game, the safe would remain in the smaller of the two bedrooms of the suite, which Jamison used as an office. It secured the fifty thousand-dollar buy-ins each player was required to bring with them, as well as any other collateral they may have brought to cover any losses or additional chip purchases during the game. Though most of the players didn't walk around with the actual cash—it was usually in the form of a cashier's check—the safe was a necessity if for no other reason than to provide at least the appearance of extra security.

There was a loud rapping on the door, and Evie opened it to two guards with the hand truck. They headed directly to the bedroom, where the safe would stay until it was retrieved sometime the next morning.

Evie walked over to Jamison at the bar. "We're anticipating a busy evening downstairs, so I'll be at the concierge desk most of the evening. But I'm only a call away should you need anything."

"No problem," he said. "But you'll want to get back up here if you can. You didn't hear it from me, but your special friend might be in attendance." He winked and she smiled, reading his signal perfectly, resulting in a tiny flicker of anticipation in her stomach. She was a huge fan of BBC detective shows, and one night, completely star-struck when the lead in one of her favorites had been at the table, she had felt compelled to mention this to Jamison. He had promised to let her know if the actor ever planned to return.

"I'll be sure to come up as soon as I can to check on things," she assured him and he chuckled knowingly before stepping off to the bedroom that held the safe. Evie departed the suite, her steps buoyant as the door latched behind her with a loud click.

Her favorite actor. Here again.

Almost giddy, her heels fell soundlessly on the thick carpet as she headed to the elevators, wondering how much time she could get away with spending in the suite tonight before anyone downstairs noticed she was gone.

5

Evie was standing in the twenty-fifth-floor elevator vestibule at the end of the hall, congratulating herself on counting down to precisely zero as the car arrived, when the door opened and her heart skipped a beat. Kieran Carr, one of the game regulars for the last couple of months, stepped out, smiling broadly when he saw her.

Kieran Carr was the first and only person that had sparked anything in Evie marginally akin to romantic interest in the years since Mark had passed. Not that she would have acted on it, or that Kieran felt the same, but the spark of something was there for her nonetheless. It was both disturbing and comforting. Disturbing because it suggested that someday, with someone, she might be able to move on. Comforting because it suggested that someday, with someone, she might be able to move on. Fortunately, with him being a player in the game, there was no chance of anything happening between them, and it took the pressure off her somewhat. Jamison had made it clear in the past that, though he didn't mind her becoming friendly with the players, he didn't want it to go any further than that. He didn't need to worry.

Kieran's bespoke blue-gray suit, fitted as it was, stylishly outlined what Evie guessed was around a six-foot frame. He had no tie—as a contemporary art dealer he had no need for something so stuffy. Instead, beneath the jacket he wore a charcoal, crew neck T-shirt that hit right at his collarbone. A pair of burnished loafers, Prada or Louboutin or an equally expensive brand by the looks of them, completed his ensemble, which was high fashion by any standard. Some might wear an outfit like that to project confidence, but, in Kieran's case, it wasn't necessary. He exuded confidence all on his own.

"Hey, Evie. How's it going tonight?" he asked.

"Going well, Mr. Carr," Evie replied, using his surname for propriety's sake. This drew a look of mock disapproval from him, his barely lined brow furrowing, crinkling his bright hazel eyes. They were a few shades richer than his ash-brown hair, neatly coiffed in an Ivy League crew cut.

"How many times am I going to have to tell you, Evie? It's Kieran."

"Once more, I guess," she answered. Jamison had a strict rule against her calling a player by their first name unless they specifically invited her to do so. Even then, he preferred that she start each subsequent encounter by reverting to formal names, just to preserve the polish of the experience.

Kieran crossed in front of her, moving toward the hallway on the right. She turned to watch him go. Suddenly he stopped, twisting back in her direction.

"Will I see you inside later?" he asked, one eyebrow slightly raised.

"Absolutely. I'll stop by to check on everyone."

He nodded and started walking down the hall toward suite 2500. "Wouldn't be the same if you didn't," he called out, this time without looking back.

She pivoted to the elevator and pressed the call button once more, grateful Kieran could not see the pleased grin that had lit up her face.

6

Saul Kozlowski groaned, low and deep, as he ran a stocky finger around the rim of his glass.

This was not good. Not good at all.

His guys had identified Catcher as soon as the kid left his apartment. They had tailed him successfully for two blocks before he made them. Then Catcher had sprinted down into one of the busiest stops in Midtown where he had somehow lost them, probably jumping on a train or squirreling unseen up the stairs with the surfacing masses.

Saul fidgeted in his rolling chair, positioned behind the chunky desk made of red oak that he had been using for decades. It had once been his father's, all the way back to when Saul was little and used to hide toy soldiers in the drawers for Pop to find. So, when Saul finally took over the business all those years ago, he moved the desk here, into his office in the loft above his auto garage in Greenpoint, Brooklyn. The space was rough, smelled like engine grease, and offered nothing to suggest the seven-figure income Saul pulled in annually from his other, less public enterprise.

"Saul, I swear. We had him. I'm sorry." The apology was just as shaky the third time around. It came from the skinny, shaggy-haired twenty-three-year-old sitting across the room from Saul on a worn leather sofa. He looked nervous as he spoke, the aged, cracked cushions nearly swallowing him up, making him look even more pitiful.

The chair creaked as Saul leaned back and exhaled like a man in need of a ventilator. "It happens, Matty."

"Not to me," grunted a second man, hunched on the sofa next to Matty. He was older, in his mid-thirties, with muscles that tested the boundaries of his army-green windbreaker. He sounded annoyed, not scared.

Saul nodded. "Yeah, Kimball. I know." He tapped a forefinger on the note where he had written Catcher's address. "You got nothin' from the roommates?"

Kimball shook his head. "Nothing we didn't already know. Got a feeling Catcher told them about what he did to that Mueller kid, so they weren't anxious to talk." He frowned. "What do you want us to do now?"

"I'll keep reaching out. See if we can get a lead. In the meantime, go back to the apartment. Take it apart. There's got to be something there."

Kimball ran a hand over his buzz cut, nodded, and walked out. Matty followed him silently.

Saul sat alone in the room, contemplating. He felt stupid, and he didn't like feeling stupid. He had trusted Catcher because they had a long history, a good one, and though the guy was constantly scheming—you could just see it behind his eyes—Catcher had never given Saul pause, at least not when it came to his loyalty to Saul. He had never given Saul a reason to believe Catcher would cross him. Honor among thieves was a relative term, but in this business, not paying your partner's share from a job was the fastest way to find yourself in a world of hurt.

That is, of course, *if* you were allowed to remain in the world at all.

7

Four hundred sixty thousand and change. That was what the pot held as the clock ticked over to one a.m. and the last card, the "river," was laid down in the center of the table.

There were six players at tonight's game. The English actor, Thaddeus Dale, was the most famous, widely known among the masses, from suburban dwellers to the ranks of the Hollywood elite. He was the "special friend" Jamison had tipped off Evie about. But he was simply a dabbler, and this was only his second time at Jamison's table. To his right sat Chris Crosby, pitcher for the New Jersey Colts who was on a two-game no-hitter streak. Crosby frequented the suite whenever he was in town, but was down several hands tonight, putting him in the red by about forty thousand.

Beside Crosby was Henry Forrester, a Manhattan real estate developer in his late forties. Though not quite Donald Trump, he definitely held his own with a nine-digit net worth, according to the internet. Forrester was a regular, and had been attending the game since its inception. For the last few months he hadn't missed a Tuesday night, sometimes winning, sometimes losing. Tonight he was struggling, having lost a number of hands in a row.

Continuing around the table was Art DeVries, easily the oldest player there, probably around sixty, by Evie's estimation. She had no idea what DeVries did for a living, but she got the distinct impression that asking about it, or anyone even mentioning it, was a huge no-no. From one or two offhand comments in the later hours—always after DeVries had left for the night—she deduced he had something to do with bookkeeping, and not the Ernst & Young variety. As far as categories of players went, he fell into the more shady of those, and although he had never been anything but pleasant to her, something about him—possibly the fact that he looked like an extra from *The Sopranos*—rattled her. DeVries usually made a showing once a month, and he would typically break even, give or take a few thousand. Tonight was no different.

Another actor, Hudson Masters, sat next to DeVries. Masters was a heartthrob of the small screen, the star of a teen vampire melodrama on a premium cable channel. In his late twenties, the kid had more money than sense, but seemed to have a good bit of luck. Tonight he had been doing well and was responsible for the losses sustained by Crosby and Forrester. Finally, there was Kieran Carr, who had only been gracing the game for a couple of months, but, like Forrester, hadn't missed a single one in that time. Initially he had won big, but in the last weeks had finished with hefty deficits every game.

In this hand there were two players left battling it out for the gigantic pot: Forrester and Masters. It was unusual for the stakes to go that high on a single hand, but there had been a lot of losses in the last hour, and both Forrester's and Crosby's bad runs had exhausted their initial supply of chips, prompting them to use collateral to buy more. This had exponentially increased the total amount being played with at the table and had resulted in the fortune currently up for grabs.

The sheer amount being tossed around was beyond Evie's reckoning, but the add-ons—these chip buys during the game—were what really blew her mind. Jamison refused to extend credit without collateral. That meant if someone wanted to buy more chips at some point during the game, they would have to provide security for the "loaned" chips to cover the cost in the event that they didn't win enough to pay for them. So, these men actually came here, with extra thousands and thousands in value, *knowing* they might lose the fifty grand they began with, ready to spend even more to continue playing. It was hard to imagine being in possession of that kind of wealth—wealth you could just throw away, when Evie was doing everything she could to make ends meet.

The variety of the collateral for chip purchases was as interesting as the players themselves. Of course, Jamison never discussed any of this with Evie. But after a few drinks, or when they were too tired to think better of it, the players sometimes talked to her about it, and over time she had also observed a lot.

Some of them kept it simple, bringing extra cash or cashier's checks, which they would turn over to Jamison if and when they decided to buy more chips. That was Crosby's preferred method, and he had had to turn a check over a little while ago just to stay in the game. Vehicle titles had also been used—on one occasion, to a Ferrari that one of the players had driven to the Wexsor for the game, but had to surrender to Jamison by morning. Then there were financial instruments—stock certificates or bonds—or the unique items, such as jewelry or fine art. Just as the game afforded her opportunities to mingle with people she would never otherwise meet, Evie's exposure to these priceless objects was something she would have never experienced outside the game. One player, who wasn't here tonight, sometimes carried in a five-by-seven original oil painting by Leo Dupree, the pop-art genius. Forrester always brought along the same rare coin. Others brought jewelry or gemstones, like DeVries, who often carried in a velvet bag of cut diamonds.

Occasionally she got to handle these objects. Once, at a player's insistence, she had worn an emerald necklace crafted for the Vanderbilts one hundred and fifty years earlier, though just for twenty minutes while he played out a hand that would determine whether he or Jamison was leaving with it at the end of the night. At another game, before handing his rare coin over to Jamison to be held as collateral, Forrester showed it to Evie, pressing it into her open hand. She had almost dropped it when he casually asked her what it felt like to hold four million dollars in her palm.

These people simply lived in a different world. Certainly not one she would ever be a part of. But here, in this job, she got to stand on the edge of it and peer inside, like a little girl with her nose pressed to a shop window staring at dollies she would never own.

In this particular moment, she was being allowed to witness the absurdity of either Forrester or Masters becoming half a million dollars richer upon the turn of a single card. DeVries, Dale, and Crosby remained at the table, close to the action, gleaning whatever information they could to put themselves in a better position during the next hand. Kieran Carr, however, who had been the first to fold, had sidled up to Evie by the bar, where he continued chatting her up, something he had been doing most of the night, and much more than usual. Between that and Thaddeus Dale's presence, Evie had found plenty of reasons to linger, somewhat shirking her responsibilities downstairs.

"What do you think, Evie?" Kieran whispered, leaning into her, his scotch on the rocks clinking as he moved. "Think he's got him?"

"We'll have to see," she replied, mindful of Jamison's insistence that the staff do nothing to affect the game—including voicing opinions about the current play.

"Very diplomatic answer, Ms. Diaz," Kieran drawled appreciatively, the last syllable slurring a bit.

Kieran had been downing the drinks, and it was starting to show. It also explained his less-than-stellar performance.

If she had learned anything over the last two years from watching this game, it was that poker wasn't about playing the cards. It was about playing the players. And too much alcohol made that difficult to do. Kieran's judgment was possibly on the verge of being compromised, not to mention his balance. Right before this hand, when stepping away for a restroom break, he had turned too quickly and barreled into Jamison, nearly knocking them both to the floor. If Kieran wanted a shot at winning back his money, he would need to lay off the booze.

Jamison walked over, his eyes on the table, but his attention zeroed in on her. "Any issues here?"

"None," Evie replied, and she meant it. Jamison locked eyes with her as if to disagree, twitched his head toward the bedroom that served as his office, and started in that direction. She followed.

"You've had quite a night," he said, once they had stepped through the doorway.

He wasn't wrong. Thaddeus Dale had arrived late and had to sit out a full hand before jumping in. He had spent the entire wait talking to Evie, and to her surprise, had remembered her from his last time there. He even asked about Gabby, so she asked about his family—no names, just generics. She didn't want to seem like a freak fan, after all. He mentioned that summer in New York was broiling compared to London this time of year, and when she said that she had never been there, he had told her that she should visit and that if she ever did, he and his wife would be glad to show her around.

"You're right," Evie told Jamison. "I really have. One for the books. I can't believe Mr. Dale remembered Gabby."

"No. Not him. I was talking about Mr. Carr." Jamison's words were not sharp, but they were stern, and Evie sensed a reprimand coming. She straightened up, squaring her shoulders.

"I don't understand. Mr. Carr?"

"He's been very focused on you tonight."

"I think he's just had a couple of bad hands and wanted someone to talk to."

"I think he's a bit taken with you, Evie."

They stood together, right inside the bedroom, looking out at the sitting area. On the far side, Kieran remained at the bar, animatedly speaking to the bartender and laughing vigorously, apparently finding his own comments irresistibly funny. His head swiveled as he cast around the room, his gaze landing on Evie. He smiled invitingly.

"He can be charming, that one," Jamison muttered, crossing his arms. "I need to know that you understand the rules where Mr. Carr and his intentions are concerned."

Evie's eyes narrowed in amused disbelief. He actually believed Kieran was interested in her. "It's the liquor and the losses talking," she assured him. "He's only flirting. It doesn't mean anything."

His eyes looked her over appraisingly, a twinge of disappointment furrowing his brow. "You may be more naive than I thought."

She swallowed uncomfortably. "Sorry?"

"Romantic entanglements would complicate things for the game. I don't need players wreaking havoc with my staff and vice versa—"

"It's not an issue, Mr. Jamison."

"Because you two have been awfully chummy lately, and tonight—"

"*Nothing* will happen there." She said it with finality, a grim hardness punctuating both her words and her countenance, her soft features taking on a drawn, sharp quality. "Nothing," she repeated adamantly.

Jamison sniffed. "Good, then. Good," he said, and nodded toward Dana, who was depositing a prime rib sandwich at the elbow of one of the players. "Check with Dana before you go, just to make sure she's got everything she needs."

Out in the hall minutes later, Evie's lips clamped together tightly, her stomach hard as stone. Though Jamison hadn't explicitly used the words, he had made it clear that it had been time for her to leave. James Jamison had, in his own smooth and subtle way, kicked her out. And that was a first.

What if he doesn't let me come back?

She took a deep breath, telling herself to slow down. He hadn't said or done anything that suggested that was a possibility. In fact, him questioning her about his rules suggested he *did* plan to have her continue on, but needed to be certain that she would not cause him any issues. What *was* abundantly obvious was that he did not appreciate the type of attention she was receiving from Kieran Carr.

I'll have to keep my distance from him in the future, she thought. *Distance without being rude.* It wouldn't be an easy balance to maintain, especially if Jamison was right and Kieran did have some interest in her. She would have to find a way, though. Because she needed this little side gig. She needed the extra cash for her and for Gabby and for all the changes coming their way soon.

She pressed the elevator call button for what seemed like the hundredth time that night. Only, instead of playing her counting game as she waited, she began planning how she would separate herself from Kieran Carr without it looking like she was trying to.

8

As the door to the suite closed behind Evie, wild clapping ensued, along with a few woofs from Crosby. Forrester grinned, his smile as wide as the black-rimmed glasses he wore as he reached out and drew in toward himself the pot of chips totaling nearly half a million. Masters slumped in his chair, defeat etched into his features, looking as if he had just lost all eight hundred thousand of his Twitter followers.

"Way to show that boy something," Crosby guffawed, slapping the table. DeVries said nothing, but nodded enthusiastically. He had lost a lot on that one hand. Dale looked amused, but simply said, "Nicely played, Forrester."

"Thank you," Forrester replied, as Kieran stepped over to them.

"About time," he said, placing a hand on Forrester's shoulder. "Somebody here deserved a change of luck. Wish it could've been me, but..." He splayed his hands before him in a gesture of surrender.

"Jump back in," Crosby egged.

"Nah. It's not my night, boys." Kieran shook his head

dismissively. “I wanted to see that last hand through, but since I'm nearly out of chips, I'd better hit the road. But next week? Same time?”

The others waved him off as the dealer began another hand, and Kieran moved toward the door. Jamison stepped lively to meet him, reaching Kieran as he clasped the handle.

“Sorry about tonight,” Jamison said, a slight edge to his voice.

Kieran shrugged. “Unfortunately it's starting to be a pattern. Seemed best to walk away with what little I had. Maybe I need to take a few weeks off. Adjust my chakra or karma or whatever. See if I can't change my luck.”

“I understand.”

“Besides, if I leave now, maybe I can catch up to Evie.”

Jamison tensed at the mention of Evie's name. “If you need something from the hotel, Dana can help you.”

Kieran chuckled meaningfully. “Uh, no. It's not that kind of request.” He tipped his head at Jamison. “See you in a few weeks.”

~

“I PROMISE, Mrs. Beasley, I'll look into this immediately,” Evie vowed for the fourth time. She stood at the doorway to suite 2510, conferring with an older woman standing inside the threshold, dressed in black loungewear from head to toe. The outfit matched the severe black bob framing her bony face, still covered in this hour with an excessive amount of caked foundation.

Five minutes earlier, Evie had been stepping onto the elevator when Mrs. Beasley exited her suite with her teacup poodle curled in the crook of her arm. The woman had called her over, insisting that Evie inspect the state of the room service that had been delivered.

"I just don't understand. How hard is it to follow simple directions?" Mrs. Beasley bemoaned, noiselessly tapping one foot sheathed in a fluffy Ugg slipper.

"I sincerely apologize—"

"I have insomnia," she said, carving her tongue around each word. "*Insomnia.* Some nights I don't fall asleep until two or three—"

"Mrs. Beasley, I'm so sorry—"

"—and Pepper keeps me company, but if he's going to stay up then he has to have his steak and it has to be medium rare." She reached over to the linen-covered rolling table, snatched the steak knife from where she had already stabbed the slab of meat and jabbed it again. More bright red blood dribbled out. "See? *Rare.* I said medium rare. Not rare. Not medium. *Medium rare.* How is Pepper supposed to eat this?"

Evie wasn't quite sure how Pepper could have eaten the ten-ounce sirloin regardless of the temperature it had been cooked to. The thing was as big as the dog. Evie exaggerated her tight smile. "Did they offer to bring you another one when you called room service? Who did you talk to?"

"I talked to no one because no one answered. Really, a hotel of this alleged caliber and no one answers when you call room service? I mean, what is the point of room service, then?"

Evie was about to answer, when someone else did it for her. "I wholeheartedly agree. This is no way for our hotel to treat a patron such as yourself."

Evie turned around to find Kieran Carr standing so close to her that she could have touched him. Mrs. Beasley's eyes narrowed suspiciously as she took in his attire.

"You work here?"

"I do. I'm one of the kitchen managers. They sent me straight up to apologize personally."

What was he doing?

Heat flushing her neck, Evie prepared to call him out, when

she cut her eyes to Mrs. Beasley. The woman's shoulders had dropped, and her gaze had latched onto Kieran with a sort of vague interest. Evie snapped her mouth shut.

"Finally," Mrs. Beasley chided, though her tone was noticeably less rancorous than the one she had been using with Evie.

"Yes, ma'am. I'll remove that," he said, stepping between the women to pull the table out the door, "and have another brought up right away." Mrs. Beasley jerked her foot back to avoid having her toes rolled over as little Pepper barked, possibly unhappy about his midnight snack being taken away. Evie was fairly certain he didn't care whether the steak was well done or ice cold.

"Medium rare," Mrs. Beasley quipped.

"Medium rare," Kieran echoed obligingly.

"And for your trouble," he continued, "we would like to offer Pepper one of our premium doggie spa sessions. On the house."

Mrs. Beasley's chin jutted out as she momentarily considered this, followed by a crisp nod. "We'll be waiting," she said, and closed the door in his face.

Kieran pushed the table against the wall, then smugly winked at Evie.

"What in the world?" Evie asked, moving to keep pace with him as he walked past her to the elevator.

"I was coming down the hall and heard her carrying on," he said, pressing the call button. "Thought you needed an escape route."

"Okay, but," she spluttered, "we don't have a doggie spa service."

"Well, you'd better come up with one before tomorrow."

Evie choked back a snort at the sheer magnitude of his chutzpah. "I guess I'd better. And what if she asks for you?"

"Tell her I was fired over the steak mishap. It'll thrill her to think she has that kind of power."

Evie laughed outright, drawing a satisfied smirk from Kieran. The elevator door opened and he extended a hand, inviting her to enter first. She did and he followed her inside.

"You're leaving early tonight," she noted, then quickly pinched her lips together. She was supposed to be talking to him less, not more.

"Yeah, well," he said, shrugging nonchalantly, "it wasn't my night. Thought I'd better go while the getting was good. And besides," he continued, his sparkling eyes locking onto hers, "I wanted a chance to say goodnight to you."

"WELL, that's the first time anybody's made change for a nickel and gotten half a million dollars," Crosby observed wryly. He leaned back from the game table, puffing on the Cuban he had just lit during a short restroom break for the dealer. The smoke floated up and over his head, shimmering in the glare from the canned lights above.

"What's that?" a bemused Thaddeus Dale asked, wiping a bit of au jus from the corner of his mouth, a remnant of his prime rib sandwich.

Masters leaned forward, his face sour. "Forrester gives Jamison a rare coin as collateral whenever he needs to buy more chips," he grumbled, still stinging from the loss Forrester had inflicted.

"And with hands like that, I'll easily be collecting it back from him at cash out," Forrester said, stacking the mountain of chips he had won, the red, blue, and green plastic discs clacking against one another.

"Let's hope I can say the same," DeVries grunted, referencing the three diamonds he had surrendered to Jamison to finance his additional buy-in, most of which he had lost in the last hand.

Jamison stood near the bar, observing from a distance. A taut smile stretched across his face as he slid his hands in his pockets. "I'm sure you both will. Till then..."

Forrester chuckled as the dealer returned, but Jamison's expression caught, then hardened. The dealer called for the blinds to be placed and started the round. As the cards flew, Jamison glided from his spot to where his security man, Thompson, sat on the far couch, leaned over his shoulder, and began whispering in his ear.

9

"...I wanted a chance to say goodnight to you."

Kieran had leaned in a bit and now was far too close. Heat crept across Evie's skin as she took a half step back. "Well, that was...kind of you, but, honestly...there was no need."

"Aww," he started as the elevator door began to close. "Are you saying you weren't going to miss me at—"

Before he could finish, a burly hand shot between the door and the elevator's frame, causing the automatic safety feature to retract the door, revealing Thompson, Jamison's security man. He wedged his foot against the door, preventing it from closing again.

"Mr. Carr?" he asked, his gravelly voice devoid of humor.

Kieran cocked his head. "Yes?" he drawled.

"You need to come with me. Mr. Jamison needs to see you."

Kieran blinked a few times in rapid succession. "See me? Why?"

"If you'll just come with me," Thompson insisted.

"Well," Kieran said, and in a shocking move snaked one

arm behind Evie's waist, pulling her to him, "we were talking about heading out for a drink—"

The heat Evie had previously felt blossomed into a full-grown blaze. She pulled back from his embrace, knowing her face must be ten shades of red. "Uh, Mr. Carr," she stammered, "I don't think—"

"Just come with me," Thompson barked coldly, ignoring both Kieran's flirtatious display and Evie's embarrassed response. Though Thompson's face was impassive, his jacket seemed slightly more taut, as if he were tensing up in preparation for something. The elevator's alarm started pinging annoyingly as he persisted in holding the door open.

"Fine," Kieran said, expelling an annoyed sigh as he stepped out of the elevator and turned. "Sorry about that, Evie. Couldn't resist. But hey," he continued, flashing another grin as Thompson finally removed his foot, the alarm ceased, and the door began to shut, "I really would like to get that drink sometime. What do you say?"

Her brain and tongue were both tied in knots, and before she could manage an answer, the door had closed completely.

10

Evie replaced the handset at the concierge desk after ordering another steak for Mrs. Beasley in 2510. Though during the day the manager usually stayed behind the scenes in the back offices, as night manager, Evie floated between there and the concierge desk, sometimes performing concierge tasks as one was not on duty from midnight to five a.m.

Her cell rang, and, extracting it from her pocket, she saw a photo of Eleanor and Gabby displayed on the screen. The older woman's lined, rosy face was squished next to Gabby's chubby one in a selfie they had taken in the snow last winter. Gabby's hair, the same rich brown shade as Evie's, reached down to just below the shoulders of her pink dress. Thick bangs formed a blunt line above her light blue eyes—the same color Mark's had been.

Evie's chest contracted as if a rope had been cinched around her. It was much too late for Eleanor to be calling. Pushing down the threatening panic, Evie answered.

"Hello? Eleanor? Everything all right?" She was unable to keep the note of concern out of her voice.

"Yes, yes, dear. Fine. Really. It's just, well, Gabby's asthma. It started acting up. I think she was playing at the back of the closet and dust got stirred up—"

"But she's okay?"

"Yes, fine. I gave her a nebulizer treatment and she's down now. Her breathing is nearly normal."

"Okay. Good. Thanks for letting me know." The tightness in Evie's chest relented. Asthma was a battle they had been fighting since Gabby was two. Most of the time her maintenance medicine was enough to keep it under control, but when her allergies were bad—dust, grass, pollen—her asthma would be triggered, and she would need a breathing treatment to open her lungs. The treatment typically resolved the condition in less than ten minutes, but Evie was always on edge until Gabby was breathing without difficulty once more.

"Well, also," Eleanor continued, "I called because I pulled out her inhaler to check it, and tried to prime it, but couldn't get it to work. I think the mechanism is jammed or something."

Evie's stomach plummeted. The albuterol inhaler was their last line of defense. If there was ever a time Gabby's nebulizer wasn't working, or if they weren't near it when an attack happened, it's what they would use to get the asthma under control. It went everywhere with Gabby. In an emergency it could save her life. *What if this had been one of those emergencies? What if, tonight, the nebulizer hadn't worked and Gabby had needed the inhaler?* The possibility sliced her insides. "Oh, Eleanor, I had no idea. We haven't needed it in a while. I haven't looked at it lately. I'll call in a refill right now—"

"Already done, dear, at the Duane Reade near you. They said it should be ready in about a half hour." A twenty-four-hour branch of Evie's pharmacy sat only five blocks from the hotel, right on her walk back to Grand Central Station where she would catch the 7 train after work. Evie used the pharmacy whenever she had to pick something up for herself or Gabby before heading home. It was more convenient than trying to do it in Queens after taking the train back in the morning. Eleanor knew this.

Eleanor knew everything. Evie rubbed the heel of her palm against her chest, a sadness settling there at the thought of things to come.

"Thanks, Eleanor."

"No problem, hon. She's sleeping so I'm headed to bed now."

"Okay, see you in a few hours."

Evie let Eleanor go, sliding the phone into her pants pocket. She hated that Gabby had an episode tonight. It was not only scary for the adults, but it threw the child off for days, resulting in sporadic temper tantrums and nightmares. Inhaling and exhaling slowly, she registered that she would probably have to extend an excessive amount of grace to her daughter until her system calmed down.

Evie glanced at the clock. It was 1:45 a.m. and quiet in the lobby. Most of the wedding reception guests had departed, leaving just a few stragglers who had made their way to the bar. Only one clerk, Jayda, manned the front desk. She was focused on her computer screen, and though it looked as if she were working, Evie knew it was more likely that she was web-surfing. This was generally the dead period for the front and concierge desks. As a rule, nothing much ever happened until a little before four, when travelers taking early flights began making their way downstairs looking like extras from *The Walking Dead.*

Evie considered the pharmacy, and how much busier it would be after her shift than it was now. And how tired she would be then, and how she would want to get home as quickly as possible to check on Gabby rather than waste precious time standing in line at Duane Reade. *I could be back in less than an hour,* she calculated. *Fifteen minutes there, a short wait, and fifteen minutes back.* She was due for a break anyway, having missed the one she normally took around one a.m., because of her extended visits to the poker suite.

Technically, she wasn't supposed to leave the premises as they were short-staffed during the night, but she had done it before without any problems. They could call her cell if they really needed to find her. She walked over to Jayda, who was still consumed with whatever was on her screen, and explained that she had a little crisis and was going to run to the pharmacy. Jayda promised to cover for her, returning to her screen as Evie slipped through the door behind the desk and into the rear offices.

11

The sound of low breathing at Kieran's back confirmed that Jamison's man was sticking uncomfortably close as they walked down the hall, back toward the poker suite.

"So, uh, it's 'Thompson,' right?" Kieran asked amicably, trying to diffuse the tension. Thompson didn't answer, and they continued moving in silence toward the suite. When they neared it, Kieran reached for the door handle, but Thompson grabbed his shoulder.

"Uh-uh," he grunted, "not there."

Kieran's jaw stiffened. "Well, where—"

"There," Thompson said, nodding toward the stairwell door at the end of the hall, about ten feet away.

"The stairs? We're taking the stairs?" The hairs on Kieran's arms prickled.

Thompson nodded again.

There were only a couple of reasons one would use a stairwell this high up. Kieran didn't like any of them. "You do know we're on the twenty-fifth floor?"

Thompson held him with a blank stare.

"Okaaay," Kieran drawled. His steps hesitant, he crossed to the stairwell door and slipped inside with the low, ominous breathing at his back once more.

~

"WE FOUND SOMETHING."

Saul held the phone to his ear as he rose from his desk chair, wincing. The arthritis felt like fifty-grit sandpaper in his knees. "What?" he asked, hoping they had finally gotten a break that would lead them to Catcher.

"Well," Kimball said, "when we pointed out to his roommates that they oughta be more concerned with what we might do to them now rather than what he might do to them at some undefined point in the future, they started talking."

"And?"

"He spends a lot of nights away from the apartment on a regular basis." Kimball cleared his throat, a constant habit of the smoker who typically lit one up at least every hour. "One of them got curious. Wanted to know what he was up to. I think he was thinking he would have leverage against him, in case he ever needed it."

"Okay."

"The roommate started following him on the nights he'd leave, simple as that. He's got an idea where he'd be now, and that's where we're headed."

Saul dug a yellow pad out from under a stack of invoices and snatched up a cheap, plastic ballpoint pen with "Messinger Meats, 1007 66th Ave, Queens, NY" printed on its side. He pressed his hefty thumb down on the top, clicking it as he leaned over the pad.

"Gimme the address."

Room 1804 of the Wexsor Hotel was nice enough, Kieran thought. Not nearly as extravagant as suite 2500, but certainly upscale with its floor-to-ceiling windows, cherry furniture, and crystal bar service in the small sitting area. They had tromped down seven flights of stairs to reach it. When Thompson ushered him inside, Kieran wasn't surprised to see Jamison, arms crossed, standing with his back to the expansive view of the island of Manhattan, at this hour a collage of thousands of multi-colored lights glowing against the inky night.

"What's with the change of scenery?" Kieran quipped as he heard the door shut behind him, the click of the lock sending a wave of apprehension through him. He fought it back, forcing himself to focus.

Jamison said nothing, instead waiting silently as Kieran stepped further into the room, prompted awkwardly by Thompson, who continued bumping his shoulder into Kieran every time he stopped. Finally, Kieran stood within a few feet of the game host. When the aggressive nudging ceased, Kieran turned just long enough to toss Thompson a look of perturbed disdain, then directed himself to Jamison. "What's with your man, here? You wanna call him off?"

When Jamison didn't answer, Kieran felt his composure falter. He raised his voice. "I was in the middle of something when the Hulk here interrupted. What am I doing here? And what's with the cloak-and-dagger routine—bringing me to another room?"

"Trying to be discreet, Mr. Carr. Trying to have some consideration for my players."

"Well, I'm one of your players, and I have to say, I'm not feeling very considered."

"I'm sorry about that, but there's been a development I need to handle, so I asked Thompson to bring you here."

"What development?"

Jamison nodded, and suddenly a thick hand closed around the back of Kieran's neck, ruthlessly shoving him toward the wall. He slammed into it with a resounding thud, barely turning his head in time to avoid his nose being smashed.

"Hey! What th—"

"Don't move," Thompson said as he kicked Kieran's legs apart. He grabbed one of Kieran's hands, and then the other, pressing them palm-first against the wall. "Hands up here. Stay put," he ordered, and began patting Kieran down.

"You need to do what he says. Thompson can get a bit rough with noncompliant subjects," Jamison advised. The warning was unnecessary. The harsh way Thompson jabbed and slapped at Kieran's body made it clear he wasn't going to tolerate any resistance.

"I'm not carrying, if that's what you're worried about," Kieran grunted.

Thompson finished the pat-down, then went through each of Kieran's pockets, even turning them inside out where possible, dropping the contents—a wallet, keys, cell phone—onto the floor. Apparently satisfied, he pulled Kieran back from the wall, turning him so that he was facing Jamison again.

"You could've just asked," Kieran said, delivering what he hoped was an impudent smirk as Thompson released him, picked up his wallet, and rummaged through it.

"No gun in there, man," Kieran taunted as his credit cards and cash were removed and each wallet slot inspected. Thompson tossed the wallet back on the floor and shook his head.

Jamison breathed in and out, seemingly contemplating something. His eyes flicked to Thompson then back to Kieran.

The dark understanding that passed between Thompson and Jamison made Kieran feel like a rabbit trapped between two wolves. He held his hands up. "Look, I really don't know what's going on, but I can tell you it's bad for player-host relations."

Jamison's gaze rested on Kieran a few seconds more, before a grim determination flashed across his face. "Use it, Thompson," he snapped decisively, followed by Thompson whipping something from his waistband and stepping toward Kieran.

12

"Whoa, whoa!" Kieran yelped as Thompson pulled a black metal detector wand from his jacket. "Wait...you just searched me! What's *that* for?"

"Don't move," Thompson barked, shoving Kieran's arms up and out. Starting at Kieran's head, he ran the wand slowly over the length of Kieran's body, front and back.

Kieran could feel the rage rising in him like the night tide on a shore. "You carry a metal detector on you?" he asked.

Jamison nodded. "We've found it useful in games from time to time. I've got a strict no-weapons policy. Sometimes we've felt the need to check."

"Well, you've already checked, so lay off!" Kieran shouted, but did not move, allowing Thompson to finish his scan. He knew there wasn't anything to find, and that they were wasting their time, but this would be over more quickly if they just got on with it.

The wand beeped only once, right above Kieran's belt buckle. Thompson told him to remove his belt, and with an aggrieved huff, he did as he was told. He handed the belt to

Thompson, who inspected it, then tossed it on the floor with the other items.

"Nothing," Thompson reported, stepping back from Kieran.

"'Nothing' is right!" Kieran said angrily, dropping his arms so that they slapped against his legs loudly. "Now are you going to tell me what's going on or what?"

"Why were you so chatty with Evie tonight?" Jamison's voice remained coolly even.

"What?" Kieran asked, hearing the disbelief ringing in his own voice. "That's why you dragged me down here? To ask why I was flirting with a beautiful woman?" He rocked back and forth, jamming his hands onto his hips. "Gee, I don't know. It's a complete mystery!"

Jamison raised his eyebrows and pulled a face, as if sending the message that he was prepared to wait on an answer.

Kieran snorted. He was going to have to verbalize it for them. "I like her, all right? I *like* her. You got a problem with that?"

"I don't allow fraternizing between players and staff. It complicates things."

Kieran snorted again. "Uh, okay, fine. Whatever. Then I guess you've just lost a player."

Jamison appraised Kieran for several seconds, then inhaled deeply through his nose as, in a full reversal, a contrite pleasantness washed over him and his stance relaxed. "I hope that's not true. I'm truly sorry about this, but it was unavoidable. I trust you've been with us long enough to accept that this is not a reflection on you, but rather how seriously we take security and look after our players' interests."

Thompson held Kieran's personal articles out to him. Kieran snatched them from him, tucking the wallet, cell, and keys away but holding onto the belt. He briefly imagined smacking Thompson with it. "You're telling me this was for my benefit?"

"Well, for the benefit of the game, so, yes, for you too. Can I rely on your discretion to not share this...meeting...with the other players? It might give them the wrong impression."

"Yeah. We wouldn't want them to get *the wrong impression* now, would we?"

Though Jamison's expression remained stoic, he swallowed hard, the Adam's apple in his throat undulating. "There will be a ten thousand-dollar credit for you at the next game. For your trouble. I ask you to please believe me when I say this was a necessary evil."

"Mmm-hmm," Kieran murmured, making sure the derision in his tone was obvious. "Is that all?"

"Have a good night," Jamison answered dismissively.

Kieran glared at him briefly, turned on his heels, and walked out, slamming the door behind him.

"WHAT DO YOU THINK?" Jamison asked Thompson, falling into one of the plush chairs in the sitting area of room 1804.

Thompson folded his arms across his body. "There wasn't anything on him. So, maybe it wasn't him."

"Maybe." Jamison drummed a finger on the arm of the chair. "I don't think we can take that chance."

"You've still got players upstairs. Could've been one of them."

"But if it is Carr, and he disappears..." Jamison groaned. "I've got two, three hours max before this blows up in my face," he said. "You'll need to follow Carr." Jamison took out his phone and started texting. "I'm calling in some backup, so you can go after him now. We don't want to lose him." He kept his eyes on the screen after pressing the send button, as if willing a reply to appear.

"Who you bringing in?" Thompson asked, tilting his head.

"Nobody you know," Jamison answered, not looking up. "Heavy hitters. They work for an associate of mine."

"And you want me to leave to follow Carr *before* they get here?" Thompson asked, a note of surprise in his voice. "You won't have anybody in the suite if a situation arises."

"If you don't leave, we won't know where Carr's headed. I won't be alone for long. Wait until I hear back from them. Then you should go on down—but stay out of sight. I don't want him to realize that he's being followed. You may need to take the stairs for the last floor or two. That way you won't meet him at the elevators in the lobby if he happens to be slow getting out of here, although I'm betting he won't want to stick around. I'll have our man in the hotel security office watch the front entrance so we know which way he goes when he leaves," Jamison said, then started texting again.

"Okay," Thompson confirmed.

They waited silently for another couple of minutes before Jamison's cell finally buzzed. He glanced at it, then looked up at Thompson. "They'll be here in twenty. You can't wait that long. You'll lose him. Go on and go."

Thompson shrugged resignedly. "It's your call."

"Just in case, give me that thing," Jamison said, nodding at Thompson's jacket. Thompson pulled out the metal detector wand and handed it to him. "I may need it upstairs," Jamison explained.

"They won't like that," Thompson noted.

"They'll like it better than the alternative."

Thompson nodded, then moved to open the door.

"Hold on a second," Jamison said, placing a hand on his arm. "Carr said he was in the middle of something when you found him. What was he talking about?"

"I don't know. I caught him in the elevator with Evie."

"With Evie?"

"They looked pretty cozy. He said something about meeting up for a drink later."

Jamison's eyes darkened. "He say where?"

Thompson shook his head. "Nah."

Jamison paused, seeming to deliberate for a moment. "Okay. I'll let you know when I know which way he headed—if you miss him."

As Thompson disappeared through the door, Jamison leaned back in his chair. Placing his hands tent-like over his nose and mouth, he sucked in a cleansing breath, then exhaled slowly. He dropped his shoulders, repeated the exercise, then picked up his cell and dialed.

~

KIERAN LEANED COMFORTABLY against the front desk, as the porter handed him a black leather messenger bag.

"Thanks for hustling, that was quick," he said appreciatively, slipping the man a five-dollar tip. As the porter left, Kieran returned his attention to the woman behind the desk and flashed a grin. "You have a spare envelope, Jayda? Preferably a padded mailer?"

Her eyes sparkled with eagerness. "I'm sure I do. Just a second." She marched over to the concierge desk and opened a drawer. She withdrew a letter-sized padded manila envelope, then walked back, handing it to Kieran with the air of someone who had found a long-lost treasure. "Will this work?"

"Perfect," he said, taking it, then kneeling down. He set his bag on the tile, rifled through it, then moved something from the bag into the envelope, licking and sealing it shut as he rose. Borrowing a pen from Jayda, he scribbled a note on the envelope, then held the package out to her. She grasped it, bending toward him ever so slightly.

"Jayda, I know you said Ms. Diaz is unavailable at the moment, but I need her to get this as soon as possible."

"She shouldn't be long—"

"The thing is, I really can't wait. Would you give this to her as soon as you can? It's very important," Kieran insisted.

"Sure," she replied, squaring her shoulders. "Of course."

"Thank you, Jayda," Kieran said, and leaned in closer, almost whispering. "Now, I have one more little favor to ask..."

~

NEARLY TEN MINUTES had passed since Carr left suite 1804, when Thompson finally rounded the next to last landing of the stairwell, Jamison's voice blasting through his cell, sharp and urgent.

"Where are you?" Jamison barked.

Thompson gripped his phone hard as he tromped down the flight of steps to the first floor, his breathing fast and labored. "I'm about to exit the stairwell to the lobby. Took the elevator to the third floor, then took the stairs the rest of the way."

"Our guy in security finally picked up. He just saw Carr on CCTV leaving through the hotel's front doors, then turning left."

"On it," Thompson said, ending the call and quickening his pace.

13

Kieran's quick strides had already put several blocks between him and the hotel. He pulled his cell from his pocket, checked it again, and groaned.

Why wasn't she calling him back?

He didn't know why he kept looking at it. It would buzz if she called. But it surprised him that she hadn't called him back yet, and he kept thinking that maybe, somehow, she had called and he had missed it. If she didn't get in touch soon, he would have to try again, but if she didn't answer then—well, he didn't know what. This really wasn't something he wanted to leave in a message. But he would if he had to.

Though his steps were driven, he was unsettled, his nerve endings tingling since the encounter with Jamison. A loud squawk of laughter erupted from somewhere to his right and his heart jumped in his chest. Jerking toward the sound, he saw a posse of rowdy college-aged kids on the other side of the street, hooting and slapping one another on their backs as they went. He exhaled a staggered breath, pausing briefly to gather himself as cars rolled past, their headlights glaring on the pavement.

"Get it together, man," he mumbled to himself as he resumed his former pace, his brain humming furiously as he strode. He stepped over a subway grate, the ground beneath him trembling as a train cut through one of the subterranean tunnels beneath him.

Something must have happened in the suite after he left. Something bad and something that made Jamison think he was responsible for it. Because getting dragged into a private room like that with the host of a high-stakes poker game and his gorilla of a security man was not the norm. The fact that Jamison chose to handle it that way was an ominous sign. And if Jamison truly believed Kieran had tried something, there was only one explanation for why Jamison had let him walk out of that hotel.

Because he didn't find the proof he needed. And accusing a player without evidence would be devastatingly bad for the game.

If Jamison had pushed things any further without having real evidence, and Kieran ratted him out to the others, Jamison would lose credibility. His standing in the private poker community would suffer great harm. The bottom line was that it would hurt his bottom line.

Kieran's stomach turned as his thoughts drifted to another question. *Why had they asked him about Evie?*

There was no reason for them to bring her up, yet they had, and they were clearly suspicious of his interest in her. Why? Just because he had flirted with her a little that night?

If they were harassing him, it was possible she was next. Did they go looking for her as soon as he had walked out of the Wexsor? On the whole, Jamison had a reputation for being a fair and reasonable game host. He wasn't prone to dramatics or power plays even when he needed to collect, but if he was having serious trouble, and he thought either Kieran or Evie had something to do with it, all bets were off. People in Jamison's position were not typically known for showing mercy when it came to their money and the loss thereof.

A stab of certainty gutted him.

I have to find her before Jamison does. Even if it means risking running into Jamison.

Reversing course, he turned in the direction of the hotel, pulled his cell out, and dialed.

14

Bruno Agnellini stood beside the black Lexus GX parked in front of the Wexsor, holding the rear passenger door open for a line of several thirty-somethings piling in one after the other. They had requested that the car take them to a bar near Times Square, hoping to squeeze in one more drink before closing time. They were loud and obliviously obnoxious, clearly continuing a party that had been going strong for hours.

The last woman tripped trying to step up into the SUV. Bruno's quick reflexes prevented a tumble, and over her cackled "thank you," he closed the door behind her. As he turned to go, he caught sight of Evie leaving through the employee exit and turning left, walking briskly down the sidewalk.

Something about her seemed harried. And he would know. He had been watching her for four months. Yes, they had hardly spoken in that time, trading only a few words in passing here and there. But that didn't matter. Because her face and frame, he knew.

He had studied her while she conversed daily with Wilson at the front entrance, often laughing, her apple-red mouth turned up, framing that smile of perfectly straight, white teeth. Sometimes she was more serious. Almost somber. Maybe talking about her late husband or an issue with her child. On those occasions her forehead would wrinkle, the slight divot between her eyebrows would deepen, and her posture would sag, as if draped in a melancholy blanket. But tonight, she had her intense game face on. She had some kind of mission to complete, and she was in a hurry.

He did not like the idea of her walking alone at this time of night. It was safe enough in this area, as far as that goes in New York after midnight, but still. Things happen.

A gale of laughter and a playful scream from inside the SUV snapped him to his present circumstances. He walked around the front of the vehicle and slid in. The engine purred as, spying a break in the traffic, he drove forward and cranked the music up to drown out the juvenile revelry going on in the back.

He would have offered Evie a ride, even though it was against hotel policy to chauffeur the staff. Not that she would have accepted his offer. In her mind, they were basically strangers, which was entirely his fault. She had tried talking to him, but he just got so nervous whenever she was around. It was frustrating because normally that was not a problem for him. But something about her was different. Maybe it was just that this time it wasn't some girl his mother had invited to Sunday lunch in an effort to match-make over osso buco, or one of the blind dates his roommate had set him up on. Maybe it was because this time it really mattered. Because he *wanted* this one to go right. And he didn't want to screw it up by doing or saying the wrong thing at the wrong time, given the situation and her state of mind.

She was a widow and, as far as he knew from discreetly asking around, she had not been involved with anyone since her husband's death or even mentioned seeing anyone, even though the man had passed several years ago. Of course, Bruno had observed hotel guests flirting with *her* sometimes. Though she was polite, artfully playing it off, she never reciprocated. She was smooth that way—not participating but not embarrassing them either. He liked that about her. Her consideration for others. She just had a way. And so, he was patiently waiting for the right moment.

It would only be a matter of time.

~

"SHE'S NOT at the desk and she's not answering the hotel's calls to her cell," Jamison groused. "Where is she?"

He stood in the security office of the Wexsor, a small room in the back offices that, at eight feet by eight feet, was more of a closet, really. Three computer monitors were lined up on an elevated shelf mounted six inches above a long metal desk pushed against the wall. The monitor in the center, with the keyboard placed beneath it, was devoted to the management of the system. The others were for viewing whatever footage—live or recorded—happened to be pulled up at the time.

Evan Glick, the hotel security officer on Jamison's payroll, sat in front of the monitors, his charcoal gray uniform amply filling the plastic, overtaxed chair positioned at the middle of the console. His curly hair, much in need of a cut, flopped down on either side of his square black glasses. A number of discarded bags, emptied of nacho chips and cheese curls, were scattered across the desktop, explaining the pungent odor permeating the room.

"I don't know. I don't see her anywhere," Glick replied. "What did the front desk say?"

"That she must have taken her break. When was the last time you saw her?" Jamison asked, waving a hand across the spread of screens.

"I didn't. I wasn't looking for her. Why don't you just call her cell?"

"I already texted her. She didn't respond. If I keep trying to reach her, it might scare her off." Jamison bit his lip, closed his eyes in frustration, then opened them. "She left the suite at about one thirty. Start there with the footage."

"Okay, hold on…that helps." Several minutes passed as he browsed multiple recordings from different cameras spaced throughout the hotel. "Okay, yeah, I got her," Glick finally said. "Look over there," he directed, pointing Jamison to the monitor on the far right. A new window opened on the screen, showing a view of the twenty-fifth floor from the vantage point of the elevators. It panned down the hallway leading to suite 2500, showing Evie walking toward the camera. After she reached the elevator, the interaction with Ms. Beasley followed, as well as Carr's interference, culminating in Thompson eventually collecting Carr. Glick shrugged. "That's it."

"What about after that? Where did she get off?"

Glick pursed his lips and started scrolling through thumbnail screens of more footage on the primary monitor in the center. The keys clacked as he worked, moving between typing and clicking the mouse. Eventually he inclined his head toward the side monitor again.

"There, see…she's off the elevator and," he opened a new window on the screen to display a recording from a different lobby camera, "there she is at the concierge desk. At…1:44 a.m." He pressed a key and fast-forwarded through Evie placing a call on the hotel phone, receiving and ending a call on her own phone, and then stopping by the front desk before leaving through the back office door.

Jamison nodded at the monitor. "Where did she go after that?"

Glick shook his head. "We don't have cameras in the back offices. At least not that I can access. We've got them on the exterior of the building, though." He pulled up footage of Evie exiting the building by the employees' entrance and turning down the street. "Look at the time stamp," he said, aiming a chubby finger at the right corner of the video window. "She didn't do much back there. Pretty much left right away. That's it, man. That's the best I can give you."

"Does she usually leave like that? In the middle of a shift?"

Glick eyed him cynically. "How would I know? You think I just sit here and watch people?"

Jamison fired a caustic look at him and exhaled loudly. "Go back to her at the concierge desk. Right before she left."

Glick wordlessly retrieved the requested footage, letting it play at regular speed as he leaned back in his chair. Jamison bent closer to the monitor. The video offered a panoramic shot of one entire wall of the lobby, including the front and concierge desks, with Evie standing at her post. Despite the width of the angle and the distance, it still captured the concern that contorted Evie's face when she took out her cell and glanced down at it.

"Something's wrong," Jamison observed keenly, as the video continued to play. It showed Evie speaking with someone on her cell for nearly a minute before hanging up. Afterward, her shoulders remained tense and she cast about the room, apparently mulling something over. She walked to the front desk, spoke to the clerk, then exited through the door behind the desk.

"I need to talk to that clerk again," Jamison snapped. "I want to know exactly what Evie said to her."

"Okay, well, she's right out there. Just go talk to—"

"And I want to know why Evie looks so nervous," Jamison said, suspicion ripe in his tone. "Who called her? And why did she go AWOL right after getting that call?"

"Beats me," Glick replied unconcernedly, shoving an orange-powdered triangle into his mouth and crunching.

Jamison peered at the shot of the empty concierge desk, until finally stepping back and crossing his arms. "That bit at the elevator. When my guy stopped Carr. Go back to that."

Glick groaned and hunched over the keyboard again, his fingers leaving orange-dusted prints on the keys. He rewound the footage to the spot where Thompson arrived at the elevator, then clicked play. When Thompson turned down the hall, following Carr, Jamison tapped Glick on the arm.

"No, no...what about inside the elevator?"

"Um, yeah, but you won't really be able to see your guy. It's pretty much a straight overhead shot." Another half minute of keystrokes and mouse-clicks brought up the elevator footage.

It started with the elevator opening and Carr and Evie entering together. The door had nearly closed when a hand burst through the narrow gap between it and the frame. The video continued until Jamison gripped Glick's shoulder.

"There! There!" he exclaimed. "Stop it!"

Glick obeyed, freezing the video.

"Now, go back, just a little. And slow it down. And...stop."

Glaring at the frozen screen, Jamison pulled out his cell and dialed. After several seconds of waiting, he spoke. "Thompson. New plan..."

15

"Eleanor."

The hushed whisper pierced the dreams of the seventy-six-year-old, slowly ushering her back to reality. Her eyelids fluttered, then opened to the tiny, dark-haired girl standing beside Eleanor's twin bed in Evie Diaz's apartment.

"Eleanor, I can't sleep." Gabby Diaz held a soft, chenille blanket to her face, its pale pink a striking contrast to her tawny skin even in the darkness of her bedroom, lit only by a nightlight plugged in near the armchair in the corner. She wore fuzzy, peach-colored footie pajamas with miniature rosebuds arrayed in diagonals across the fabric. Her long dusky hair was mussed, bunched and flying out at every angle, her bangs a thick fringe over her pleading eyes.

Eleanor's bed was in Gabby's room, on the wall opposite the girl's bed, conveniently close in case there were any nighttime issues. Pushing herself into a sitting position, Eleanor reached for Gabby. The little girl climbed up next to her, and Eleanor squeezed her tightly.

"Well, now, child, why can't you sleep?" she asked, kissing the top of Gabby's head.

Gabby pressed into Eleanor beneath the woman's arm, gathering her blanket protectively around her. "I'm skittery," she said, her voice just a squeak.

"You are?" Eleanor asked kindly, squeezing her tighter.

"Yeah. The neb-lizer made my insides all jumpy."

Eleanor smiled at Gabby's description of one of the side effects of the albuterol delivered by the nebulizer. "Your bones are doing somersaults again, huh?" she teased, giving a playful pinch to Gabby's tummy, causing the girl to giggle and press harder into her. "I'm sorry the nebulizer does that. But we want those lungs of yours to open big and wide when you breathe."

"I heard you call Mommy." Gabby's lip turned down a bit. "She'll worry."

Eleanor stroked Gabby's hair, smoothing wayward strands as she marveled at the five-year-old's perceptiveness. "All mommies worry. She knows you'll be fine."

"But what if she can't work like I can't sleep?"

"Is that why you can't sleep? Because *you're* worried?"

Gabby was slow to answer. "Maybe. A little," she admitted tentatively. Gabby routinely exhibited anxiety about her mother being away during the night, a fear that was heightened whenever she woke in the night or was plagued with an asthma attack. This instance had brought both.

"Well, my dear, you have nothing to worry about because your mommy is fine at work and you are fine here, safe and sound. And because you know the secret to not worrying."

A knowing grin stole onto Gabby's face. "We say our prayers."

"Exactly. We say our prayers," Eleanor agreed. "You take those worries, you hand them to Jesus, and you go back to sleep. Right?"

"Right," Gabby echoed.

"How about you start and I'll finish, and then we'll get you snuggled in that bed," Eleanor suggested, gently tapping Gabby's nose.

Gabby nodded, then folded her hands, bowed her head, and started to pray.

16

"Take him back to your office? You're sure?" Thompson grunted as he continued down the sidewalk, his head lowered, his ear pressed against his phone. He had kept half a block between him and Carr since following him from the Wexsor. Now they had ventured into a less lit, more residential area of Thirty-Fifth Street, and Carr had just taken a left at the intersection ahead and disappeared around the corner. Thompson hustled to keep up.

"I'm sure," Jamison confirmed in a steely tone. "Where's he headed?"

"Nowhere as far as I can tell. He just keeps moving, making a big loop every coupl'a blocks. Almost like he's—"

"Circling the Wexsor," Jamison finished for him.

"Exactly. No taxi, no Uber. Hasn't gone into a subway station."

"Grab him. And get him back here ASAP."

"And the woman?"

Jamison sniffed. "I can't find her, but now we know she's involved. Bring him back here and then she's next."

"Got it. I'll be there as quick as I can." Thompson glanced

down to end the call, barreling around the same corner that Carr had gone around a minute earlier. Eyes on his phone, Thompson ran full force into a pedestrian striding with equal intensity in his direction, who also had his head down. The collision sent the men bouncing off each other like two rams headbutting.

"Watch it," Thompson growled, bringing his gaze up.

"Watch yourself," the pedestrian muttered, and likewise looked up, glaring at Thompson.

Both men froze, as Thompson and Carr found themselves staring directly into the face of the other.

~

EVIE SIGHED HEAVILY and cocked her hip, shifting her weight to her other foot. She had been standing in this line for over fifteen minutes and was now stalled in the second place position. At this hour, there was only one pharmacist on duty at the all-night drugstore, and her attention had been completely devoted to the forty-something man at the counter who refused to accept that his cut-rate insurance company was not going to pay for his prescription refill. Harsh fluorescent lights glared down on them as she listened to the increasingly heated discussion in front of her.

"I don't care what your computer says," the man barked. He was dressed in jeans and a wrinkled red T-shirt, his shoulder-length dishwater-blonde hair askew. "I get this every thirty days. I'm out. I need it. They have to pay for it."

The young pharmacist sighed, the unforgiving lighting exaggerating the dark circles beneath her eyes that had seemed to grow over the last several minutes. "Sir, I don't know what to tell you. You need to contact your carrier in the morning and have them explain it to you. I can't do anything about it."

"So, I don't get my medicine? Seriously?"

"You can pay for it yourself, if you like, and seek reimbursement from your insurance. Again, it's ninety-four, thirty-eight...."

This conversation had been going on for most of the time Evie had been in line, and at this point she was almost ready to pay for the man's medication herself just to get him out of there. She suspected that the three customers in line behind her had probably also thought the same thing.

Her phone vibrated in her pocket. Nervous that it might be Eleanor again, calling about another episode, she pulled it out to check.

"Next?" the pharmacist called, and Evie jerked up to see that the disgruntled man had finally stalked off. Evie's eyes shot down to the phone. It wasn't Eleanor.

"Ma'am, please? There's a whole line behind you."

It was the Wexsor. Again. *Shoot,* she thought, and groaned. She had been ignoring their calls in the hopes that she would get back to the hotel quickly, and be able to gloss over her absence. This wait was making that impossible.

Pushing that concern aside for the moment, she stepped to the counter, sliding the phone in her pocket. Whatever it was would have to wait. She was not getting in the back of this line.

~

TIME SEEMED BRIEFLY SUSPENDED as both men stared at one another, surprise apparently curbing their ability to react. Then Thompson reached out and grabbed Kieran by the lapel of his jacket.

Kieran pivoted, first pulling away from Thompson, then, using the man's own heft and force against him, shoved his body hard in Thompson's direction—the same direction in which Thompson had been pulling with all his strength. The abrupt change in momentum caused Thompson to stumble backward, giving Kieran an opportunity to wrench himself from Thompson's grasp. Kieran sprinted down Thirty-Fifth Street as Thompson scrambled after him, surprisingly much faster than would be expected from a man of his girth. The two sped past the street's brownstones and iron railings, Thompson thrusting his arms out in front of him, trying to grab some part of Kieran.

Finally he landed a claw-like grip on the tail of Kieran's jacket and jerked down. Against the sound of ripping fabric, unable to continue forward, Kieran tripped on his own feet, face-planting on the gritty sidewalk. Before he could recover, Thompson stepped over him, yanking him up as he twisted Kieran's right arm behind his back in a dislocation-threatening fashion.

The few pedestrians in the area had crossed to the opposite side of the street and, other than cautious glances, had left the two men to their private business. Thompson gripped Kieran tightly, the shadows of this dimly lit section of the street swathing his face as he grunted in Kieran's ear through rough breathing. "We—" he started, then cut himself off to suck in a lung full of sultry night air before continuing, "—have got a problem."

17

"How much longer?" Matty asked, turning off of FDR Drive and heading west.

"A coupl'a blocks," Kimball answered. Hunched over in the front seat of the black Chevy Traverse, a mid-sized SUV, he checked the magazine of his semi-automatic pistol again, releasing it, then popping it in with a click.

"Why's Saul meetin' us here?" Matty asked, changing lanes to go around a cab stopped against the curb, waiting for its passengers to enter. "We could just take him to Saul's once we grab him."

"Saul wants to be on hand. Increase the pressure and such. Doesn't want to wait for us to bring him to his place. Time is money, and all that."

Matty sniffed and wiped his nose with the back of his hand. "What if we don't find him?"

"It's Tuesday. The roommate said this is where he is on Tuesdays. And we gotta try something. If he's not there, then maybe somebody there'll know where we can find him."

Traffic, still plaguing the streets in this section of Manhattan even at this hour, had caused a jam somewhere up ahead. The cars in front of them were slowing to a roll as a line formed. Matty tapped the brakes. "Man, I need a cigarette," he whined.

"Do *not* light up in here," Kimball warned, shooting him a nasty glance. "You know how Saul is about his vehicles."

"Yeah, yeah," Matty said, taking advantage of a break in the gridlock to swing into the far right lane and move up half a block. They cruised through the traffic signal, but only got partially down the next street before slowing again. This area was residential, and without the storefronts there was less light, leaving their surroundings in shadow, the curtain of night draping the doorsteps of the brownstones and their tree-lined sidewalks.

After a delay of several minutes, the line of cars advanced, creating a gap in front of their SUV. Matty stepped on the gas, propelling the car forward, but as he did, something caught his attention about twenty yards up and to the right. Something in the vague shadows.

"Hey, stop! Stop, you idiot!" Kimball bellowed, looking up from his phone just in time to see they were about to rear-end the white delivery van ahead of them that had come to a full stop. Matty slammed on the brakes, a high-pitched screeching filling the air as they avoided a collision by mere inches.

"What are you doing!" Kimball yelled.

"Look, over there! You see that?" Matty exclaimed, and flung his arm out, pointing a bony finger at the sidewalk.

KIERAN'S HEAD WAS SPINNING, blood dripping from his nose after striking the pavement. His hands stung like they had been dragged over broken glass as Thompson breathed menacingly on the back of his neck.

"You're coming with me to see Mr. Jamison."

"No, no...you're making a mistake," Kieran protested, shaking his head, squeezing his eyes shut against a building dizziness.

"No, you're the one making—"

Kieran felt a rush of air and movement as Thompson suddenly released him mid-sentence. He opened his eyes to find Thompson engaged in a scuffle with another man. The other man shoved Thompson hard and he stumbled backward, tripping on the low, wrought iron landscaping fence surrounding one of the sidewalk trees. Unable to catch his balance, Thompson fell flat on his back, striking his head on the curb. He moaned, writhing weakly before going limp.

Kieran stepped back, ready to run, when a hand crashed down on his shoulder. He spun to find a scrawny twenty-something grinning at him malevolently. Recognition registered just as Kieran sensed that the other man was standing right behind him. That man gripped Kieran's arm in a vise-like hold and whipped him around.

Kimball and Kieran locked eyes, the corner of Kimball's mouth turning up in a sneer as he spoke. "Long time no see, Catcher."

18

Evie bolted from the Duane Reade, glad more than ever that she had changed into her running shoes before leaving the hotel. Between the disgruntled customer and the pharmacy's computer freezing as Evie was trying to check out, she had been away for nearly forty-five minutes, almost the full amount of her allotted break. She had been gone too long. Gerald was most likely going to hear about it, which meant she was most likely going to hear about it from him. Though he often bellyached about her being late or forgetting something, the truth was that she was almost never guilty as charged. So, this time, when it was true, she expected he would milk the misstep for all he could.

The late-night summer wind fluttered across her face as she turned a corner, now just a few blocks from the hotel. She regretted not taking a cab, and not only because her calves were beginning to ache at this power-walk pace. As a general rule, walking a few blocks in Manhattan was much faster than driving, especially given the one-way streets and ever-present congestion down the avenues. But at the moment, traffic was lighter, and she probably could have saved time and her feet by hailing one.

She skirted to the left as two couples stepped out onto the sidewalk, emerging from a subterranean stairwell that led to the door to a little French bistro. A green canopy over the stairwell read "La Petite Oie." The couples laughed behind her as they whistled for a cab.

It's crazy that they're leaving a restaurant at two thirty in the morning.

An odd pang of jealousy struck. Evie normally wasn't prone to fits of wishing she were other people, but they sounded so carefree, so delighted with life that, for just a second, she wished that were her. What she wouldn't give for a night out with friends. She *did* have friends. But they were moms who got together for playdates, not nights on the town. And anyway, she barely had any time with Gabby in the evenings. She wouldn't want to spend her only free ones out with someone else. No, her nights were reserved for Gabby and the Wexsor.

The Wexsor.

Her arm swept across her stomach, an attempt to still the dread percolating there. In addition to the hotel calling her cell multiple times, Jamison had actually texted her, something he had never done before. She had given him her cell number years ago, when she started working with him. But, respectfully, he had not used it, instead always contacting her through the hotel line.

Even with this disquieting departure from routine, she had ignored his text, because she couldn't say anything to excuse the fact that she wasn't there. She had, however, returned the hotel's calls as soon as she left the drugstore, and was relieved to find out that there hadn't been an emergency; the calls were just to let her know that Jamison was looking for her. Even so, that still might mean trouble. At a minimum she would get another lecture from Jamison. At worst, she might lose her position as liaison to the game.

She took a deep breath. Maybe she was overthinking it. It wasn't ideal that she hadn't been there to take Jamison's call and fulfill whatever request he or one of his players must have had. But between Dana and the front desk, surely it was handled.

Surely that would have satisfied him.

She hoped so. The last thing she needed was to be fired from her role as Jamison's go-to person at the hotel. Not only would that be embarrassing, but it would cost her so much. The most important of which was the tips.

The tips I probably won't be getting tonight.

She reached the next intersection and stopped, waiting for the pedestrian signal to change. From behind her on the sidewalk, a man darted past her into the street, crossing against the light. A bus ambled through the intersection just in time to meet him in its lane. Angry honking ensued as the bus came to a stop to avoid flattening him. The man ignored it all, continuing to wherever he was going in such a hurry.

The bus continued on, and the red hand displayed by the pedestrian signal was replaced by a white walking figure. Evie stepped out into the street, increasing her speed with each step, her thoughts turning quickly to another problematic issue, which was that Kieran Carr had also called her cell and left a message.

She didn't even know that he had her cell number. She hadn't given it to him, and it didn't make sense that Jamison would have, in light of his warning to her earlier that evening to stay away from Kieran. After calling the hotel back, she had listened to Kieran's voicemail, in which he had simply asked her to call him on his cell as soon as possible. She hadn't. He had called one more time after that without leaving a message, but she had ignored that call too. She didn't know what to do.

She didn't want to give Jamison any additional grounds to be annoyed with her. But getting a call—*calls*—from Kieran...

What in the world was that about?

Her mind raced, drifting back to the elevator. Kieran had taken her by surprise, grabbing her like that. But would it have bothered her as much if Jamison hadn't insisted that Kieran was off limits just minutes before? She searched her feelings and found the answer.

Probably not.

Yes, Kieran was forward and, yes, there was a bit of bravado about him, but there was something very charming about him too. Like it or not, she had to admit that she was drawn to him.

Could that have been why Jamison was trying to reach me? To warn me that Kieran would be calling? To repeat his concerns and demand I ignore Kieran? The image of them in the elevator, interrupted by Thompson, flashed in her mind again. Her mouth went dry. *I'll bet Thompson went right back and told Jamison what Kieran did in the elevator. What if he took it the wrong way? What if he thought I encouraged Kieran or was egging him on?*

Evie groaned. This was extra drama she did not need. What she needed was to be back at the hotel already. Kieran Carr, his phone calls, and his flirting would have to wait. Grateful once more that she was not wearing her Jimmy Choos, she charged on toward the Wexsor.

19

The leather of the Traverse's back seat was cool against Kieran's face as he fell onto it after being tossed inside by Kimball. He pushed up into a seated position, but before he could even think about hopping out, Matty had hit the door locks.

"Don't try anything," Kimball ordered from the front passenger seat as Matty drove the SUV forward, making a left on Park Avenue to head downtown.

Kieran shook his head one more time, blinking rapidly. Focusing on Kimball, he realized that he had on the same army-green windbreaker Kieran had spotted on one of the men tailing him after he had left his apartment.

So, I was right. It was them.

He also noticed that Kimball held a pistol in his lap.

He was baffled. He had no idea how they could have found him. That apartment was something he had kept to himself. A safety net, a hiding place just in case one of the high-end scams he regularly ran went bad. And even then, there was nothing in it—no paperwork, no mail, no bills—that could have led them here, to his activities at the Wexsor. Saul had never known about those. Or at least, that was what he had thought.

Blood oozed down Kieran's nasal passage, and he sniffed deeply. "How did you find me?" he asked, pinching the bridge of his nose.

"Your roommates in Hell's Kitchen were more curious about you than they let on. You should've been harder on them," Matty answered, unable to disguise the self-satisfaction dripping from his words.

"Lesson learned," Kieran grumbled.

"Anyway, we found you. Now Saul wants to see you," Matty said.

"I was coming to see him."

"Sure you were," Kimball groused doubtfully. Matty scoffed.

"Seriously. Tonight. I was just getting my ducks in—"

"Save it. You'll have plenty of time to explain why you robbed Saul when you see him."

"I didn't *rob* him!" Kieran insisted, scooting forward so his head was between the front bucket seats. "I had a delay. That's all. A—"

Without warning, Kimball lifted his left arm from the armrest and ruthlessly drove his elbow backward into Kieran's nose. Kieran sucked in a sharp breath, shooting back in his seat and grabbing his face. Blood seeped from between his fingers. He squeezed his eyes shut tightly, then opened them, tears gathering in their corners.

"Hey!" Kieran bellowed nasally, his hand muffling the sound. "Not cool, man. Not cool!"

Kimball offered no reaction to Kieran's complaints. Instead he calmly pulled out his cell and tapped on it. Kieran leaned forward far enough to read Saul's name on the screen. His heart dropped ten stories within him, and he rocked back, his mind racing, desperately scrambling for a plan as the sound of expectant ringing filled the car.

There she is again.

It had taken Bruno a little more than forty minutes to make the trip from the Wexsor to the bar and back to this point, only two blocks from the hotel. Navigating anywhere near Times Square, regardless of the hour, meant long delays, slow driving, and lots of red lights, and this occasion had been no different. The timing was apparently providential, though.

Evie was practically jogging, her arms swinging awkwardly by her sides the way they do when someone is speed walking, but doesn't want it to look like they are. If she was in that much of a rush, maybe she would consider letting him give her a lift.

Maybe.

He was already positioned next to the sidewalk, having maneuvered into the far right lane in anticipation of making a turn one block ahead to get to the hotel. Stepping on the gas, he closed the gap between him and the car in front of him, pulled even with Evie, and slowed to a roll, just fast enough to keep up. She was so consumed with whatever was preoccupying her that she didn't seem to notice him tracking her, a dangerous state of mind for a person to be in when walking alone on these streets at night.

She definitely should not be out here walking by herself.

He depressed a button on his armrest, causing the passenger window to slide down noiselessly. "Hey there, Evie," he called out, leaning on the center console, one arm draped over it. He projected his voice as much as he could, alternating his gaze between her and the traffic in order to avoid rear-ending the car in front of him.

At his call, Evie's head jerked sharply to her left, stark apprehension clouding her visage as she seemed to realize someone was following her. That quickly changed when she met his gaze, her eyebrows rising in mild surprise, and a fleeting shadow of something that looked like...discomfort, passing across her face. The latter caused his heart to sink as she stopped, then came to him, leaning in through the open window.

"Bruno—what are you doing?" She glanced at the line of cars forming behind him. A honk issued from one of them, promptly echoed by several more in a variety of piercing tones. She tipped her head in the direction of the aggravated drivers to the rear. "You're holding up traffic."

"They'll live. You want a ride? I'm going there anyway."

Please say yes.

"Um...no. Thanks, but, I'm in a hurry—"

"That's why I'm offering. And look...it's late. You shouldn't be out here by yourself."

"I'm fine," she protested. "It'll be faster to walk. It's only a couple of blocks and you could get stuck in traffic. And I'm already in enough trouble. If I step out of this car at the Wexsor's entrance, I'll never hear the end of it. But thanks," she said, patting the top of the doorframe as she straightened up and stepped back. She waved, then resumed walking.

He rolled up the window. She was wrong about the traffic. It wasn't *that* congested. If he had driven her, at best, he would have had her there in less than a minute. At worst, they would arrive at the same time as if she had walked. As though proving him correct, the cars in front of him began moving faster, creating a gap that allowed him to roll right past Evie. He resisted the urge to look at her, instead keeping his eyes straight ahead.

He sighed, his shoulders caving slightly. *I've really screwed this up.*

How much did she have to *not* like him in order to justify refusing a ride when she was in that much of a hurry, at that time of night? *And the look on her face when she realized it was me in the car*!

Now he was certain he had handled this badly. He had just wanted to be respectful, take his time. Knowing her background, he had been determined to not overstep, to be mindful of her feelings. He had seen her situation as a minefield and had been so afraid of saying the wrong thing that he hadn't said anything at all. And now, she had the wrong idea. Her expression had said everything. She couldn't believe he was talking to her.

She thought he didn't like her.

"Idiot," he snapped at himself, smacking his forehead, then running a hand over his thick auburn hair, then down the well-groomed stubble of his boxed beard. He squeezed his eyes shut for a split second, causing him to miss that traffic had halted abruptly, nearly plowing into a taxi before slamming on the brakes. The SUV jolted to a standstill, followed by another series of angry honking behind him. His face grew hot, and he was preparing to honk back when, from the corner of his eye, he saw Evie about to pass by on the sidewalk again, having caught up to his vehicle in this incessant street game of leapfrog. She walked past his window, giving no indication that she had noticed him. He felt the sting of it acutely.

His eyes stayed trained on her till she turned the corner at Thirty-Fifth Street, headed down the last stretch toward the hotel. He had had such high hopes, had believed that his considerate approach would make her like him. But, apparently, it had the opposite effect. As he stared at the spot where she had passed from view, disappointment coursed through him, assaulting his gut.

Well, if you don't like the way this is going, don't whine about it. Change it.

The thought resonated from deep within him. From the same place that all notions that require committed resolve come from. The place that birthed his decision to pick himself up off the playground at eight and beat the stew out of Chris

Bleecker for pushing him down and stealing his Pokémon cards one too many times. The place that spawned his determination to keep taking the ACT—despite his dyslexia and urging of his counselors to settle—until he had earned a score high enough to qualify for a full scholarship to Rutgers. And the place that had driven him to get up off the tear-stained carpet of his room two years later, and march out to assume the role of man of the house after his father died unexpectedly, leaving him the sole protector of his mother and four sisters.

He would find a way to talk to Evie. To explain without sounding like an idiot. Or a nutcase. He would bring her around, convince her to change her opinion of him. And he would start tonight.

But for now, he would try to catch up and stay with her all the way to the hotel to make sure she arrived safely. *But not like a crazy stalker or anything,* he told himself, completely aware that that sounded exactly like something a crazy stalker would say.

20

"Younger, where are you?" Jamison said, speaking in hushed tones into his cell. He stood in the office bedroom of the poker suite, watching at a distance as the players, tensely enthralled in the current hand, waited for the river card to be dealt. The game was still going strong. Aside from Carr, all the players remained. Forrester was back in the hole, DeVries had never climbed out, and Dale and Crosby seemed to be holding steady at breakeven. Masters was the big winner and the others couldn't stand it. They were all playing with an eye toward taking the young brat down. Fortunately, it was prolonging the game—something Jamison desperately needed.

"Me and Richards are walking up to the lobby now," the gruff voice on the other end of the line reported. "There was a wreck on the FDR—"

"I don't care. Listen. The front desk told me Evie should be back any minute. They said she was on her break. At first they said she was unavailable, but when I pressed, the girl let it slip that Evie had stepped out to the pharmacy."

"Okay—"

"The closest one is just north of here. Turn left out of the hotel, then left at the light and straight up four blocks. Thirty-Ninth and Fifth. That's the most direct route. Follow that, and if we're lucky you'll head her off. Meanwhile, send Richards up to the suite."

"All right."

"Call when you've got her. Hotel security will let you in the back entrance. Take her straight up the service elevator to Room 1804. Got it?"

"Yeah, boss. Got it."

"Have you heard from Thompson?"

"No, why?"

Jamison sighed darkly. "He was following Carr. Last we spoke he was going to bring Carr back here, but I haven't heard back from him since and he's not answering his cell."

"You want me to go looking?"

"No. No, he'll turn up. If Evie's not lying about intending to come back here, then we've got a pretty good idea of where she is. Pick her up first. Then we'll deal with Carr."

"Why is she heading back to you if she's mixed up in this? Seems stupid."

"I think she's keeping up appearances. Now, go. I need you to move fast. I'm running out of time."

"Got it. I'm on my way."

~

EVIE TURNED the corner at Thirty-Fifth and basically began sprinting the last half block to the Wexsor. She hadn't been gone that long, but it *felt* like forever. Which meant it probably felt that way to Jamison.

Maybe I should have accepted Bruno's offer.

The SUV had not passed her yet, so unless he zoomed by in the next minute or so, he wouldn't have gotten her to the hotel any faster. Even so, she felt bad about refusing him. There was something in his expression, something...sad...when she had said no. Perhaps he wasn't as apathetic about her as she had come to believe. Riding with him for a couple of minutes might have given her a chance to break the ice with him. With the exception of Gerald, she generally had a warm working relationship with her fellow employees. She didn't like the awkwardness between her and Bruno, and frankly, didn't understand why it existed in the first place. Bruno asking her if she wanted a ride was the only exchange he had ever initiated. Maybe he was attempting to mend fences. Or build a bridge. Or whatever construction metaphor applied to a guy who had never paid her any mind suddenly taking such an interest in her personal safety and comfort.

Evie was still questioning whether or not she had made a mistake with Bruno when she noticed a man ten yards ahead, standing in her path, with a chest as broad as a bull and hair as dark as one. An odd sort of pleased recognition shone out from his stare as he narrowed his eyes, as if locking in some kind of targeting system. Adrenaline coursed through her veins, speeding her heart, her intuition firing on all cylinders. Everything about him screamed *run.* She stepped one foot back as the man's supple black leather jacket seemed to flex even wider.

Then he shot like a bullet toward her.

Evie pedaled backward, nearly tripping on her own feet. She flung her arms out wildly to steady herself and turned to run, the man's footsteps pounding in her ears as he hurtled closer, closer—

A gut-wrenching screech cut the night air as Bruno's SUV revved its engine and plowed onto the sidewalk just behind her. She yanked her head around, to see the front end slam into her pursuer, sending him flying across the width of the sidewalk into the adjacent building, where he crumpled to the ground, limp on the concrete.

Evie shrieked, then gasped for air as Bruno jumped out of the SUV and ran around the rear of it to her, grabbing her by the upper arms.

"Are you all right?" he yelled.

She barely heard him, even though he was inches from her face. She continued gasping heavily, her mouth wide, unable to draw her gaze from her motionless, would-be attacker, whose jacket lay open, revealing a shoulder holster bearing a gun.

"Evie?" Bruno said, shaking her gently. "Are you all right?"

Her focus dragged reluctantly off the man onto Bruno's forest-green irises. Dazedly, she registered that Bruno was there, talking to her, shaking her. *I never noticed his eyes were green before,* she thought oddly, as his voice rose in her ears, like someone had just pulled wads of cotton from them.

"Are you okay?" he demanded.

She sucked in a trembling breath and stepped out of his grasp. "Uh, I'm..." Her stare flashed between the man on the ground and Bruno, a wave of sick rolling over her. "What did you do?"

"I stopped him. He was going after you."

"But, but—you ran him over!"

Evie started to twist to look at the man, but Bruno grasped the bottom of her chin softly, stopping her. "Don't. Look at *me.*" She stopped trying to turn. "He was coming for you, understand?"

Evie nodded, his thumb and forefinger still holding her chin. "Yeah. Okay." She took a deep breath. "You're right. You're right," she agreed, stepping back from him. She turned away from the scene and put her hands on her hips, supporting herself as she bent at the waist, inhaling several steadying breaths through her nose.

She looked up again. Down the sidewalk, a few onlookers had begun to gather. Though they kept their distance, they pointed and gestured animatedly. Multiple cell phones were out, held chest high, presumably recording video or snapping photos.

"We need to call the police," Evie said, swiveling to Bruno.

"Okay, yeah. But first, you should get in the car," he said, taking her forearm. She pulled away.

"I'm fine, Bruno. Really. It just...shook me for a minute." Evie took her cell out. "I'm calling 9-1-1."

Bruno began to nod, then stopped, a puzzled look washing over his countenance as something drew his attention from her. Evie followed his gaze, and saw that the gathered spectators were pointing even harder in their direction, shouting words she couldn't decipher. She snapped her head to the right, following the trajectory of their gesturing, and an electric jolt reverberated through her.

The man was moving.

He had managed to sit up and was grabbing at the vehicle's grill, struggling to pull himself to his feet. Bruno dashed toward him, but before he had gone two steps, the man had righted himself and, wobbling slightly, reached beneath his jacket and whipped out his gun. Bruno skidded to a stop, his hands splayed out in front of him as a shield against the weapon aimed at his chest.

"Hey, man," Bruno said, as he took a step backward. "Don't be crazy. Just...don't, okay?"

The man stepped backward too, again and again, until he had put several yards between him and the SUV. Then he turned, ran through traffic to the opposite side of the street, and bolted down the block, until finally disappearing around the corner.

"WHERE ARE WE GOING?" Kieran asked, letting go of his nose to test the bleeding. It seemed to have stopped. He threw the wadded-up, bloodied napkins on the floorboard.

They had driven into the Murray Hill area, a part of Manhattan replete with townhouses, apartment complexes, and tree-dotted sidewalks. Cars were parked bumper-to-bumper against the curb wherever the drivers could get away with it.

"You got bigger things to worry about right now," Kimball muttered, his eyes glued to his cell phone. "Matty, right here. Slow down."

Kieran looked out his window as the Traverse slowed, staying in the right lane. Twenty yards ahead, Saul Kozlowski exited one of the parked cars, shut the driver's door, and stepped into the small gap between his car and the one in front of it. Matty pulled up to him and stopped.

Kieran tensed and scooted to the far left of the rear seat as the lock popped on the rear passenger door and Saul climbed in next to him. Matty rolled the SUV forward again as Saul turned toward Kieran, leaned against the locked door, and sighed heavily.

"You've been a hard man to track down, Kieran." Though Saul's words were metered and even, uttered without a trace of anger, the lack of emotion was more unnerving than if he had yelled at Kieran while waving a gun in his face.

"What happened to 'Catcher'?" Kieran asked. "We go way back, Saul."

"Nicknames are for friends. I don't think you're my friend anymore. And don't think some stupid nickname's gonna keep me from taking care of business."

"You gave me that stupid nickname."

"The fact that you played ball with my kid twenty years ago isn't going to help you if you stole from me. You steal from me, you pay."

Kieran rolled his lips inward, pinching them together as he

weighed how to proceed. Finally, his words spilled out in a torrent. "I swear, Saul. I didn't rob you. I didn't try to make off with your share. If I was going to do that, I wouldn't have stayed here, right? You get that?"

"What I get," Saul growled, "is that you've been holding on to three-quarters of a million dollars that you owe me. *Have* owed me, for almost two months."

"Hey—not two months," Kieran protested, shaking one hand vehemently. "The first few weeks we said 'no contact,' remember? That was your idea. No communication, no deposits, no nothing. Too much heat, too soon. You didn't want to draw attention."

"Yeah. For two weeks. We're seven weeks out now, Kieran. Where's my seven hundred fifty thou?"

"It's okay, all right? I just...needed some time."

"Why?"

Kieran swallowed, the grinding of his Adam's apple sounding loudly in his ears as it rose and fell. "You're not going to like it."

"Not a great start, kid."

"I've always been good at cards. Texas Hold'em if I can get it. In between con jobs, if I can find a decent game, I like to play. Most nights I end up leaving with more than I came with. It's legal, it's quiet...and it's not like I can put all my earnings from my con jobs in the bank."

"Okay."

"My cover as a gallery owner is perfect for playing cards—art dealer, lots of cash, bored, rich kid serving the one percent, yada, yada. I met Jamison at a charity gala thing where I was targeting one of my marks. Jamison's the guy that runs the table. Anyway, he invited me to play. So, I did."

"I'm still not hearing the part that tells me where my money is."

"I lost it."

"You what?"

"There was a game, the night after the job. I played—"

"You gambled with *my* money?" Saul said, his face turning to stone.

Kieran held his hands up. "No, no...not...just wait. I had a bad night. Lost hand after hand. I bought back in with the rest of my share from our job and lost most of that, too. I left that night five hundred K in the hole. I thought it was a fluke, you know? I rarely lost, and never that much. The next week I figured I could win it back. And I did. I started winning."

"Then, where—"

"Then, I started losing again. And I just...I just couldn't walk away. I thought that if I borrowed your share of the take from our job—only temporarily to stake another buy-in—I could make it all back and it would be like nothing happened."

"But you lost."

Kieran bit his lip and nodded. "Not all of it. Not all at once. I even came out ahead a couple of nights. But, eventually, yeah, I lost everything."

"So, pay me yourself. Out of whatever you've got lying around. With interest."

Kieran held Saul's gaze without answering.

"You don't have anything left, do you?"

Kieran shook his head. "I spent every dime I had trying to win your share back."

"Then you got a problem, kid."

"No, I *had* a problem. But I've fixed it. Really. I've got it all worked out *and* I was on my way to dealing with it, when *they* came along," Kieran explained, jerking a hand at Matty and Kimball.

Kimball grunted sourly. "You had *nothing* fixed when we found you. You were gettin' kicked around when we drove up—"

"That was temporary. I would've—"

"So, what's the fix?" Saul bellowed, interrupting their bickering, his glare betraying that the last of his patience was evaporating.

An alarm went off in Kieran's head. Saul losing it would be a very bad thing. Squashing any hint of nervousness, wanting to sound supremely confident, he said, "A few weeks ago, right after I lost the last of the cash, I came up with a way to get our money back, and then some. We're going to come out even better than before."

"And how's that gonna happen?"

Kieran stared him down. "With one little phone call."

21

"What now?" Bruno asked, staring at the spot down the street where the attacker had gone around the corner.

Evie shifted her focus from the SUV to where the man had lain on the ground, then back to Bruno. Her body felt like lead, sapped of all its energy in one fell swoop. "Let's just go to the Wexsor," she said, flinging a hand in the direction of the hotel further up the block. "We can call the police from there."

"Are you sure it's worth reporting at this point? I mean, he's gone." Bruno craned his head around the front of the SUV to get a better look at it. "There's no damage to the car. The hotel doesn't need to know."

Was he really worried about getting in trouble with the hotel at this point? "We have to report it, Bruno. In case."

"In case of what?"

Evie sighed loudly and heard the smack of exasperation in it. "In case he comes back or makes something up—says you hit him while he was crossing the road. The SUV might be fine, but he wasn't. Plus one of those people watching may have called already. How would it look if we didn't? Why wouldn't you want to report it?"

He tilted his head and huffed. "I just thought...it might create problems with the hotel, but—yeah. You're right. We should report it. Come on," he said, stepping to the rear passenger door and opening it for her.

Evie held her place for a second, even now considering refusing him and walking instead, though she wasn't sure why. Maybe out of habit. But then, exhaustion nudging her, she gave up the notion and climbed inside. Bruno shut her door, went around to the driver's side, and slid in. When he reversed the SUV, it bounced sharply as the front tires dropped off the curb and onto the pavement with a vibrating clunk, jarring Evie in her seat.

While they rolled toward the Wexsor, she studied his profile from her position in the back seat. His eyes were scrunched, so that tiny lines fanned out from the corners, and his short-trimmed beard didn't hide his well-defined jaw, which was set tight. *Was he angry? Nervous?* She couldn't pinpoint the feelings responsible for his clouded features.

"Are you sure you're okay?" His words cut the silence, and in a quick flash, he glanced over his shoulder at her, then back at the road. But it had been long enough for her to see that the emotion pooled behind his green eyes was not anger or nervousness. It was worry. Genuine worry. *For her.*

A flicker of shame nipped her insides.

He isn't stuck up or disinterested or whatever I presumed him to be. Maybe he was just really shy.

Her phone buzzed in her pocket, but she chose to ignore it, feeling an overwhelming need to right this wrong immediately. "Bruno, listen," she said, clearing her throat. "I really, *really*, appreciate what you did back there. If it weren't for you, I'd be in a bad way right now."

He shuffled one foot. "It's no problem. I'm glad I was there."

"Still. If they give you any grief or if you, I don't know, *need* anything because of what happened—"

The corner of his mouth turned up slightly. "Like what?"

"Like, I don't know, if you have to talk to the police and you need an attorney or anything—I'll pay for it."

He held up a hand to stop her. "I'm not going to need an attorney, and you wouldn't be paying for one if I did." She caught a glimpse of him in the rearview mirror, smiling warmly at her. A wry glimmer shone from his eyes as he spoke. "I wouldn't be much of a hero if I made the damsel in distress reimburse me for expenses."

She chuckled softly, returning his smile.

Half a minute later they were pulling into the SUV's reserved space in front of the Wexsor. Evie stepped out, meeting Wilson as he strode over from his post by the revolving doors, a confused expression on his face.

"What in the world, little girl?" Wilson said, his eyebrows knitted together so that they practically touched. "What're you doin' in there?"

"Bruno gave me a ride. I had some trouble down the street."

His gaze darkened. "What kind of trouble?" he asked, a note of protective concern in his tone.

She squeezed his arm and leaned in. "I almost got mugged," she whispered, then released him as she started for the employees' entrance.

This time he grabbed *her* arm, halting her. "You got what?" he said, his deep voice rising in pitch. "Is that what all that noise was down there? Are you hurt?" His neck stretched as he straightened to his full, towering height and peered down the block, as if trying to get a look at the person who had attacked her.

"I'm fine, Wilson. Bruno came along. He, um...stopped the guy."

Wilson's stare flicked to Bruno, who was coming around the

front of the SUV, then back to Evie. A knowing, borderline smug satisfaction crossed Wilson's visage. "Well, good for him. Good for you kid!" he bellowed as Bruno approached. "D'you call the police?"

Evie shook her head. "I'm going to in a minute. I wanted to get back here first. The guy ran off, so time wasn't of the essence."

"You should do it now. Don't wait. He get anything from you? Your wallet or anything?"

"No," she answered. "He didn't get a chance, thanks to Bruno. Didn't even touch me."

Wilson smiled approvingly at Bruno. "Nice."

Bruno inclined toward Evie, as if to be discreet. "I'll be out here, if you need something—when you talk to the police, I mean," he said. "If I get a call for a ride, I'll give you a heads up. Just so you know where I am."

Evie nodded. "All right. And I'll let you know what they say—whether they want to take a statement from you or whatever."

"Okay."

"And, hey," she said, her gaze softening as she gently laid a finger on his forearm, "thank you, again. Seriously. I don't want to think about what would've happened if you hadn't been there."

A faint blush rippled beneath Bruno's fair skin, but he shrugged nonchalantly. "No problem. Anytime."

Evie pretended not to notice Wilson's reaction to this, a subdued grin that made it clear he was amused by their little exchange. She offered Bruno one last appreciative nod, then walked to the employees' entrance and slipped inside. Before the door shut behind her, she heard Wilson's deep chuckle, followed by Bruno's exasperated, but good-natured, reply.

"Shut up, man. Just shut up."

"MR. JAMISON, WE'VE GOT A PROBLEM." Younger's voice rang out of Jamison's phone, followed by a sharp intake of breath.

Jamison stood near the bar, nursing a drink as he watched another high hand play out in the suite, this one cleaning out the last of DeVries's chips. DeVries's shoulders slumped as he raised his gaze to the ceiling and ran a hand over his balding head. Jamison set his glass down on the bar top and walked into the empty foyer. "Where are you?" he whispered harshly.

"I had to take off."

"You what?"

In gasping phrases, Younger rehashed the run-in with Evie and Bruno on the street. "I'm carrying, so I got out of there. I didn't think you'd want questions." He moaned again and sucked in air, cursing. "I think I might have broken a couple of ribs."

"Where is she now?"

"Um," Younger groaned, "I don't know. Should I come back to the hotel?"

Jamison squeezed his eyes together tightly. "No. Just stay where you are. If either of them sees you again it'll create too many issues." He looked over at Richards, the man who had arrived at the hotel with Younger, but had come upstairs instead of going to look for Evie. "Richards is here, but don't go far. I still can't reach Thompson and I may need you."

"What about my ribs?" Younger asked. Jamison heard a deep sucking sound on the other end.

"Can you deal with it a little longer?"

Younger sniffed and paused, apparently mulling it over. "Maybe. Yeah."

"Okay. Stay near your phone," Jamison ordered, then hung up and dialed another number.

It picked up on the third ring.

"Glick, here."

"It's Jamison," he said, clenching the phone. "I need you to do something for me..."

~

EVIE CAME through the door that led from the back office into the lobby to find the space exactly how it usually was on most weekdays at this time. At a little before three in the morning, only two people occupied the welcome area, huddled together in plush seats in a far corner by the window. A round of whooping laughter sounded in the bar across the way where several stragglers remained, likely from the wedding or some other gathering, pounding back one more before crashing into bed upstairs when the bar closed in a few minutes. Jamison was nowhere to be seen.

"You made it," Jayda called to her from the front desk, her eyebrows raised in faint chastisement. "I held Jamison off, but he wasn't happy."

"I'll bet. Thanks for covering for me."

"No problem," Jayda said. "You can return the favor sometime."

Evie nodded. "Absolutely." She sidled up to the concierge desk and moved to pick up the phone, when she spotted the manila envelope propped on her keyboard.

"Oh, yeah, I almost forgot," Jayda said, an amused smirk blossoming on her face. "*Someone* left that for you earlier."

Evie picked up the envelope, studying the note scrawled on it.

For Evie Diaz. Open ASAP. KCarr

The envelope was heavy and had a lump in the bottom. She set it back down.

Why in the world would Kieran leave her a package like this? Maybe she should just return it to him—unopened—at the next game he attended and put a stop to whatever *this* was. But curiosity begged her to peek inside. While weighing the two opposing considerations, dread pinged her gut as she imagined how Jamison would react if he saw the envelope—

Oh, no. Jamison.

What was she doing, standing here, pondering Kieran Carr and his odd behavior? Jamison was still waiting to hear from her. Pushing aside all thoughts of Kieran's envelope and whether or not she should open it, she dropped the envelope back on the desk, picked up the desk phone, and dialed the game suite directly.

~

"SHE'S BACK," Glick said. "In the lobby."

Holding his cell tightly against his ear, Jamison signaled to Richards, seated on the couch farthest from the game table. He popped up and followed Jamison, already barreling toward the foyer.

"Is she with anybody?"

Glick mumbled something, but Jamison couldn't make it out over Masters yelling at him, "Hey, Jamison, what's got you in such a hurry?"

Jamison turned back. Masters, a huge grin plastered on his face, was raking in yet another pile of chips, his luck having returned a few hands ago. Jamison covered the phone with his palm. "I've got to take care of something," he announced to the room. "I'll be back in a minute. In the meantime, Dana will get you whatever you need." After a quick nod from Dana, Jamison bolted out with Richards, the door swinging shut behind him.

"Glick, is she with anybody?" Jamison repeated, as he

hustled down the hallway to the elevator, his and Richards's shoes pounding with muffled thumps on the carpet.

"Nah, like I said," Glick answered, "she's by herself."

"How does she look? Is she nervous?"

"I don't know, man. She looks busy."

"Do not let her out of your sight," Jamison ordered as they reached the elevator vestibule, and he slammed a hand on the call button.

STANDING BEHIND THE CONCIERGE DESK, Evie replaced the phone's receiver into its cradle with a clack. She looked up at Jayda and bit her lip. "Dana said Jamison stepped out for a minute."

Should I stay here and wait for his return call, she wondered, *or track him down? Which would he appreciate more?*

"Maybe I should just go up there and find him," she finally decided, rounding the concierge desk. "If Jamison calls or comes down here—"

"I'll let him know you're on your way," Jayda offered quickly.

Evie smiled. "Thanks."

She was headed for the elevators, planning in her head what she was going to say to Jamison once she caught up to him, when she sensed that something wasn't quite right. At first she couldn't put her finger on it, then it struck her. The familiar click-click of her heels on the tile was absent.

Her heels.

She gaped at her black running shoes, horrified. In all the commotion, she had neglected to change back into her Jimmy Choos. She turned around, darting back to the desk, and as she reached it, realized with consuming dread that her heels weren't the only thing she'd forgotten. That call, the one she had ignored in the SUV as she was talking to Bruno—she had never checked it to see who it was from.

What was wrong with her? Had that near-mugging really thrown her off balance that badly? She ripped her cell phone from her pocket. *What if it was Eleanor who had called?*

She pulled up the log of recent calls and heaved a sigh of relief. It hadn't been Eleanor. She stared at the number. Though she didn't know it, she thought it might be the same one Kieran had called from earlier. He had left a message. She pressed play and held the cell to her ear.

"Hey, Evie, this is Kieran Carr again—"

Evie's heart gave a little kick at the sound of his voice, and she wondered once more exactly how he had gotten her phone number, a question immediately answered by Kieran himself.

"Look, I'm sorry. I know this is your private cell, and I convinced the front desk clerk to give me your number—"

"You gave Kieran Carr my number?" Evie snapped, spinning to Jayda.

"Sorry," Jayda mouthed, her face screwed up in embarrassment as she shrugged. "He's so cute and he begged me. He said he wanted to ask you out. I thought it would be good for you—"

Evie rotated away from Jayda, rolling her eyes as she refocused on what Kieran was saying.

"—not supposed to but it's very important. You've got to listen to me." His voice was stern, demanding her full attention. *"Something's happened tonight and...I don't understand it all...but I think Jamison believes that I tried to pull something over on him. At the game, maybe. I don't know. But whatever it is, it's bad. Really bad—"*

Evie's mouth grew dry as every concern she had dismissed over the last two years, every unheeded worry that the game wasn't completely on the up and up, every repressed fear that she might be playing with fire, collided in her stomach in a singular sickening implosion.

"—and he thinks it's my fault. He questioned me tonight after having that goon of his, Thompson, pull me out of the elevator. He let me go, but it was obvious he didn't believe me when I said I had no idea what he was talking about. Then he sent Thompson after me again once I left the hotel. He attacked me, Evie. Right on the street—"

Evie gasped involuntarily, the sound echoing through the nearly empty lobby.

"What is it?" Jayda called out, apprehension rippling her words.

Evie threw a hand up to stop her from speaking as she continued listening to the message.

"—beat me and was going to drag me back to the hotel, but I got lucky and got away. I'm okay, but Evie...he thinks you're in on it, too. Whatever 'it' is. I don't know if it's because we were talking or flirting tonight or whatever, or maybe it was something Thompson told him after seeing us in the elevator together, but you have got to get out of there. He's going to send someone for you just like he did for me. He's not going to believe you, Evie."

Images of the man stampeding toward her on the sidewalk right before Bruno hit him with the SUV flashed strobe-like in her mind.

"Don't wait for him to come for you, okay? I left an envelope for you with the front desk. Get it and leave right now, then call me back. We can figure this out, but you can't do this alone. And for reasons I can't get into, you can't call the police. Please trust me. I know Jamison seems like a good guy—"

From somewhere behind Evie, across the quiet lobby, foot-steps slapped on the tile. She swiveled, and saw James Jamison and another man exiting the elevator vestibule, headed straight for her.

"—but if there is money involved in this problem he's having, and I'm sure there is, Jamison will not play nice. He will hurt you to undo whatever it is he thinks we've done. Do not talk to Jamison. Do

not take his calls or respond to his texts. He'll try to manipulate you, threaten you. Call me as soon as you get this—"

As the last of Kieran's message played out, her gaze still fixed on Jamison, Evie took several hurried steps backward. Then she turned and sprinted for the concierge desk, grabbing up Kieran's envelope and speeding to the closest exit—the revolving front doors. The footfalls of Jamison and his companion thundered behind her as Jayda called after her again.

Evie charged through one of the revolving doors onto the sidewalk, frantically looking left and right like a trapped animal. Wilson, standing at his post by the entrance, was visibly startled by her abrupt appearance and moved toward her, one hand outstretched as if to calm her.

"Evie?" he asked, concern twisting his dark features as he bent lower to see eye to eye with her. "What's the matter?"

She didn't answer. Instead her brain whirled, seeking an escape, a way out. She spotted Bruno's SUV still parked in front of the hotel. He was leaning against the rear passenger side door, holding his cell phone as though he had just been looking at it, but now was staring at her.

"Did you reach...the...cops?" His words faltered, his tone rising in pitch as she ran at him.

"I need you to drive!" Evie yelled, pulling him off the door and ripping it open. "Now! Go!" she barked, climbing inside.

"Hey, what are you—"

Jamison burst through one of the revolving front doors, fury ignited in his cheeks as he skidded to a stop and zeroed in on Evie in the SUV. Bruno's gaze panned quickly from Jamison to Evie, then he took off running for the driver's side and jumped in.

The SUV's engine revved and the door locks popped just as Jamison got to it. He swung out, landing one palm on the window beside Evie, causing her heart to skip a beat. The SUV pulled into traffic, prompting the car behind it to slam on its brakes, its tires squealing on the pavement as the driver laid on the horn.

The traffic light was with them. Bruno sped across the intersection, changing lanes and leapfrogging vehicles, as Evie twisted in her seat and watched through the rear window as the Wexsor passed from view.

22

"What's going on?" Bruno snapped, desperate concern shadowing his face as he looked back at Evie in the rearview mirror.

She was perched on the edge of the middle row of the SUV, her cell and Kieran's envelope in her right hand, her left clasping the shoulder of Bruno's seat for stability. She breathed heavily and saw in her reflection that her eyes were wide with fright.

"It's Jamison."

"What do you mean?"

Evie blinked, set the envelope and cell on the seat, and brought her hand to her mouth. She rubbed it vigorously before answering. "Jamison—he's the man who runs the poker games that I manage for the hotel—he's the reason that guy came for me on the street. Jamison sent him."

The yellow signal at the next intersection was about to change to red as Bruno flew through it. He barely got down the block before he was forced to brake at the end of a line of cars awaiting a green light. He twisted around to look at her.

"What—why? Why would he do that?" he asked, his voice dubious.

Evie launched into the story, explaining Kieran's message, his warning, and how Jamison had come into the lobby right in the middle of her listening to it. When she got to the part about the envelope Kieran had left her, her gaze shot to it, still lying unopened beside her. She snatched it up, tore the top open, and turned it over. A small smartphone fell into her waiting hand.

"What? Why would he leave me a cell phone?"

Bruno shook his head. "I don't know, but I don't like it. Or this Kieran character—leaving you here, to take the brunt of whatever Jamison's dishing out."

He stepped on the gas as the signal changed, the SUV rolling on as he spoke, now entering the area of Midtown that constituted Times Square proper. Neon lights, the artificial midnight sun of Broadway, flooded the SUV's cabin and dispatched reds, greens, and blues off every reflective surface. The pedestrian traffic was at a low now, though people were still milling about on the sidewalks of the Great White Way even at this hour. Though Evie stared out the window, she didn't really register any of it, too consumed with the churning of her insides and racing thoughts as she tried to make sense of what was happening.

"Is there any truth to it?" Bruno asked. "Any truth in what Kieran is saying? I mean, you've been working with this poker guy for a while, right? Would he be capable of what Kieran says he's done?"

She snapped her attention back to him. "Well, I wouldn't have thought so. But after what happened to me, and apparently to Kieran, I just don't know." She racked her brain, searching for a morsel of reason to cling to. "He *was* acting differently earlier."

"Who? Jamison?"

Evie nodded just as her cell buzzed. "It's Jamison," she said, reading the screen. She let the call go without answering it.

"Should you maybe talk to him?"

She shook her head sharply. "Kieran said not to."

"How was Jamison different tonight?"

"Different in how he acted around me. He was unhappy about how much time Kieran had spent talking to me during the game tonight. He actually told me to stay away from him." Her phone finally ceased buzzing.

"Don't you have to talk to the players?"

Evie shrugged. "I guess he thought it was too much. He said it wasn't good for business for me to get involved with a player."

"Are you? Involved with this...Kieran person?" Bruno bristled as he said it.

"No," Evie said, slightly annoyed by his question. "I'm not. And I thought Jamison was overreaching, but then, after we left the suite, Kieran did sort of...I don't know, flirt with me, so maybe Jamison was right. But that doesn't explain what's going on or why he would think I'm part of whatever he's upset about. Or why he would send that guy after me."

Bruno switched lanes to speed past a taxi that had stopped to pick up passengers. "Were the police sending anyone over to deal with the guy that came after you? What did they say when you called them?"

Evie's gaze flipped up to the mirror. "I didn't call. I didn't have a chance. I wanted to touch base with Jamison first. I was planning to call after that, but then I got the message from Kieran."

She saw Bruno grimace in his reflection in the mirror. "Are you sure you shouldn't have just talked to Jamison in the lobby? What's he going to do to you in public, there in front of everyone?"

Her cell buzzed again. She lifted it to see who the caller

was, then dropped it back on the seat. "Now it's the hotel. Jamison probably asked them to call."

"You're positive you shouldn't talk to him?"

"You didn't see the way he was looking at me. Like he was going to eat me alive."

"I thought the poker game was legit."

"It is," she protested. But even as she said it, she knew that now she didn't completely believe it. "Or, at least, it's supposed to be."

"You sure? These things are always sketchy on some level."

Always sketchy. The words sounded in her ears like faint echoes of a warning bell she herself had rung before. He was right. There were times in the past when she had had her own suspicions, but she had dismissed them because it was, well, just easier.

"Yeah, maybe," she conceded, then began tapping on her cell.

"What are you doing?" Bruno asked. "Are you calling the police?"

"No. Kieran."

"You *need* to call the police."

"I will. I just want to understand what's going on first." She paused for a second in mid-dial, realization striking her. "And you shouldn't be here."

"What?" Bruno exclaimed, as a text from Jamison appeared on her cell.

Come back now.

Evie ignored it, instead replying to Bruno. "You shouldn't be here. You're probably in enough trouble after ramming that guy with the car—" She cut herself off and peered out the window. "Look, there's a spot there," she said, nodding ahead to an opening along the curb. They had moved beyond Times

Square and were driving east, somewhere near Park Avenue. It was darker, less populated, and plagued with significantly less traffic. They had left most of the revelers behind, and here shared the streets primarily with cabs and tourists walking back to their hotels after stretching the night as far as they could stand.

"Just let me out there," she told him, pointing to the space. "I'll grab a cab, figure this out and..." She stopped speaking when she met his green eyes in the rearview mirror, which were screwed up in complete disbelief. "What?" she asked.

He snorted. "Yeah, that's not happening. I'm not dropping you off in the middle of nowhere at three in the morning."

"It's not the middle of nowhere. It's off Park. I'll be fine."

"You'll be fine because you'll be with me. I'm not leaving you here." He sped past the open spot and she groaned.

"Bruno, come on—"

"It's Rune."

"What?"

"Rune. My friends call me Rune. If I'm going to be your getaway driver, I think that qualifies you."

She frowned at the slip of a smile on his face. "This is serious, Bruno."

"Rune. And, yeah, I'm aware. That's why I'm not letting you out. Call Kieran, find out what the heck is going on, and then we're calling the cops, whatever he says."

Evie's phone buzzed. She saw that it was Jamison again and her grip on it tightened. "What are you gonna do—just keep driving around till I get some answers?" she asked.

"Unless you have a better plan."

Evie sighed. She didn't want to admit it, but he was right. Not only was it unsafe to stand out on the street with no place to go, but something told her she didn't need to try to unravel this alone.

"Okay. We'll do it your way," she said reluctantly, then

tapped on her phone screen, putting it to her ear as it began to ring. The SUV raced across First Avenue and Bruno suddenly cut hard to the right, changing lanes and taking them onto the on-ramp for FDR Drive, the thoroughfare that hugged the eastern edge of Manhattan. The unexpected shift jolted Evie to the left, and her hand shot out against the door to brace herself.

"Where are you going?" she questioned, her puzzled stare reflecting back to him in the rearview mirror.

"Don't worry about it. Just make the call to Kieran. I've got an idea."

"SAUL KOZLOWSKI" might not be exactly a household name, but those who engaged in a certain type of enterprise in Brooklyn were definitely familiar with it, and likely fell into one of three categories: they either knew of him, did business with him, or were afraid of him. He was the third generation heir to a commercial legacy that included a wide variety of both legitimate and not-so-legitimate interests, and maintained a subtle notoriety, one that extended beyond the borough. Even though Saul's stomping grounds were in Brooklyn, he had plenty of contacts in Manhattan who owed him favors. Including Bill Muzzo, owner and operator of the Lucky No. 7 Lounge on the Lower East Side.

While Matty navigated the Manhattan streets, Saul reached out to Muzzo, looking for somewhere to wait until Evie Diaz called Kieran back. Now Matty pulled up to the Lucky No. 7, housed in an older brick building on Shelby Street between a cupcake shop and a dry cleaners. Though the bar had probably been closed for hours, at a little past three, Muzzo, heavyset and balding, met Saul, Kimball, and Kieran at the door in his ragged T-shirt and boxer shorts. He let them in and, without asking any questions, traipsed back upstairs to his second floor apartment. Matty stayed in the car, parked down the street.

The interior of the establishment was long and narrow. A dull, worn wooden bar extended the length of the space, ending just before a short hallway leading to the bathrooms at the rear. Suspended brass light fixtures, several of which were missing bulbs, cast a dim glow about the room, sending thick shadows across the three of them, now seated at the bar on red pleather-covered stools. They were the only people in the place.

The odor of bleach, stale rags, and spilled beer floated up to Saul from the bar's surface, mixing with the acrid aroma of the cigar he had lit. He timed his puffs so evenly, it was almost like a dance, the curls of smoke ribbons twirling above his head. The sheet mirror hanging on the wall behind the bar, somewhat obscured by shelf after shelf of bottles filled to varying degrees with gold, brown, and even green and blue liquids, offered a hazy reflection of the whitish vapors as the men stared and waited.

Saul cut side glances at Kieran as he puffed in silence. Kieran sat loosely on his stool, one foot resting on a spindle, the other planted on the floor. He leaned heavily on the bar top, his head propped up nonchalantly on one elbow. To the casual observer, it might appear that Kieran was completely unfazed by this turn of events, but Saul knew different. He could see it in Kieran's right middle finger, tapping incessantly against his tumbler so slightly that Kieran himself probably didn't notice it. But Saul did.

He didn't blame the kid for trying to give off an air of confidence. At this stage, confidence was one of the few plays he had left in the game. A game which he was currently poised to lose unless this woman picked up the phone and dialed him. Soon.

Saul set his cigar on the counter. "It's been a while, Kieran. You sure she's gonna call you back?" he groused. Though he didn't turn to look at Kieran, his gaze flashed to the kid's reflection in the mirror in front of them. Kieran glowered back.

"She'll call," he answered assuredly. His finger—momentarily stationary while he spoke—resumed tapping nervously.

"I don't know why she would," Kimball mumbled caustically, the words barely slipping between his lips.

Kieran's eyes narrowed and his nose scrunched. "Because she's into me, all right?" he said, his body snapping to attention, his limbs rigid. "Because she's going to get that message and want to know what it's all about, and she's not going to be okay just ignoring it. I'm telling you, when she hears that message she'll call."

"Maybe Jamison got to her first."

"Nah. This is gonna wo—"

Kieran's phone buzzed violently, jiggling across the bar top. Shooting a victorious glare at Kimball, he snatched it up and pressed the answer icon.

23

"Evie?"

"Kieran?" Evie replied, noticing her voice sounded higher pitched than usual. She straightened up in her seat, then leaned slightly toward the center console. Rune's eyes flashed to the rearview mirror, connecting with her briefly before returning to the road.

"Evie! I was getting worried," Kieran said, his voice filtering through her earpiece, ripe with relief. "I'm so glad you—"

"What is going on?" she snapped before he could finish. "Some guy came after me on the street, then I get this message from you, and your envelope, then Jamison comes into the lobby, looking like he wants to kill me—"

"Wait—are you okay? What guy came after you?"

"I don't know. I mean, yeah, I'm fine. But I don't know who it was on the street. He ran off."

"Ran off where?"

"It doesn't matter. Tell me what's happening. Why does Jamison want to talk to me? What does he think I've done? What does he think *you've* done?"

"Hey, slow down, okay? It's gonna be all right."

She could picture his hazel eyes narrowed, small furrows in his forehead as he tried to soothe her. But she didn't want soothing. She wanted explanations. Heat flushed through her as she laid into him. "*Hey*, start explaining." Her words were sharp and demanding, and the moment she spoke them, she felt slightly embarrassed by her lack of reserve. But he wasn't getting to the point, and she was running out of patience.

"Yeah, okay, sure," Kieran answered, a modicum of surprise in his tone, "but calm down, all right? I'm not the enemy here. I called to warn you, remember?"

She sighed, squeezing her eyes tight and forcing herself to inhale deeply through her nose. "I know. I'm sorry, it's just...this is ridiculous. You need to tell me what's—"

"Did you talk to Jamison?"

"No. I just ran."

"Good girl."

"Kieran, seriously, tell me what's going on."

"Where are you?" he asked.

"We're driving around."

"Who's we?"

Evie's gaze shot sideways to Rune, who was rapidly maneuvering the SUV south on FDR Drive toward Downtown. His green eyes were dialed into the traffic, his mouth fixed as he concentrated.

"I jumped in a cab parked outside the hotel to get away from Jamison," she lied. Rune's eyes flashed questioningly to hers in the mirror, then darted back to the road as she continued. "I didn't know where to go, so I'm just having him drive me around until I figure out what's next."

What? Rune mouthed in the mirror, squinting as he eyed her reflection again. Evie pursed her lips and shook her head, waving a hand at him to hold him off.

"Come meet me," Kieran pushed. "I'll explain then, but not over the phone like this."

"No, tell me now."

"I can't do that," he said. "I don't even know everything, and I don't want you talking about this in front of the cab driver."

"You can tell me *something*. Tell me something now or I won't meet you."

Kieran exhaled. "I think someone stole from Jamison tonight. And for some reason, he thinks it was me."

"Was it?"

"What? No! Evie come on, you know me."

She sniffed, killing a few seconds while she thought. In truth, she didn't really know Kieran Carr that well. Yes, she had spoken with him more than she had with any other player during the time that he had been attending games. And yes, there was a certain connection between them. A certain... potential. But there was still so much she didn't know. Even so, what she had learned made it exceedingly difficult to imagine him pulling anything like what Jamison was suggesting. Or needing to. Kieran was quite well-off, the owner and operator of his own private art gallery in Brooklyn. She had Googled it, even gone by there out of curiosity for a peek one Saturday before realizing it had limited hours and was accessible by appointment only. He was legitimately wealthy. And smart. Too smart to try to steal from James Jamison.

"What was stolen—and why does he think I'm involved?"

"I told you on the phone earlier, all I can figure is that he's seen us together and has made the leap from that to assuming that we are working together in whatever he's upset about."

"Why did you leave me a cell phone?"

Kieran sucked in a breath. "I'm not sure, but I think it's possible that Jamison could track you by your cell. He's got connections, you know, given the kind of players that come to his games, that could possibly make that happen. We don't want to give him the chance to find you before we go to the police."

"Whose cell phone is this?"

"It's a prepaid burner. I grabbed it near the hotel at one of those all-night convenience stores when I realized that Jamison might go after you. This way you can stop using yours. I put my number in it. You should take the SIM card out of your phone and turn it off, that way Jamison can't use it to find you."

"*If* he can track it."

"Is it worth finding out whether he can?"

Evie exhaled, overwhelmed by the course of events and the inexplicable game of chase she now found herself in. She knew what the prudent thing to do was, and she was going to do it.

"I want to go to the police," she told Kieran matter-of-factly, rubbing a palm along the fabric of her pant leg nervously. "Now."

"Yeah. Okay."

His easy capitulation surprised her. "Really?"

"Yeah, sure. But together. Let's go together. It'll make more sense that way. We can each tell our side of it. Look, I've got my car. Let me come pick you up."

She looked at Rune again. It was better this way. She shouldn't have involved him in the first place.

"Fine," she agreed. "I'll text you an address."

24

One minute after Evie hung up with Kieran, Rune pulled into a rare open parking space on a side street off Sixth Avenue in Greenwich Village. As he shifted into park and turned in his seat to face her, Evie worked to remove the cover from the back of her phone.

"What are you doing?" Rune asked.

"Removing the SIM card," she explained, extracting the tiny electronics card that dictated the phone's number and service. "Kieran thinks Jamison might have contacts he could use to track me by my cell phone." Pulling the battery out also, she slipped both into the right pocket of her pants.

"He might be right about that," Rune conceded.

She looked up, taking in the view around them. "Why are we here?"

He pointed to a diner on the street corner. "That's where we're headed. I know it. It's quiet this time of night. A good place to meet." He frowned, doubt creasing the corners of his mouth. "Are you sure about meeting with Kieran? You're not worried about...I don't know...his part in all this?"

She couldn't keep skepticism from crinkling her eyes. "He's

my friend, Bru—Rune. It's fine. Whatever his part is in this, I don't think it's what you're thinking."

"Evie, you're wrong about him being your friend. If he was your friend, he wouldn't have overstepped the mark, putting you in a bad position by always flirting with you, and now dragging you into this." His gaze fell on Evie's phone, now untraceable. "It seems to me that Kieran is working awfully hard to keep you from talking to Jamison."

His words carried an unmistakable distaste for Kieran, and her blood curdled a bit in reaction to them. Okay, yes, Rune was more than going out of his way to help her. But his ire toward Kieran, this second-guessing her when he didn't even know her —and his comment that Kieran had flirted with her? *He* was overstepping.

"You're concerned about Kieran *keeping* me from Jamison? Jamison? The same man who beat Kieran and then sent a guy to do who-knows-what to me on the street? The same guy that chased me out of the hotel? That guy? You're concerned because Kieran wants to keep *that guy* away from me?"

Her words cut through the cabin, leaving a hollow silence in their wake.

Rune swallowed, gathering himself, then spoke carefully. "I just...I just think he's not telling you something."

She took a deep breath, trying to calm herself. "Yeah, you're right. He's not," she agreed, sounding less hostile, though her aggravation still seeped through her tone. "But that doesn't mean he's wrong about Jamison."

"I just don't see what it could hurt to talk to Jamison."

"And I don't see what it could hurt to wait to talk to Jamison until we get the full story from Kieran."

Rune looked away, staring out his window as he leaned back in his seat and rubbed his stubbly beard. Evie collapsed into her seat as well. "Rune, I'm not saying that I trust Kieran completely, or that something isn't wrong here. But I genuinely don't think he's out to get me. I think he wants to help. And I don't want to talk to Jamison until I've had a chance to see Kieran face-to-face and get a read on the whole thing. Okay?"

He nodded without turning. "Okay."

That settled, her thoughts returned to his earlier comments, and she inclined her head slightly. "What did you mean a minute ago, when you said Kieran was 'always flirting with me'?"

Rune's focus slowly swiveled to her. He drew his shoulders up and shrugged. "Only...that I've seen him doing that before. In the lobby when you've been there with him. He flirts. With you."

"I don't remember that."

"It happened," he insisted staunchly. "Happens. I remember because every time I think how inappropriate it is."

Evie felt her eyebrows rise. It sounded a little as if he was admonishing *her* for her role in this alleged flirting. She opened her mouth to defend herself, but he pressed on, overriding her.

"And I was right, wasn't I? Because Jamison didn't like it either."

"I wouldn't go comparing myself to Jamison right now," Evie said.

"No. But still."

He grew quiet, his face falling down toward the gearshift, which seemed to have suddenly become very interesting. Something inside Evie softened.

"Rune, I appreciate where you're coming from. I do, really. But Kieran's coming to get me. You should go back to the hotel, and maybe you can talk your way out of this—tell them that you didn't know what was going on, which you didn't. That I just asked you to drive and that you don't know where I am."

She started to type a text message into the phone Kieran had given her when Rune reached out, gently squeezing her wrist. "Wait. Okay? Just hold on."

She jutted her chin out and cocked her head. "What?"

"I drove down here for a reason. A buddy of mine's a patrol officer. Night shift right near here in the Village. Talk to her. See what she thinks."

"Kieran's waiting for me to give him an address so he can meet me."

"So, let's get in touch with Layla now. Then when Kieran shows up, the cops are already here. No more delay. That's what you want anyway, right? To go to the cops?"

"Of course—"

"Then there's no reason not to reach out to her. If Kieran's on the up and up, I mean."

"He is."

"Okay, so we get her here, and you tell her your story. Then she can connect you to the right people, and you won't have to wander into some precinct and try to convince someone to take you seriously."

Evie considered his suggestion. It would save time. And hassle. She exhaled in submission. "Yeah, okay. Fine."

He bit his lip as a thin, sheepish grin emerged. "Good, because I texted her on the way over. She'll be here any minute."

25

Jamison rubbed the back of his neck, watching from the bedroom doorway as the game officially shut down for the night. It was 3:20 in the morning, and Forrester had just won the last hand, finally cleaning out Masters in one fell swoop, but leaving the others with a respectable result. Jamison's chest sagged with dread. He was out of time.

"And that's why you gotta watch the old guys," Crosby chortled, leaning back and nodding at the now-empty space where Masters's chips used to be.

"Quite a turn around," Thaddeus Dale agreed, his clipped accent rising above the clinking sound of glasses being removed by Dana as she worked to clear the table.

Masters glared at Crosby, cursing him as he stood.

"Respect your elders, kid," said DeVries, a pleased note in his tone as he tapped a finger on one of the stacks he had managed to amass during the last hour of play.

"Yeah, yeah," Masters groaned in a thick voice, shaking his head as he made his way toward the front door. "I'm out." He turned to Jamison, his posture sagging and his eyes noticeably bloodshot. He gave a little nod and a deflated two-fingered salute. "Jimmy. See you next week."

Jamison returned the nod and watched the kid go. The others were rising from the table, leaving their chip stacks to be counted by Jamison, then cashed out. He coughed into one hand, then folded and unfolded his arms, shifting in place while the others stepped back.

"Let's get this going, Jamison. I'm ready to head home," DeVries barked, stifling a yawn. "I got a killer migraine and sleep's the only thing that'll get rid of it."

"Sure," Jamison replied, slowly walking to the table. Each player's chips were stacked neatly at their spot, waiting to be tallied and exchanged for a check. He placed his fingertips on the edge of the table, rubbing them on the padded rail.

"Yo, Jimmy. You awake over there?" Crosby asked before downing the last of whatever was in his tumbler.

Jamison exhaled. "Sorry, gentlemen," he said, and began counting their chips. After about fifteen minutes, he had closed out Crosby, Dale, and DeVries, who promptly left once he handed them their checks. Only Forrester remained.

"Saved the best for last, eh?" Forrester asked, sparing Jamison a tired, but amiable, grin. He was seated on the couch near the bar, reclining heavily into its plush cushions. "I gotta tell you, I am glad this one wrapped up when it did because I am bushed."

Inhaling through his nose, Jamison sat down across from Forrester on the other couch and leaned forward, propping his elbows on his knees. He squinted tensely.

"Henry, we need to talk."

"TWENTY-FOUR HOURS," Jamison barked into his cell phone. "That's all we've got."

"Is the game over?" Younger asked.

"A little while ago. We've got to find her." Now alone in the suite with Richards, Jamison had opened the blinds and was pacing in front of the window. He looked out on the miles of blackness peppered by the glow of the city lights hundreds of feet below him. In the expanse, between buildings, he could see where the western edges of Manhattan met the charcoal waters of the Hudson River. In the vicinity of Thirty-Seventh Street, a steady parade of red taillights snaked toward the Lincoln Tunnel, which would carry the vehicles into New Jersey.

"You want me to head over there? I took four Advil to stave off the pain from the ribs. It's bad, but manageable for the moment."

"Maybe. Thompson's still MIA, and I may need at least two of you to help me handle this."

Younger paused. "Did you let him know?"

"He doesn't need to know. Not yet," Jamison insisted.

"He keeps a pretty tight rein on the payroll—"

"You'll get paid. Don't worry."

"And what about the medical bills?" Younger pressed.

"What medical bills?"

"A dude hit me with a car an hour ago, man. On your clock."

"We'll deal with it. I promise. But right now—just sit tight."

"You sure? If you have any leads on her I could try to find her."

"No. She took off with the hotel driver, but she could be anywhere by now."

"What about him? You got any way to find him? What if you told the hotel you needed a car?"

"Nah. They'd see through that. The woman at the front desk saw me chasing after her. I had to come up with a story about her being upset about a player that gave her a hard time.

I think they bought it. They tried calling her for me, anyway, but she didn't pick up."

"Well, is there anyone she'd turn to—anyone she would talk to about where she's headed?"

"Ahhh," he groaned, lowering his head and passing a hand through his hair. "I don't know."

"What about the cops? You think she'd go to them?"

"If she's involved? No. Not a chance. If I'm wrong and she's not involved? What would she tell them? 'Some guy approached me on the street and the hotel driver ran him down'? I mean, you didn't do anything, right?"

"No. I went for her, but the guy hit me before I could get there."

"So, even if she's innocent, there's nothing for her to tell the police. You have more to complain about than she does. But her running out like that when she saw me?" He shook his head. "No. The only reason she would do that is if she's in on it. Which means she definitely won't be approaching the police."

"Okay, then, where do we start?"

Jamison stared out the window, watching as a yacht, maybe a party cruiser or a private vessel, navigated the Hudson with lights strung from bow to stern. He traced it with his gaze as it cut through the black water, his stare drifting along with it until it disappeared behind a building. Jamison's eyes followed the lines of the building to its rooftop, where antennas, fixed with blinking red and white beacons, stretched toward the heavens.

"Jamison?" Younger prompted when he didn't get an answer.

"Yeah, I don't know."

"What about focusing on the driver? Maybe somebody at the hotel is friends with him, connected to him on Snapchat or Geobuddies or whatever? Ask around at the hotel. Then maybe you track him through one of those apps or through—"

"Wait, wait, wait," Jamison sputtered. His eyes flicked to the wall, where he unseeingly studied it for several moments, zeroing in on a thought. Then he jerked, and stepped quickly toward the door, motioning for Richards to come with him. "I've got it," he announced triumphantly to Younger. "Just stay near the phone, in case I need you," he said, and hung up as they left the suite.

FIVE MINUTES LATER, Jamison was back in the security office with Glick, the monitors before them displaying the video feeds from various cameras on the property.

"...like I told you when you called, he's not answering his phone," Glick said, reclining so far back in his chair that it threatened to crash backward onto the floor. "I don't know how else to reach him."

"I understand that," Jamison reiterated from where he stood behind Glick. "But I'm not here to ask you to call him. I want to know if you can track the hotel's SUV through the manufacturer, with some kind of satellite service that the hotel pays for monthly, or whatever."

A phone rang somewhere down the short hall that linked the spaces that made up the offices. Currently Glick was the only member of security personnel present and he ignored the call. Jamison presumed the others were dispatched to duties in other parts of the hotel.

"No. That wouldn't work." Glick shook his head, his curls flopping around. "We'd have to file a police report before they would access it. And I'm assuming that's not something you want to do."

Jamison frowned, shifting his weight to his back foot while he closed his eyes and rubbed his thumb repeatedly across his left lid. He had to find this driver. He had to find Evie. "We'll have to check her home, then," he mumbled.

"What?"

Jamison exhaled sharply. "Nothing. Just...let me know if he calls in or comes back—"

"Now, we may not be able to use the manufacturer's locator service, but we could check the GPS tracker *we* installed. I mean it's not the same as the manufacturer's and probably not as precise—"

Jamison turned on Glick, his expression incredulous. "You've got a tracker on the SUV? Why didn't you say something?"

"I *did* say something. Just now. You came in here asking about the Lexus people, not—"

"Forget it, it doesn't matter. Just find it."

26

In keeping with its name, the Midnight Diner was open twenty-four hours, seven days a week. It sat on the corner of a quiet street on the east end of Greenwich Village, its red neon sign wrapping around the outside roofline, burning the diner's name into the dark of night. Booths upholstered in pumpkin-orange vinyl lined the windows. Tables filled the dining space, separated from the kitchen by a long, chrome-trimmed bar with matching orange vinyl stools.

A perky jingle from the bell suspended by a cord over the entrance greeted them as Rune pushed it open. He and Evie stepped inside just as a waitress hustled out from behind the bar carrying a tray laden with coffee and plates stacked with pancakes. She moved past them without making eye contact as she headed for a table in the far corner, but did abruptly shake a hand around the room, as if to say, 'take any seat.'

At three thirty in the morning the place was still about a third full and serving up orders from a greasy laminated menu to anybody hungry enough to be hunting down food at that hour. The patrons were spread out, leaving Evie and Rune several seating options that would offer them a modicum of privacy. After a brief survey of the room, Evie turned to the right, zeroing in on a booth by the front window that wasn't near anyone else and slid in. As Rune took the opposite side, a text alert sounded from the phone Kieran had given Evie.

"Is that him?" Rune asked. She nodded as she read the text. "What did he say?"

"He'll be here in fifteen minutes," she answered, setting the phone on the table and looking up. A sense of calm settled in her chest. Kieran would arrive soon and he would give them answers. "I didn't tell him about your police friend. I didn't want to scare him off."

Rune's face darkened in concern. "It bothers me that you think that he would be put off by that. There's no reason calling the police should scare him off."

Evie's jaw clenched. "He just...seemed to have a set idea about how he wanted to do this."

"Well," he started, shrugging unsympathetically, "he'll just have to adjust."

"You really don't like him, do you?" Evie asked pointedly.

"Never met the guy."

She sensed there was more he wanted to say. "But?"

He cocked his head and sniffed. "It's a vibe he gives off. Like something's just not right."

Evie was about to reply, when she noticed his phone on the table. Jamison knew she was with Rune. And the hotel knew Rune's cell number. "I think you should take the SIM out of yours too," she said. "Jamison knows you drove me away from the hotel. If he hasn't already thought of using your phone to track me, he will eventually."

"He doesn't have my number."

"He'll get it. It's not hotel policy to give numbers out, but he'll flash some cash and make it happen."

Rune seemed to consider this for a moment, then picked up

his cell. "I'll need a paperclip." He eyed the waitress across the room. "Maybe she can get me one."

Cool air blew through rattling vents in the ceiling, sending the scent of high-octane coffee, brewing somewhere by the bar, wafting over the table. The aroma was rich and soothing, and Evie breathed it in deeply. It pricked her senses, causing her stomach to rumble. She had missed the light meal she typically ate during her mid-shift break, usually around one in the morning.

For the first time that evening she took stock of herself. Her legs ached a bit. And her neck was tight. She reached up to rub it, beginning to truly feel the weariness setting in. Normally she had no problem remaining at full power throughout her shift. She was used to working nights. She had done it for a long time. But tonight's events were taking a physical toll, and Evie found she was craving the jolt of energy a stiff cup of coffee would provide.

Fortunately, the waitress was making her way over. She sidled up to their table, tall and thin, her stark-straight blonde hair pulled back in a severe ponytail, her nails painted a charcoal color. Her white plastic name tag with gray engraved letters read, "Allison." Faint freckles dotted her young face. "What can I get you?"

She had looked to Rune first, but instead of answering, he nodded toward Evie. At the gesture, Evie felt the corner of her lip pull up in the beginnings of a soft smile. Deferring to her and allowing her to order first was something Mark used to do.

She lifted her face to Allison. "Coffee, please. Thanks." When Evie looked at Rune to signal that he should order, his eyes were narrowed quizzically.

"That's it?" he asked, surprised. "You're not going to eat? You've got to be starving."

Evie sighed. "A little, but I don't know if I could eat."

"Try. You'll be sorry later if you don't."

"Um, okay. Toast, I guess? Maybe an egg—scrambled?"

Allison scribbled on a small pad. When Evie didn't ask for anything else, she pivoted toward Rune. "And you?"

"Coffee."

Allison raised her eyebrows, as though cuing him to continue with the rest of his order.

"Just coffee."

"Ohh-kay. Got it," Allison replied, jabbing her pen on the pad as she finished, then swept away from the table.

"Oh, uh, and a paperclip?" he called out after her. "If you've got one lying around?"

Allison's brow furrowed at the request, but then she shrugged. "I'll see what I can do," she said, before continuing into the kitchen.

"So, I should eat, but you don't need to?" Evie asked, echoing his question to her.

"Nah. Had a sandwich in the car earlier. I do that most nights around ten or so, in between runs. But you skipped lunch. Or, I'm guessing you did, with everything that's gone on tonight."

He said it with the air of someone well acquainted with her schedule, enough to know that she was off of it tonight. She stared across the table and for the first time, under the meager glow from the globe pendant hanging over their table, finally got a good, solid look at Rune Agnellini. Aside from the last hour, their interactions had been so brief because of his apparent disinterest, and because they happened right in the middle of work, that she had never stopped to do more than take vague note of his features. Now she registered that his reddish hair stuck up a bit at the crown, quirky spikes that teased that a devil-may-care attitude might reside somewhere beneath his reserved exterior. The groomed scruff of his beard—a sculpted five o'clock shadow that perfectly highlighted his cheekbones when he smiled—

projected a measure of self-possession. Confidence. The combination was undeniably attractive. And his eyes...Rune had always avoided her, leaving her with the impression that he was somewhat cold. At least toward her. But at this moment, those green eyes opposite her held something else. There was warmth there. A certain—gentleness. And another...quality... she couldn't quite place. But before she could discern what it was, he broke the connection and glanced away.

"Rune," she said quietly, "why are you helping me?"

He blinked back to her, a small grin erupting. "Because... you jumped in my car like a crazy person and told me to drive."

She chortled softly. "Yeah. Yeah, I know, but...I mean, you could've dropped me off, you could have taken me to a police station, but all this?" She gestured at the restaurant. "Why?"

Once again he looked away from her, out the window that separated them from the street beyond. She followed his gaze so that they were both staring out at the city through glass marred by hazy streaks left behind by poor attempts to clean it. The glare from the overhead lighting revealed a spot just above the top of Rune's seat, where a tiny, smudged handprint rested, probably slapped there by a toddler corralled between the window and a parent at some point in the past. Four little fingers and a thumb, like the colorful poster-paint handprints Gabby brought home from preschool.

"You needed help," he said, interrupting Evie's brief reflection on Gabby and drawing her focus back to him. "I wanted to help. Simple as that."

Despite his words, something in his demeanor suggested otherwise. The slight, questioning flicker in his eyes; the infinitesimal drop of his head. It was as if he were evaluating her reaction, waiting to see whether she accepted what he said at face value. But no matter what he said, "simple" wasn't a word she would use to describe what was going on.

"But," she pressed, leaning in, "you've hardly ever spoken to me. Every time I tried, you just sort of—"

"Blew you off. Yeaaaah," he drawled, grimacing, "that was pretty stupid." Her mild surprise at his sudden confession must have shown on her face, because he continued, "Aww, don't look at me like that. I wish I had some really slick reason to give you to explain why I acted that way, but..." He trailed off, shaking his head.

"Slick's overrated," Evie said. "How about just honesty?"

"Okay," he said, sitting up straighter and folding his hands in front of him on the table. "The truth? I just wasn't sure how to behave around you. I asked Wilson about you early on, and he told me your situation and that I should be sensitive to it. He said you didn't need anyone coming on real strong. So, I don't know, I just didn't want to overstep. I didn't want you to think I was...coming on to you or something, so I went full on in the other direction."

That explains it. He wasn't the first guy to act strangely around her because she was a widow. It had happened occasionally, when someone would meet her for the first time and, somehow, the fact that Mark had died would come up. At that point the person's whole affect would change, and they would begin treating her *more* kindly—excessively so—like she was a blown glass ornament that couldn't be dropped. She detested that part. The way the tragedy would define her in the person's mind after that. A label she couldn't shake. Rune's approach wasn't much better, but at least he hadn't turned her into an emotional charity case.

"But you've been there for months now," she protested.

"I know. But I just couldn't find the right time, or the right way...and then so much time had passed it felt weird saying anything. Later, once Wilson got to know me, he said I wasn't paying you *enough* attention..."

Allison returned to the table with their coffee. She set an

off-white mug before each of them, steam spiraling up from the ebony brew. "Thank you," Evie said.

Allison gave a sharp nod. "Food'll be right up," she said. "And," she continued, slapping a paperclip on the table, "here."

"Thanks," Rune replied. Allison walked away, and he used the clip to make quick work of extracting his SIM card. He slipped the card, phone, and clip into his pocket, as Evie reached for the individual cylinders of cream in a ceramic dish by the salt and pepper shakers. She promptly peeled the lids off of four of them and dumped them in her coffee, turning it the color of caramel. She ripped open three sugar packets and poured them in as well. As she stirred the concoction with a spoon, she glanced up and saw him eyeing her with amusement.

"Like a little coffee with your cream and sugar?" he asked, his hands wrapped around his own steaming mug.

"Fully loaded," she said and took a sip. "Only way to have it." The heat of the drink coursed through her, settling her nerves and anchoring her. She sighed and extended a hand across the table to him, leaving it hovering expectantly.

"So, how about we try this again? Start over from scratch?"

Rune's lip curled in a crooked smile. He reached out to clasp her hand in his and shook it. "Nice to meet you."

"And you."

"I'm Bruno Agnellini. But my friends call me Rune."

"Evie Diaz. Pleasure's all mine," she said. They both laughed as they dropped their hands. Rune lifted his cup, as Evie continued. "And I'm going to have to have a chat with Wilson. He shouldn't have warned you off like he did. He seriously overreacted." Her belly plunged. "Ugh. I wonder who else he's done that to."

"No, don't worry about it. I get it. He's just looking out for you. He cares. My dad passed when I was nineteen—"

"Oh, I'm sorry," Evie interrupted gently.

"Thanks. It was nine years ago. But at the time, all I wanted to do was protect my mom. Make sure no one tried to take advantage of her, you know? Wilson's only doing the same for you. It's nice that he cares."

"If he's scaring people off, though, he might ought to dial it down. I can't imagine why he thought he needed to do that with you."

He wrinkled his nose sheepishly. "It...probably had something to do with the fact that, on my first day, I mentioned to him how...pretty you are."

"Oh." Evie felt her cheeks flush and pictured the faint pink coloring that was likely spreading over her skin. She stared down at her coffee before meeting his gaze again. "That might've done it."

"So, um, where were you going when you left the hotel earlier?" he said abruptly, changing the subject. "You looked like you were on a mission."

"Pharmacy. My daughter needed some meds."

Concern flitted across his face. "Is Gabby all right?"

She leaned back in the seat, suddenly feeling like a project he had studied. But it didn't make her uncomfortable, just playfully curious. "Okay...you know Kieran was flirting with me, you know I didn't get to eat because I was out when I normally take my break, *and* you know my daughter's name."

"Yeah, when I hear you say it out loud like that, it does sound a bit stalker-ish."

She chuckled. "A little bit."

"Maybe Wilson was right to wave me off," he suggested, a twinkle in his eye.

She snorted amiably.

"Okay, honestly, I swear I'm not a stalker. But, I mean, come on—you've looked in a mirror before. Any guy around you five days a week—or nights, rather—would have to be blind not to notice you—or the other guys noticing you."

Her nerve endings tingled, and she felt herself growing red again.

"And as for the lunch thing," he continued, "you eat at the same time every night. After four months of being in and out of the break room, a person starts to recognize a pattern. Unless you're a person that's just not aware of what's going on around you."

"And that's not you."

He tipped his head. "Devil's in the details. So, I try to be aware of the details."

"And Gabby? How did you know about her?"

Rune smirked timidly. "That was Wilson again. He's mentioned her more than once. Thinks the world of her, FYI."

A grin parted her lips. "When she met him, she asked if he was my bodyguard."

"I think he may have taken her suggestion a little too seriously."

She chuckled. "Maybe so."

The waitress swept in, clanking a plate down in front of Evie. "Your egg and toast," she announced before disappearing again.

Rune nodded toward the plate. "Dig in."

Evie picked up a fork and pierced some of the fluffy yellow scramble. The eggs were savory and hot, and one bite made her realize just how famished she was. She hastily scooped up more.

"See," Rune said boastfully. "I told you you were hungry."

Evie swallowed. "You sure know me pretty well for someone who's never had a real conversation with me."

"Well, I'm glad that's changed." He pressed his lips together. "And I'm sorry it took so long. I guess I was just too nerv—"

The bell on the front door trilled, snapping their attention to the entrance as a uniformed police officer walked inside.

Upon spotting Rune, the officer smiled widely and moved toward them.

"Hey, Layla," Rune said, rising to greet the officer with an enthusiastic hug when she reached their table.

"Geez, Rune," Layla said, snorting as she wriggled out of his embrace and stepped back, "still working out much?"

"Every day." Rune scooted into the booth, allowing room for Layla. She fell in next to him, her polyester uniform scratching against the seat.

"If you'd seen him in high school, you'd get it," Layla told Evie, drawing her thumb and forefinger together. "Scrawniest thing you'd ever seen."

"Really?" Evie said, her eyebrows rising. That was hard to imagine. Rune was lanky, but far from scrawny, given the way his shirt fit across his chest and upper arms.

"Officer Layla Driver, this is Evie." He gestured between the two women. "And Evie, this is Officer Layla Driver. Exaggerator and twelfth-grade beauty queen."

"Prom queen, thank you very much," she corrected, leaning forward as if about to share a secret with Evie. "He always does that because he hopes it'll embarrass me, cause I'm a big ol' tough cop now. But prom queens can kick butt too."

Evie didn't know about "prom queen," but the woman sitting opposite her could have been a model as easily as a police officer. Even with her flat shoes, Layla Driver had to be somewhere in the range of five-eight or nine. Her black hair, long with very tight curls, was gathered in an elastic band just below the base of her neck. Her brown skin had not a blemish on it, and her eyes, large and also brown, had a smile all their own.

"Beauty, brains, and butt-kicking," Rune said, rolling his eyes.

"You know it," Layla replied, punching him in the arm.

"You two went to high school together?"

"Fort Hamilton High," Rune offered.

"Bay Ridge, Brooklyn, baby," Layla countered, then bent in even further, her expression growing heavy. "But enough about us. Rune tells me you're in a bit of trouble," she said, her gaze fixed on Evie. "Lay it on me."

27

"What is she doing?" Saul snapped. He stared at the Midnight Diner from their SUV's parking spot across and down the street from the restaurant's entrance. "She's sitting with a cop!"

Kieran leaned forward in the back seat so that he could see past Saul and get a better look through the large plate glass window of the orange booth holding Evie, a female cop, and some guy. Kimball cursed and Matty ran a nervous hand over his forehead.

"Who's the guy?" Saul demanded.

Kieran narrowed his gaze, focusing on the man sitting opposite Evie. He only had a side view, but the man looked vaguely familiar. Still, he couldn't place him. "I don't know. He looks sort of familiar, but...I don't know."

"You said she was in a cab," Saul grunted.

"So, maybe it's the cab driver," Kieran speculated and cleared his throat.

Saul squinted at him dubiously. "The cab driver? The cab driver went in the diner with her? Really?"

Saul's mocking tone made Kieran's blood simmer. He forced

his voice to remain steady. It wouldn't be helpful to lose his temper. "I don't know, man." Kieran splayed his hands. "Does it matter?"

"Yeah, it matters. I want to know what we're dealing with. And we've got to pick her up before she does something stupid and we miss our chance to turn this around. Could he be working with Jamison? Maybe he got to her before we did."

"Since I talked to her ten minutes ago? No. I gave her a clean cell, told her to take the SIM out of hers so Jamison couldn't track her, blah, blah. She bought it. So, he's got no way to contact her now."

"Unless he already had her when she called you."

Kieran shook his head. "No. I don't think so. If Jamison had her, he wouldn't let her talk to the cops. The last thing he'll want is police attention drawn to that poker game." Something about the face of the man in the booth tugged at him, a truth just out of reach. Suddenly his chest lightened as realization struck. "Wait, I do know him! Yeah...he works at the Wexsor. I think he's their driver. I've never used him, but I've seen him there before—"

"Now the hotel driver's involved?" Saul said through gritted teeth.

"Hold on," Kimball interrupted, glaring at Kieran. "I don't get something."

Probably not the first time you've said that, Kieran thought.

"You told her that you picked up that phone at a convenience store, but your story to us didn't include that little detail."

"That's because it didn't happen, I just told her that. I already had the spare phone with me," he said, giving his messenger bag a tug. "I'm a con artist, Kimball. A professional. I make sure I'm prepared at all times with anything I might need in any situation, and that means having an extra phone on me. In my line of work, you never know when you're gonna have to make a call from a number that won't be recognized."

"I still think you're not telling us something."

"Whatever," Kieran said, shrugging.

"Shut up, the both of you," Saul said. "Every second she sits there with that cop puts us one second closer to losing control of this thing."

"Evie talking to that cop is not going to change anything, okay? She doesn't even know what's really going on," Kieran insisted.

"Well, she knew enough to call the cops," Saul shot back. "She said that some guy came for her on the street? That was probably Jamison's doing. After that, and what you told her about Jamison's man taking you down, she's got enough of a story to at least get the cops interested. Look," he said, pointing a thick forefinger at the trio in the diner as Evie set her phone on the center of the table and tapped it. "Your girl's playing something for them." He rotated towards Kieran. "I thought she cut her phone off! You think that might be your message?" he asked sarcastically.

Was he right? Was she playing his message? Kieran's stare drilled into the diner booth, the muscles in his neck contracting tightly.

"You see the problem, right?" Saul pressed. "If she ends up leaving with that cop, this whole scheme is done. We'll never get another chance at her. She'll be gone, and my money will be too."

Kieran had no answer. Saul wasn't wrong. This could go real bad, real fast. He eyed Kimball's windbreaker, knowing that somewhere under there was the gun he had seen earlier. He wondered how quickly it would come out if Evie ended up driving away with that cop. He had to get Evie out of that diner and into this car.

Ideas were spinning through his brain when Saul breathed

in deeply, sucking air in and out of his nose, like a bull preparing to charge.

"Gimme your windbreaker, Kimball," he ordered, shoving an open hand over Kimball's seat.

"What?" Kimball replied, turning toward Saul.

"You heard me."

Obediently, Kimball scooted to the edge of his seat, and after some awkward twisting and pulling, managed to wrestle the jacket off. He tossed it back to Saul, who jammed his arms into the sleeves.

"What...what are you doing, Saul?" Kieran asked, as Saul snatched the zipper up to his neck with a loud, *zzzzpp*.

"Saul?"

Instead of answering, Saul grasped the handle beside him and shoved his door open. Dropping onto the pavement, he strode away from the SUV toward the restaurant.

"Saul! Hey! Saul!" Kieran yelled through the open door, his heart hammering against his sternum as he watched Saul pull the windbreaker's hood over his head and storm the diner's entrance.

28

Layla looked up as Kieran's voicemail message finished playing from Evie's cell. The second it stopped, Evie removed the SIM card and battery again.

"Where's this 'Kieran'?"

"On his way," Evie answered. "He should be here any minute." *Hopefully sooner rather than later,* she thought.

"And you've got no idea why your boss—this Jamison person—would have a problem with you?"

Evie shook her head vehemently. "No. None."

"And Kieran didn't explain when you talked to him?"

"He said he wanted to talk about it in person."

"Mmm," Layla droned negatively. "Yeah, I'm not liking that."

"Thank you," Rune chimed in.

"If he knows something, why wouldn't he just say it?" Layla asked.

"I'm not sure he does know anything. I think he's just as confused as I am," Evie said.

Layla swiveled toward Rune. "And you're positive that the guy you hit with your car is connected with Jamison?"

"Well, after that message it sure seems like that," Rune said, nodding at the phone. "Not to mention that Jamison was chasing her while she was still listening to it. Ran her right out of the hotel. He was banging on the window when I pulled away. It all seems a little too well-timed not to be connected."

A voice squawked over the radio strapped in Layla's utility belt. She reached down without looking, twisted a knob, and turned the sound lower. "I think the best thing is for me, the two of you, and Kieran to go to the station and get this sorted out. We can reach out to this Jamison, see how he reacts, and maybe figure out what's what."

"What if he doesn't respond? What if he won't come?" Evie asked.

"Then we'll know something's up and we'll go from there. At least then—"

The front door of the diner flew open, slamming against the stopper in the wall so hard that it sent the bell flinging wildly about, jangling incessantly. All three of them zeroed in on the disturbance, Layla and Rune twisting to look behind them. Like an animal on a rampage, a man in a green windbreaker—the hood pulled up and cinched around his face, covering it in shadow—charged straight for them. He whipped out a gun and leveled it at their booth. Screams erupted from the other side of the dining room, followed by the sound of falling plates smashing on tile.

All of Evie's senses seemed to explode at once, fear traveling like liquid fire through her veins. "Get down!" Layla bellowed, pushing Rune's shoulder down with one hand while unholstering her weapon with the other. As Rune dropped below the table, Evie slid under it from her side, a sharp pain stabbing her hip as she landed on the base of the center table leg. Her eyes momentarily met Rune's wide-eyed gaze, before flashing to what she could see of Layla from her position beneath the table—just from Layla's waist down—as Layla twisted toward the attacker and yelled, "Sto—"

The gunshot boomed through the space, followed by a thunderous crash as Layla slammed backward onto the table, the impact forcing her gun from her hand. It hit the seat, then bounced onto the floor beside Evie with a clatter. Rune burst from the booth, flying at the assailant as Evie grabbed for the gun, but her hands were slick from sweat, and it slipped from her grasp. She tried once more, managing to get a finger on the grip and dragging it to her.

Crawling out from under the table, Evie saw Rune struggling with the assailant, his hands locked around the man's wrists, trying to keep them in the air, preventing him from aiming the gun again.

"Stoooopppp!" Evie screamed—a deep, guttural scream, summoned from the depths of her—as she knelt on the floor with Layla's weapon outstretched, both hands wrapped around the grip.

The man froze, his hands remaining in the air even though Rune let go of him and stepped clear, moving toward the table. An odd expression came over the little of the man's face they could see, as he seemed to take in the sight of Evie. Then his shoulders dropped.

"You're not gonna shoot," he said in a confident, gravelly voice, and stepped toward her.

The shot from Layla's gun cut through the clamor of customers screaming and racing out of the place. The bullet struck the man in his upper left thigh, high and on the outside. He roared incomprehensibly as his leg trembled, and he fell back on his right foot, shifting his weight off his compromised leg. Rune slammed into him, driving him to the floor. He wrenched the man's gun away, hurling it to the far side of the restaurant as the man snatched Rune by the collar and reared back to punch him.

"Hey!" Evie barked and both men's gazes snapped to her. She stood upright now, six feet from them in a shooting posture, Layla's gun trained on the man's chest. "Let him go!"

The man immediately released Rune, rolling onto his back and splaying his hands and fingers outward in a show of compliance. Rune scrambled up and scooted behind Evie, panting raggedly.

"What are you—" Rune started.

"Did Jamison send you?" Evie shouted over Rune, her clasped hands shaking as they held the gun.

The man said nothing, but his brow wrinkled as his eyes narrowed in response.

"Did Jamison send you?" Evie repeated, this time punctuating each of the words through gritted teeth.

He nodded.

A flash of movement outside caught Evie's attention. She glanced up and through the window saw another man barreling toward the front door, a gun extended before him.

"Go! Go!" Rune yelled, grabbing her arm and yanking her toward the table where he reached over and shook Layla. She didn't move.

"Come on, Rune. Come on," Evie urged, pulling Rune with her, away from the table to the bar counter. They darted behind it, hurtling through a swinging door that led into the kitchen. The heavy aroma of bacon grease and well done burgers assaulted Evie as they raced down the narrow space between a stainless steel prep table and a gas range, headed to the back of the room.

"There!" Rune exclaimed, pointing to a door somewhat hidden by a pantry shelf holding large canisters of dry goods. Skirting the shelf, Evie wrenched the handle and shoved. The door flung open into a poorly lit alley. She ran out, humid air bathing her as she spun to make sure Rune was following. He came through at full speed, the door shutting behind him with a loud click as he motioned for Evie to keep running.

She did, her feet pounding the pavement relentlessly, though she had absolutely no idea where in the world she was going.

29

"Wait, stop!" Rune gasped after they had run almost two full blocks. Evie slowed, but her momentum carried her forward several yards ahead of him. With blood rushing in her ears, she turned and jogged back to where he stood beside a wrought iron fence that encircled a small, landscaped park.

"Let's go in here," he said, thumbing at the park, then hoisting himself onto the fence by taking hold just below the arrow-like finials near the top. He threw one leg over and then the other, dropping out of view somewhere on the other side, behind the thick bushes that ran along the fence line.

Thank God I'm not wearing the Jimmy Choos, she thought again, reaching for the bars. She wedged a running shoe in one of the decorative wrought iron curls and used the foothold to press herself up and over, jumping down. She landed hard on her ankle and winced, but shook it off as she stepped to Rune, who was pressed up against the hedges, well out of sight of anyone on the street. He was tinkering with his cell phone, reinserting his SIM card. After a few moments, the phone registered as having service again, and he punched "9-1-1."

She thought she knew why. "Layla?" Evie asked, the word almost choking off when she inhaled another deep breath, trying to satisfy her burning lungs.

Rune nodded. His eyes were mournful. Guilty.

"She was breathing, Rune. I saw her. She wasn't completely unconscious, just stunned, I think. I didn't even see any blood. Maybe it hit her vest." Wailing sirens filled the night air, their eerie revolution of tones growing increasingly louder, signaling that the vehicles they announced were drawing near. "I'm sure—"

He held up a finger. "Yes," he said into the receiver, "there's been a shooting. A police officer's been hit..." He continued explaining to the operator what had happened, sharp concern in his voice as he dodged questions about his involvement, but described Layla's injury as best he could. The edges of his mouth were turned down as severe ruts cut across his brow.

Evie drew close, placing a reassuring hand on his free forearm and whispering to him. "A million people must have called. They're probably already there. She'll be okay." As she squeezed his arm gently, something in him seemed to ease. He dropped his shoulders as he disconnected the call, took a breath, then removed his SIM card.

"The operator said they just arrived," he said numbly.

The image of Layla, lying there on the table, and the sound of the gunshot passed through her mind, and her heart plummeted, tears collecting in the corners of her eyes. "Rune, I'm so sorry." She swallowed and bit her lip, not knowing what else to say.

"It's not your fault. I'm the one who involved her. I *did* see blood on the table, but it looked like it was coming from her shoulder, though I don't know for sure—"

"It doesn't mean she was shot there. She hit the table really hard," Evie said. "She could have hit her head on the plate, or a mug...And it's not your fault, either. You couldn't have known they would find us."

He shifted, his body tensing. "How *did* they find us?"

It was a good question. One she had no answer to. "Maybe Jamison managed to trace us before we turned the phones off—or when I turned it back on to play the message?"

"That would be awfully good timing on his part," Rune said skeptically. "What about that guy? Does he work for Jamison?"

She shook her head and shrugged. "I've never seen him before. But he nodded when I asked him if Jamison sent him, so, I guess so." Evie's eyes flicked to her fingers, still grasping his arm. She released it, letting her hand fall to her side.

"You kept it," Rune said, his eyes fixed on the gun in Evie's other hand.

She had forgotten it was there. What must she have looked like, running through the streets with that thing in her grip? "Well, I wasn't going to leave it."

Rune leaned back a bit, his eyes growing large. "You shot someone!" he exclaimed, as if only now truly registering what she had done in the diner. "Are you okay?"

"Yeah. Fine," she replied, even though her hands were still trembling. "It was just in the thigh. Just enough to keep him down."

He snorted. "You meant to do that?"

"Absolutely."

"You know how to shoot?"

She smiled faintly. "I'm from Texas. Of course I know how to shoot." She worked quickly to remove the chambered round from Layla's pistol as Rune looked on, then tucked the gun in her waistband. "We need to go to the police."

"Agreed. I'd say we could go back to the diner—it'll be packed with cops soon, if it isn't already—but, if those guys followed us, we might run into them first."

"If we can't go back, we can't get the car," she said, knowing they had parked only a short distance from the diner's front door. "We should find the nearest precinct," she said, pulling up Google Maps on Kieran's cell, "and walk there if it's close, and if not, take the subway."

"Or we could take a cab—"

"No," Evie said with finality. "I'm not involving anyone else in this. I don't want anyone else to be collateral damage."

Rune eyed her appraisingly. "If you don't want to call a cab, then we could call 9-1-1 again, get someone to pick us up and take—"

Kieran's cell phone buzzed in Evie's hand. Glancing down, she immediately recognized the number from earlier. After trading nervous looks with Rune, she depressed the answer icon.

"GRAB HIS LEG and keep pressure on it!" Kimball barked. He sat in the front passenger seat of the Traverse, while Kieran sat in the back with Saul, who lay against him, panting heavily. The wound in his thigh had bled through his clothes onto the seat and now dripped onto the floorboard.

"He's got to get to a doctor," Kieran said, pressing his wadded up jacket against the wound. "There's too much blood." It was all over Kieran's hands, warm and sticky on his skin.

"No. No hospital," Saul grunted between curses.

They rocked to the side as Matty hung a right a bit too quickly. Saul bellowed when the momentum drove Kieran's hand into his thigh.

"Sorry, sorry!" Kieran apologized.

"We can't take him to a hospital," Kimball said. "It's a

gunshot wound. They'll report it. We'll have to go to Doc Belland."

"Who?" Kieran asked, panic beginning to crawl over him like ants over a mound. The whole thing was spiraling out of control.

"Doc Belland," Kimball said. "Matty, you got that? Head to Queens."

"No!" Saul shouted. "We leave now and she's gone. They were already talking to a cop. They'll just find another one. She gives it up and that's it. We've got to get to her."

"We've got to get you patched up or you'll bleed out," Kimball said. His gaze cut purposefully to Kieran in the rearview mirror. "And if he bleeds out, you're next. This is on you." There was cold resolution in Kimball's stare, and Kieran didn't doubt for a second that he meant it.

"We get her first," Saul insisted.

"We don't even know where she is now," Kimball snapped.

"Hey, can you guys make a decision?" Matty interrupted, changing lanes. "I gotta know where we're going."

Kieran let them yammer on, bickering, while he assessed the situation. He needed to take charge. He needed a plan. His mind whirred, thinking of Evie, of the driver, of—he cocked his head, and blinked.

That's it.

"We're going to the doctor," Kieran said forcefully. "You can't spend your money if you're dead, Saul. And I think I can keep her from going to the cops. Drive faster," he told Matty, and over Kimball and Saul's angry demands for an explanation, began tapping on his phone.

~

"THERE'S THE HOTEL CAR," Richards said as they neared the

Midnight Diner, pointing at the Lexus SUV parked twenty yards or so from the front door. He slowed as the police officer directing traffic motioned him to veer toward the left lane of the one-way street. Red, blue, and white lights flashed from the turrets on top of the multiple patrol cars lined up in front of the diner, along with the red strobe lights of two ambulances. The beams filtered into their vehicle, the colors reflecting off his and Jamison's faces as well as every other surface. In addition to the police and EMTs in the immediate area, there were about a dozen civilians—probably witnesses—who appeared to either be giving information or receiving medical treatment.

From his seat behind Richards, Jamison peered out the passenger window at the scene. His nerves hummed. "This isn't a coincidence."

"Should we find out what happened?"

Jamison ignored the question, swiveling his gaze wide. "I don't see them anywhere. Do you?"

"No. So, now what?"

Jamison nodded to a group of bystanders on the sidewalk several yards ahead. "Stop when we get to them. Ask if they know anything."

Richards obeyed, stopping the car when they reached the cluster of six people hovering on the sidewalk, intently watching the happenings across the street. He lowered his window.

"Hey, man," Richards said, his words directed to a young twenty-something in jeans and a grungy T-shirt. "You know what happened?"

The kid took a step closer. "Just that a cop got shot. And maybe one of the shooters. Bunch of people ran out, but we couldn't really hear anything else." The sounds of radios squawking and orders being given floated in through the open window.

"They know who did it?"

The kid shook his head. "Nah. They've been talking about APB's and bulletins and whatever. And I ain't seen no one in cuffs, so..."

The whirr of Jamison lowering his window interrupted the kid. "Look, did any of you see a woman, a little older than him, maybe," Jamison asked, gesturing to the kid Richards had been talking to, "dark hair, dressed in a pantsuit? Any of you see anybody like that?"

They murmured negatively, shrugged, and otherwise indicated that they had not.

"Hey, you!" The officer directing traffic was marching toward their car, signaling with a two-fingered jab that they should continue driving. "Keep it moving!"

"Go," Jamison said, shrinking back from the window.

Richards stepped on the gas, rolling the car forward slowly. "What now?" he asked.

"I don't know," Jamison answered coolly.

"This might not have been them. Why would they shoot a cop?"

"With that much money at stake? Why wouldn't they?"

Richards shrugged. "Maybe you should call her again."

Jamison tossed him a dubious glare. "What...tenth time's the charm? She's not answering."

"Did you leave her a message telling her what you want?"

"Right. A message—"

"Or text."

"—yeah, that's brilliant. Text her about this and leave evidence for the police to poke through later? No. I don't think so. I've already called her more than I should have. It's going to draw attention."

"What then?"

Jamison pursed his lips together, grunted distastefully, then leaned back in his seat, watching the emergency lights strobing behind them in the side-view mirror. "Go back to the hotel. If we can't figure something out, we'll have to bring him into this," Jamison said.

"He isn't gonna like it."

"No," Jamison replied, "he's not."

30

The phone Kieran had left for her buzzed violently in her hand, sending a tingle up her arm.

"Hello?" she answered tentatively.

"Evie, it's Kieran. Are you okay? I was outside the diner when I saw everything go down. Are you hurt?" His voice was high-pitched. He sounded nervous.

"No, no, I'm fine," she replied. Rough, labored breathing filled the background of his call. "Are you okay? You sound out of breath."

"Jamison saw me. I'm running. I think I lost him, but...I'm gonna have to regroup. He has people with him." He coughed and sucked in more air. "And you called the cops? I saw that cop in your booth. Why? I thought we were going to the police together?"

"We are! I just got a jumpstart on it, that's all. I want to end this as soon as possible. I thought it would help if she was already there when you arrived."

"It doesn't, Evie. Listen, you have no idea. If it were simple, don't you think I'd tell you? You have to do this my way, or neither one of us will be safe. You have seriously complicated things."

Her head swam as the reality of what he was saying hit her.

Have I really made things worse? All because I was trying to do the right thing? "It's just...you're not telling me anything," she said. "It makes it difficult to know what to do when you keep me in the dark."

"When I can explain, you'll understand. And Evie, I need to know why the driver from the Wexsor is with you. And why you lied to me."

She sighed. "He's the one that helped me get away from Jamison. Drove me off in the hotel car."

"I thought you said you were in a cab before."

She paused, considering the irony of the fact that while she was accusing Kieran of not telling her everything, she had been doing the exact same thing.

"Evie?"

"Sorry, sorry...I...I didn't tell you because I didn't want him involved."

"And you were right. He shouldn't be involved. Ditch him as soon as you can. You have to trust me. He'll only make things worse—oh, no."

"What?" she said, her stomach diving. She gripped the phone more tightly.

"I think one of Jamison's people just saw me. Look, Evie, I'll call you as soon as I can, okay? Hang tight somewhere until I get clear and call you back. I have to go."

The line went dead.

"He wants me to ditch you," Evie said, her eyes trained on Rune's, wondering how he would react.

"Of course he does." He squinted at her. "And you really trust this guy?"

"I'm not sure I have much of a choice. I know it sounds bad, but maybe he has a good reason."

"'Ditch the driver'? What possible *legitimate* reason could he have for that?" Rune pressed.

"Maybe he doesn't want to involve anybody that doesn't have to be involved. Maybe he doesn't want to risk anyone else's safety."

"Or maybe he wants to get you by yourself."

Her insides ruffled and she straightened. "No. He's not like that. He might be flirty or forward or whatever, but that's all." But even as she said it, she could feel the doubt growing within her.

"I don't like it. And you're not ditching the driver."

His features were set in stone, a hard look that matched his granite tone. It was obvious that he had no intention of leaving her and he wasn't changing his mind. His stance was even rigid, his legs bracing as if something, or someone, was about to take a run at him. She knew she ought to fight him on this. To insist that he go for his own sake, or because it would be best for the situation, at least according to Kieran. But she didn't. Because, if she was honest, she just didn't want him to go. "If you're determined—"

"I am."

"Then I guess the driver doesn't get ditched," she said, unable to suppress the tiny hint of a smile that briefly drew up one corner of her mouth.

"Good. So, what's the plan?" Rune asked.

"He thinks Jamison may have caught up to him, so right now he's running. He wants me to lay low for a bit, till he can get someplace safe and we can meet. He promises he'll explain everything then."

"Well, we can't stay here on the street," Rune said, pivoting to take in the small community garden in which they stood. Multiple groupings of towering shrubbery planted at various spots along the fence shielded much of the garden from the outside, but the regular gaps between them left plenty of opportunity for passersby to spot them eventually if they stayed.

"Okay, come on," he finally said, motioning for Evie to follow him. "I have an idea. There's a place not too far from here where we can wait. Nobody'll bother us. And we can figure out what to do. Okay?"

Evie nodded, and he led her toward the garden's exit, a narrow gate on the opposite side. "How about we use the gate this time?" he said, running his finger along a large tear in his pants, which she guessed was the result of scaling the fence earlier. "I won't be much good to you if I impale myself."

"WHY DIDN'T you just tell her to meet us somewhere now?" Matty asked, steering the car through the light traffic headed off the island at this hour.

Kieran had to fight the urge to roll his eyes. "Because, look at me! I'm covered in blood and we've got a gunshot victim in the car with us," he said, spreading his hands as he eyed Saul. He had grown quiet, and Kieran thought he might even be unconscious. "She takes one look at me, at us, and she'll run."

"Not if we put a bullet in her," Kimball grumbled.

Kieran scoffed. "That's your plan? Shoot her? How did that work out for Saul?"

"He was getting it done," Kimball said.

"He was being an idiot. And impatient. Impatience is a con-killer."

"Well, your way wasn't getting us anywhere."

"It would have if he had just sat tight. It's not my first rodeo. And seriously, 'put a bullet in her'? What are you going to do—leave a trail of bodies across Manhattan? Yeah, that'll take the heat off." A heady exhilaration filled Kieran as he unleashed on Kimball. He had been holding back for a while, keeping his sarcasm and commentary to himself, trying to make things, well, if not amiable, at least less combative. But now, Saul seemed to be out, and it felt good to slap Kimball around a bit. "I'm a con artist, not a murderer. After what I just told Evie, she'll stay put, she'll keep quiet, and she'll meet us once we get to wherever we're going and I have a chance to set this thing up right. Unless you'd rather take the blame for all this instead of Jamison."

Kieran raised his eyebrows as he waited for an answer, but only got disgruntled silence. "That's what I thought," he said, shifting his weight and edging out from under Saul. "Just shut up and trust me. I'm working on something."

"You'd better work faster," Kimball muttered.

Kieran glared at him. "We don't need to shoot her to get her to stay away from the cops. There's a smarter way. After we take Saul to the doc, Matty and I can go handle it."

"Nothin' doin'," Saul grunted, grimacing as he shifted in his seat, causing Kieran to jump at his sudden return to the land of the living. "You're not leaving my sight. Kimball can go with Matty."

"Fine," Kieran said, a chill traveling down his spine as he wondered how much Saul had heard. "But they'll have to do exactly as I say, otherwise it won't work."

"Kimball can handle it. Can't you, Kimball?" Saul said.

"Yeah, sure. We can handle it," Kimball replied. "We can handle whatever the little con artist throws our way." He turned in his seat to face Kieran. "So, tell us already."

"You heard him," Saul said. "Explain."

31

The old church sat on a quiet corner—or at least it was quiet at this time of early morning—of a street on the east side of SoHo. Though this part of the city lacked the jungle of massive skyscrapers of Downtown and Midtown, the city had still grown up around the nineteenth-century Protestant house of worship, the umpteen-story buildings that surrounded it dwarfing the mere two-story structure. Gas lamps inside the property cast an ethereal glow across the front entrance, piercing the last shades of night. Hewn stone blocks formed the base of the building, and a pointed steeple added another two stories to the structure's summit. A waist-high wrought iron fence enclosed the modest patch of green at the church's entrance, with a double gate serving as sentinel. A brass plaque affixed to the gate read, "Life Church."

The short subway trip to get there had given Evie a moment to breathe, to slow her racing mind. Rune had shared his plan with her while the train sped through the underground tunnels, and she had thought it was a good one. She had exited the subway station feeling calmer, more in control—her heartbeat nearly normal. But now that they stood there, in front of the gate, her insides began to churn.

"Are you sure about this?" Evie asked, cutting her eyes at him.

Rune nodded. "Come on."

He unlatched the gate panel on the right and pushed it open, a shrill squeak sounding as it moved. He re-latched it after Evie came through and directed her to a narrow path between the left side of the church and the building next door. She followed him wordlessly down the path, which led to a portico-covered side entrance. The heavy oak door, criss-crossed by iron slats and rivets, was from another age, but a very modern electric lock with a keypad had been installed alongside its frame. Rune tapped a six-digit security code into it, and the red light on the lock turned bright green followed by a soft click. Rune grinned and opened the door. "After you," he said, ushering Evie inside.

The interior of the church was dark, lit only by dim sconces mounted down the length of both sides of the sanctuary and two lamps perched on a communion table at the front of the room. A high ceiling soared a full two stories, supported by lofty buttresses that stretched into the space above their heads. Without the sunlight, the half dozen stained glass windows on each side of the sanctuary were a less luminous version of themselves, though patches of color showed through where light from street lamps or other exterior sources struck the glass, illuminating the jewel tones of red, blue, and purple.

"Here," Rune said, directing her to the first pew. Evie sat, easing into the red velvet cushion and reclining into the bench's hard, wooden back, feeling the gun in her waistband pressing against her skin. At the front of the sanctuary, a podium occupied the center of a raised platform, flanked by floral sprays set atop marble plinths. Behind that, the monumental pipes of a centuries-old organ rose from the grand housing of the keyboard, shining golden vessels shooting toward the heavens, waiting for someone to release their haunting tones.

"This is beautiful," Evie said. "How long have you been coming here?"

"A while. Sorry we couldn't go to my apartment—it's only three blocks away, but—"

"No," she interrupted. "You said you have roommates. I don't want to put them at risk. Plus, if Jamison knows I'm with you, he might look there. This is the safer bet."

There was a thunk and a whirring as the air conditioning kicked on and began humming in the background. Rune fidgeted beside her on the pew, and she was suddenly acutely aware of how close he was. Something clean and fresh tickled her nose, and she wondered whether it was his aftershave, his hair product, or maybe his soap, then, feeling self-conscious, scrambled for something to say.

"Do...they just let any member have the entry code?" she asked.

"I'm sort of the volunteer fix-it man here. It's my ministry for the church. Taking care of odds and ends—you know, broken lights or chairs or painting or whatever. It saves them from having to pay for it."

"That's really good of you."

Rune shrugged. "I figure we've all got to do our part. Serve where we can."

Evie heaved a sigh. "I, um, have a church near our place in Flushing. Mark loved it. We both did. But it's been very hard for me to sit alone in those chairs where we used to sit together. I've been a few times since he passed, but most of the time I take Gabby to her group and leave, then go back for her later."

"I get it. Sometimes places make our memories more raw. My dad had a workshop behind our house, and I haven't set foot in it since he died."

Silence fell between them. Evie interlaced her fingers,

pressing them into her lap. "I wish I knew what this was all about."

"We'll know something soon. He said it wouldn't be long, right?"

"Why make me wait at all? Why not just tell me?"

"I don't know. And I don't like it either. But if you're determined to wait on Kieran, to give him a chance, then I don't see that we have much choice."

Her hands were busy, one thumb nervously rubbing circles on her palm. After she continued with this for several moments, he placed his hand over hers and patted twice before removing it. His touch was warm and strong, and her tension instantly eased, its sharp edges smoothed.

"It'll be okay," he said. "Let's distract ourselves. Talk about something else for a minute."

"Like what?"

He squinted. "Like, you said you're from Texas. Where in Texas?"

"Round Rock. Right outside of Austin. What about you?"

"Brooklyn."

"Oh, right. Layla said. Sorry."

He shook his head, casually dismissing her apology.

"Did you...like it there?" she asked weakly, struggling to keep the conversation afloat.

"I did. I'd still be there if it weren't for school."

School? That pricked her curiosity. "You're in school? Where?"

"Manhattan Institute of Hotel Management."

She felt a thin smile crease her face. "That's a great program. Congratulations."

"Thanks. I got a scholarship. Otherwise, there'd be no way I could afford it."

"That's impressive. Good for you. How much longer do you have?"

"One year. It's only a two-year program."

"So, why are you driving at the Wexsor?"

"It pays the bills. And gives me a foot in with the hotel. I'm hoping they'll move me into a position in the management office eventually. Plus it keeps me close to school, which means I have to spend less time commuting. Of course, that also means I have to split a two-bedroom apartment with two other guys, but it's not forever."

"And what's the plan when you get out?"

"Um...hotel management," he said with a gentle smirk.

"Yeah," she said, returning the look. "I figured that, but where?"

"Wherever I can get a job at first, I guess. But ultimately, I'd love to end up somewhere near home. I don't want to leave the city if I can manage it. I really want to be close to Mom. Help her out with my sisters."

"How many sisters do you have?"

"Four. I'm the middle child." He raised a hand and counted off on his fingers. "Brynn, Britta, Brianna, and Bristol."

Evie tossed him an amused grin. "All B's huh?"

Rune chuckled. "My mom's thing. She has a lot of Irish in her and insisted on naming the girls something that sounded more Celtic. She said my dad got dibs on the last name, so she got dibs on the first names, at least with the girls. I'm the only one she let Dad name. He was a full-blooded Italian, so mine sounds like it belongs to a racecar driver from Rome."

"Do you see your family a lot?"

"As much as I can between school and work. It's not always easy, but then, it's not easy for my mom either—losing your husband and becoming a widow with five kids under twenty-three."

"No," Evie said, her shoulders wilting slightly. "It wouldn't be."

Rune flinched, and pink flushed at his collar. "Oh, Evie. I'm sorry. I'm an idiot. I wasn't thinking."

"Don't be ridiculous. That's your story. You don't need to apologize for it. And you're right, it had to be terribly hard on your mom. I'll bet your help has been invaluable to her. I know I couldn't have done the last few years without Eleanor—Gabby's nanny." As Eleanor's name left her lips, hot tears collected at her lash lines. She brushed at them, embarrassed. She wasn't normally weepy. But she was so tired. So overwhelmed.

Rune squeezed her arm. "Really, Evie. This will all work out. It's all going to be okay."

"No," Evie said, wiping her eyes again. "It's not that. Well, not *just* that." She exhaled heavily. "I don't think Eleanor will be with us for much longer."

Rune's eyes narrowed. "Is she sick?"

"No, no...nothing like that. Our building's been bought. We've lived there since Mark and I moved to the city. We've been given notice."

"When do you have to be out?"

A familiar knot in her stomach tightened. "I have another four months. I think I've found a place not too far away, but Eleanor...I don't know what she'll do. She was living in rent-control, and she's been looking, but she hasn't found anything she can afford anywhere close to our new place. It kills me to think of Gabby losing her too. She's part of our world now. And our home...it's the only one Gabby ever knew with Mark. She's already starting to forget him. When we move, it'll only happen faster."

"Surely Eleanor could find a place close *enough*, though? To still help?"

"Right now, she's across the hall. It's nothing for her to come over at any time of day or night. But, at best, it looks like she'll be several subway stops away. That's two trips daily on her own, sometimes while it's still dark. It doesn't seem like a lot, but she's getting older, and if anything happened to her I couldn't forgive myself. I'm just unsure about her coming and going that much, and her sons aren't too keen on it either. I'd follow her and get something near wherever she ends up, but with her fixed income, it would be so far from where we are now, I couldn't commute to the hotel. And Gabby loves her preschool. Flushing's been great for us. I hate to uproot her. I don't want to change Gabby's world that much after everything we went through when we lost Mark. That was enough change to last a lifetime."

Rune eyed her sympathetically. "I know it would be a big thing, but could Eleanor live with you? I mean, it might be worth it for Gabby's sake."

"Absolutely. I'd do that in a second, but that would require a three-bedroom place and that's more than I can afford."

"Could you do it together?"

"I suggested that, but she wouldn't hear of it. She said that if something ever happened to her or if she had to go live near her sons because of her health, she wouldn't feel right with me being saddled with rent I couldn't afford."

"So, what'll you do?"

That's a great question. "I guess I'll have to find someone else to help out. It will devastate Gabby."

"Kids are tougher than you think." He shifted in his seat and appraised her thoughtfully. "Can I ask you something?"

"Sure." Her gaze had drifted to a stained glass window that told the story of Peter walking on the water, and she held it there, waiting for Rune to speak.

"Why are you still at the Wexsor?"

This drew Evie's attention from the window. "What do you mean?"

"I mean, you've been there for years, right? And from what

everyone says, you do your job really well. You have the experience—and Wilson said you had a degree—"

"In hospitality management, yeah."

"Exactly. So, why are you still there? You could probably get a job as a head manager somewhere and move to the day shift. Then Eleanor would be traveling to your place during the day, and it wouldn't be as much of a burden for her to live further away."

"You sound like my parents."

"They sound like bright people."

She snorted softly in amusement. "Yeah. The thing is, even in that scenario, Eleanor would still be traveling in the dark at some point. And if I'm working days, then I'd have to give up spending my daytime hours with Gabby. Yes, I'm gone ten hours out of twenty-four now, but it's mostly when she's sleeping. She doesn't know the difference. But she will if suddenly I'm working forty-plus hours a week during the daytime. I'll never see her. Right now I sleep while she's in school—it's only half days—and then pick her up by lunch. I have five whole hours with her before I have to think about leaving for work. Maybe when she's older. Maybe when she's been in school longer."

"I get it," he said, smiling. "I do. You're a good mom. You're doing the best you can."

The best I can. That's what she told herself day in and day out. But she rarely believed it. "I'm trying. I don't know about succeeding, though. I want to hold it all together the way it was before. If I can keep things the same, then at least I feel like I'm in control of the situation. That it hasn't beat me."

"I'm guessing you didn't consider moving back to Texas?"

Evie shook her head. "Not even once. My parents wanted me to, but Mark and I had plans. We had dreams about living in this city and giving our family everything it has to offer. I'd feel like I was letting him down if I changed the plan just because it's hard. After what happened, I feel I have a responsibility to him to make this work."

Rune leaned forward, resting his elbows on his knees and rubbing his hands together. Something about his demeanor suggested he was hesitant to say whatever was on his mind. He kicked at a stray pebble that someone had tracked inside, and it went rolling off, ticking across the aged stone floor toward the side aisle. "And what about Kieran? Do you like him?"

Evie looked at Rune, feeling her mouth curve. "Do I *like* him? That sounds like something you say in the eighth grade."

"No, I just mean, I don't know, when you talk about him you kind of get this look, or this tone in your voice. Like you might *like* him."

A faint heat crept up her neck. "I...I've enjoyed the time I've spent with him. I've been glad to see him when he's there at the game..." Her words trailed off as her mind spun. *Did she like him?* It was a question she hadn't even allowed herself to honestly ask, and now this person she was only beginning to get to know had bluntly confronted her with it.

She stared past the podium and sprays to the organ pipes, letting her gaze rest there. *Did she have more than a passing interest in the possibility of exploring something with Kieran Carr? Could it be that she had truly developed feelings for someone other than Mark?* Yes, she had previously admitted to herself that Kieran had given her flutters, or whatever, and that he had made her realize that maybe *someday* there could be someone... but was she fooling herself? Had it become more than that? After three years had she crossed the line into actually, well, caring for someone?

"That's an awfully long pause for a 'no' answer," Rune said, casting her a sideways glance.

"I don't think I have an answer at all. I guess the most I can say is that I like being around him. I look forward to seeing him. And I wouldn't say no to getting to know him a little better."

"So you *do* like him," Rune said.

"I think maybe I *could* like him. But I don't know enough at this point to say."

"That's fair. But I guess the real question is whether you know him well enough to be sure he isn't yanking us around? To be sure that he's not involved in this somehow?"

She sat up taller in the pew. "He's not yanking us around. No."

"But the fact that he won't explain anything over the phone. I don't know...it seems strange to me."

"To me, too. But until we know more, I don't see that we have a choice but to wait for him."

"Maybe we do."

She felt her features pinch. "What?"

"I thought coming here might be the smart move, but now I think it might be a mistake to just sit and wait." Purpose had begun to simmer in his eyes. "Let's try to figure out some part of this puzzle. Knowledge is power, right? We could use a little power."

"What are you thinking?"

He scooted to the left a bit to allow more room between them, then turned to face her, drawing his leg up and crossing his ankle over his knee. "I want you to think about what happened tonight at the game and try to pinpoint when you first noticed anything odd. What was the first thing you remember that was different tonight than other nights?"

She matched him, turning to him and pulling her leg under her. "The most obvious thing was Jamison telling me to back off of Kieran. He's never asked me to stop talking to a player. Usually chit-chatting with players is part of my job description."

"Okay, so then, what happened before that?"

Evie huffed and waved a hand in front of her. "Nothing. Nothing happened."

"Nope. Can't be. What was going on in the room right before Jamison talked to you?"

Evie paused to ponder this. "I was talking to Kieran. He'd been pushed out of the round already. He was getting a drink and was just standing there."

"Seems like Jamison realized you might have a thing for Kieran before you did," Rune teased.

"I do not have a *thing* for him," Evie said indignantly, then closed her eyes, remembering the scene. Her lids fluttered open. "That's it. After that, I left when Jamison dismissed me. I went down the hall and was dealing with a guest issue when Kieran walked up and helped me out—"

Rune's face wrinkled in consternation. "How exactly did he do that?"

Evie shrugged. "Jumped in, pretended to be hotel staff, and took the blame for the problem. It was pretty charming, actually."

"Oh my gosh, you *do* like him," he taunted, smiling as he said it, though there was something wistful in his expression.

Wistful and endearing. Evie felt the corners of her mouth turning up, but then thoughts of the man barreling toward her on the sidewalk and Layla lying broken over the table rushed in, driving the beginnings of her smile away. She sighed. "Come on. Be serious."

He leaned back. "Sorry. Bad attempt to distract you. Go back to your story about Kieran. What happened after the thing with the guest?"

"We got into the elevator, and that's when Jamison's security man showed up. He escorted Kieran to Jamison, and I went downstairs."

"Escorted? That sounds ominous."

"I don't know about that. I wouldn't say 'ominous.' I mean, it was weird, but Kieran just played it off. It was sort of embarrassing."

Rune's eyebrows rose. "Why embarrassing?"

"Because when Jamison's security man asked Kieran to leave, he grabbed me around the waist and made a joke for the guy's benefit, you know, like we were headed out together and he was interrupting."

"You didn't find that odd?"

"Well, no. Uncomfortable, maybe, but he can be flirtatious sometimes. I just thought he was taking it up a notch. He had been drinking a good bit."

"And that's the last time you saw him?"

Evie nodded.

"Are there cameras in the room where the game happens?"

"No," she said, shaking her head. "Not that I'm aware of."

"But the elevator, that would have security video, right?"

"Yeah," she agreed. "Should have."

"And the hallways? The lobby?"

Evie nodded again.

"What if we go check that out? Watch as much as we can of Kieran's comings and goings tonight, so maybe we can learn something, anything, so we aren't flying completely blind."

She locked into his gaze and pursed her lips, contemplating his suggestion. His idea appealed to her. It might put her in the driver's seat, and greater control over this situation meant ending it sooner and more safely. It was worth a try. "There's a rear entrance to the hotel in the alley that runs behind it. Jamison's never used it as far as I know and wouldn't have a reason to. If he's still watching for me at the hotel I don't think he would know to keep an eye on that door. We could get in through that alley entrance, go to the security office, and have them pull up whatever footage they have, and probably avoid Jamison."

"That wouldn't make them curious?"

"It's not that unusual for me to occasionally ask to review security footage. They'll do it. Especially if I insist that it's for something connected to the game."

"What if they know Jamison's looking for you?" Rune asked.

"After that spectacle in the lobby I'm sure they do. But Jamison's a guest like any other. The hotel doesn't hand out information about its employees to guests. We'll tell them to keep it quiet, that we're handling a problem with the game—not security related, obviously—and that we need some time."

"And you think they'll be okay with that?"

Confident they would be, she said, "The hotel doesn't pay them a lot, and in my experience, they don't worry about asking or answering questions they don't have to."

32

It only took Rune and Evie fifteen minutes to get from the church to the Wexsor by subway. Just after five in the morning, Evie pulled her keycard from her pocket and swiped it through the panel next to the door. The latch popped, and she yanked the door open and entered with Rune following.

The behind-the-scenes areas of the Wexsor were not the demonstrations of luxury that the public spaces were. Boring gray walls ran the length of long hallways that served the functional purpose of getting employees where they needed to go. The layout was much like a maze, with no signage, making it impossible for anyone but employees to successfully navigate it. Evie and Rune zipped through without trouble, turning right, right, and left again, before finally finding themselves standing in front of a door marked with an engraved plastic sign that read, "SECURITY."

Evie pressed the call button on the speaker affixed to the wall beside the door. A camera mounted on top of it fed video of her and Rune to whomever was manning the video desk.

"Hey, Evie," came a voice over the speaker.

"Hey, can you let us in?"

There was no response, but the door buzzed and Evie gripped the handle, wrenching it open. She marched through, bypassing two closed doors on her left, headed straight for an open door at the end of the hall.

"Hi, Evan," Evie said, striding into the small room filled with video monitors. Security officer Evan Glick sat in one of two chairs positioned in front of the monitoring desk, earnestly typing something on his cell. Evan had always gone out of his way to be helpful to her. She hoped tonight would be no different.

"Hey, Evie," he said, not looking up. "Just give me...one... second..." He typed out a few more characters, then with exaggerated flare, hit one last button and tucked the phone into his pocket. "Sorry about that. What's up?"

"Evan, I need your help. There's a little hiccup with the game, and I need to take a look at some security footage—"

"There's no footage of the game. We don't have cameras in the room."

"No, I know. I need to see video from earlier tonight from the hallways and one elevator in particular. Is that possible?"

Glick shrugged. "Sure." He gestured to the empty seat beside him, and she dropped into it as he turned to the monitor in front of him and began pecking on the keyboard. "Which hallways and elevator?"

"I'm looking for a certain individual. One of the men from the game. If you pull up footage from the elevator on the twenty-fifth floor around, oh...eight thirty and fast forward, I can show you who I'm talking about."

He followed her instructions and brought up the footage of Kieran arriving on the twenty-fifth floor for the game at the same time Evie was waiting for the elevator to take her to the lobby. The time stamp read "20:32:05."

The sight of him on the screen made her gut feel like lead.

There he was, all handsome and carefree—even though, in a few hours from that moment, he was going to send her world into an insane tailspin. Not that it was his fault, really.

Please don't let it be his fault.

The footage rolled, and they watched as Kieran stepped off the elevator, said something to Evie, then waltzed down the hall.

"Freeze it, please, Evan." He complied. She pointed at Kieran. "I need to see the footage of this man wherever CCTV might have picked him up, okay? Can you pull that?"

He nodded.

"And include the lobby footage of him arriving at the hotel shortly before this and then all the elevator footage of his ride up."

"Sure, okay."

"He would've been in the game room for a long time after this, but he headed out again at about one thirty. He got on the elevator with me, and I need to see that if I can."

"It'll take me a little while. Can you wait?"

Wait? She glanced at Rune and saw her concern reflected in his eyes. Time wasn't something they had a lot of. Especially when every second they spent at the hotel put them at greater risk of being found by Jamison.

She worked up a smile and tried not to sound too demanding. "This is time sensitive, Evan."

Glick's cell phone trilled in his pocket. "Sure, um, sorry, I have to get this," he said, then checked the text he had received. "They're having a bit of a problem with some guy that won't leave the lobby. I have to go help. Can you stay here, and I'll be right back?"

"I really need this quickly, Evan. Can it wait?"

"Apparently not. We're shorthanded tonight. I'll be back in a flash," he said, pushing his rolling chair back and heaving himself out of it. "I promise, if you wait here, I'll pull up whatever you need when I come back."

Glick ambled off down the hallway, and Rune slid into the seat he had abandoned. He reached over and clicked the play button so that the video of Evie interacting with Kieran during their first meeting at the elevator earlier that evening played silently on the screen.

"Look at this guy," Rune said, pointing to Kieran. "His body language completely gives him away."

Evie folded her arms and squinted at the video. "What do you mean?"

"He's totally playing you. See the way he engages you, talking but walking away at the same time? He's baiting you."

"Baiting me?"

Rune nodded. "Reeling you in slowly. Doesn't want to spook you by looking too interested."

She sighed. "You're crazy."

"I'm not. You just can't see it." His eyes darted to her. "I can't decide if it's because you really can't or if you don't want to."

Rune was wrong. He had to be wrong. Whatever was going on with Kieran, he wasn't *playing* her. Frustrated, Evie turned her attention to the far right monitor, directly in front of her seat. Several windows were open, overlapping each other so that only bits of some frames were visible. She cocked her head and leaned closer. One of the partially hidden windows displayed the left half of a woman in a navy pantsuit. *Her* navy pantsuit.

Evie scooted forward in her chair and clicked on the pertinent window.

"What are you doing?" Rune asked, leaning toward her.

She tipped her head at the screen. "That's me. In the elevator. He already had this pulled up. I wonder why?"

"Well, you did run out of here earlier and haven't

responded to anyone's calls. Maybe somebody wanted to figure out why."

"Maybe. If that's the case, it's odd that Evan didn't ask me about it."

The paused video seemed to be taken from a camera mounted high on the rear wall of the elevator car. It showed Evie and Kieran moments after they had left the game and boarded the elevator on the twenty-fifth floor. She hit rewind, and they moved backward in high speed out of the elevator. Another click, and the footage played.

"See, everything's fine," she said, pointing as they turned to face the closing elevator door. "We were coming down, and then he showed up." The video now offered a view of the back of them as a hand shot between the door and frame right before the gap closed. Seconds later, Kieran was slipping a hand around her waist and pulling her close before she severed his embrace.

She winced, watching it, reliving the awkwardness all over again. She bit her lip, expecting that Rune was about to take another shot at Kieran. "I know it looks iffy, but I think that's just his sense of humor."

Rune pulled a face. "Go back. Play it again." He chugged his seat closer and bent in, waiting, then tapped on the screen at the spot on Evie's waist where Kieran had slid his hand. Evie stopped the video.

"Did you see that?" Rune asked.

"See what?"

Rune tapped the screen again. "There. Right there, when he wrapped his arm around you?"

Evie shrugged. He took the mouse from her. "Watch," he said, then rewound the video and clicked play. This time, when the recording reached the moment when Kieran grabbed Evie, Rune hit pause, then kept double-tapping the play button so that the video only advanced a few frames at a time.

She didn't see anything. "What is it?" Evie asked.

"Just watch."

Frame by frame, Kieran's hand snaked around Evie, then she turned away and his hand slipped over her pocket—

Rune clicked the pause button.

There *was* something there. She saw it—right as Kieran's hand went over her pocket. "What is that? What's he doing?" she asked, as they both scrutinized the frozen shot of Kieran's hand as it dipped into the left pocket of Evie's blazer as she twisted away from him.

Rune zoomed in until a maximized, grainy still of Kieran's hand filled the playback window. He backed it up one frame, which clearly showed something in Kieran's fingers before they disappeared into Evie's pocket.

Evie's eyes flew to meet Rune's, then together their gazes snapped down to her front left pocket. She shoved her fingers into it, digging, and almost immediately felt it there, buried in the corner. Cold, thick dread swallowed her as she slowly pulled out one shiny, silvery coin.

"A nickel?" Rune asked. "Why would he—"

"Oh, no," Evie whispered.

"What? You know what this is?"

She nodded. "And it's not good."

33

"It's 5:20 in the morning, Jamison. I've only been asleep a half hour," Art DeVries growled over the phone. The call to his personal cell had woken the man from his Benadryl-induced slumber so that now he sat up in bed, clad in his pin-striped pajamas, still buried beneath his down comforter. His wife snored obliviously next to him.

"I know. I know. And I wouldn't have called, except we have a situation," Jamison said.

"Get to the point."

"Forrester's nickel is missing."

DeVries turned away from his wife, hissing, "What do you mean it's missing? He won tonight. What—did he lose it on his way out?"

"No. I never gave it back to him. I realized it was gone about halfway through the game."

"From the safe?"

Silence came over the line.

"You didn't put it in the safe."

Jamison sniffed. "No. I should have, but it just didn't happen tonight."

"Do you ever?"

More silence.

"I'm taking that as a no." DeVries's voice thickened, his tone growing ominous. "What's the point of the safe, Jamison, if you don't use it?"

"I do use it. For the papers, cash, and bulkier things. But with the small stuff handed over in the middle of the game—jewelry and whatnot—I just hold on to it, and give it back at the end. Or keep it, depending on how things go."

"You do that with my diamonds, too?"

"No, I don't, because that velvet bag you keep them in is too bulky for my pocket," Jamison answered. "Look, it's never been a problem before."

"Well, do you think it's a problem now?"

"Yeah, it's a problem."

"Got that right, it is." DeVries cursed as his wife moaned beside him.

"Artie, please," she whispered.

"Sorry, babe. Go back to sleep. Hold on, Jamison," he said, and climbed out of the elevated king-size bed, dumping himself onto the floor and shuffling into the hallway beyond the master bedroom. He closed the door behind him. "So then, what happened to it?"

"I'm pretty sure it was Kieran Carr. He bumped into me tonight—I thought he was drinking too much, but now I think he was pickpocketing me."

"Carr? You vetted him, right?"

"Heavily. He's clean. But I noticed it was missing right after he left. I sent my guy after him, and we interrogated him—"

"Interrogated or *interrogated?*"

"I handled it. Checked him with the wand and everything. He didn't have it on him."

"Then why are you sure it's him?"

"Because afterwards I reviewed the footage from security.

He was getting real cozy with Evie tonight. Something about it didn't sit well with me. When my guy said they were cozy in the elevator, too, I had a look. He slipped something into her pocket. You can see it on the CCTV footage if you're really looking. You can't see what he's giving her exactly, but it has to be the coin."

"Well, what's the problem then? What did he say? Does the girl have it?"

Again, silence. DeVries sucked in a dangerous breath. "You don't have him."

"I don't. He had nothing on him, so I couldn't hold him. I could have been wrong, and it would have been bad for business to take it any further if he was innocent. I didn't get a look at the footage until after we had let him go. By then he had left the hotel. I sent my man after him again, but...something went wrong. I haven't heard from my guy since."

"And the girl?"

"She's MIA. Stepped out of the hotel—just disappeared—right after connecting with Carr. At first I thought maybe Carr was just using her, but when she disappeared, I realized she was in on it. Then she showed up back at the hotel about an hour later, but as soon as she saw me, she took off. I can't think of why she would run unless she *is* involved." He explained how she raced off in the hotel car and that they tracked it, only to find it abandoned near the diner. "And apparently something went down there that also may or may not have involved Evie."

"What something?"

"A cop got shot."

DeVries groaned. "This just keeps getting better and better. I backed this game, Jamison, because you marketed yourself as a sure thing."

"I've been running this game for two years without a single

hiccup. You know I have. I've exceeded every target you set. You've made a fortune on it."

"And now I stand to lose a fortune. And have the cops poking around in my business. Who's gonna make good on Forrester's nickel if it doesn't turn up? 'Cause I'm not digging into my pockets to fix your screw up. None of the players know I've got a financial stake in this game, and they don't need to know. I don't want them getting ideas about what may or may not be fixed about it. You better find that girl and that nickel before you have to tell Forrester."

"Forrester knows."

DeVries raised a hand to his forehead and scrunched up his eyes. "Have you made any good decisions tonight? Why in the world would you tell Forrester?"

"I had to. He wanted his coin back at the end of the game. He won enough to pay back the advance. I didn't have a reason to keep it. But I convinced him it was in his best interests to give us time to get this taken care of."

"Why was that?"

"Because reporting the theft to the cops would mean cluing them in to the fact that he's been regularly playing in an illegal raked game for quite a while—doesn't matter that he didn't know it was a raked game. Plus, he's got personal reasons for keeping it quiet."

"You didn't tell him about me." It was a statement, not a question.

"No. I'm not an idiot."

"You're doing a great impression of one," DeVries snapped.

Jamison huffed. "I'll find them," he responded stoutly. "I just thought I should keep you in the loop with this much at stake. And, I might need your help. I'm out of man power. Thompson's gone missing and I called two of yours in—Younger and Richards—but Younger got hurt. I can't do this job with only Richards."

"Fine. I'll make a call. But I don't know how fast I can get someone down there, so you'd better get prepared to handle this with only Richards. You got that? *Get this handled.* I do not want to hear about it on New York One tomorrow."

"I'll take care of it. You won't—"

DeVries disconnected before Jamison could finish.

34

"Owww!" Saul bellowed, sounding like an angry bear while laid out on a table in the shed of Dr. Curtis Belland, located in the doctor's backyard on his peaceful residential street in Maspeth, Queens. From the outside, the shed resembled any other normal shed, as did the front half of its interior, which contained yard tools, storage bins, a lawnmower, and such. Across the middle, however, hung a thin plastic curtain separating the front half from the makeshift exam room in the rear half, which Kieran, the doctor, and Saul occupied as the latter received treatment for his gunshot wound.

"Stop griping, Saul," Dr. Belland grunted. "That's the last of it." The silver-haired physician looked to be in his sixties and was still dressed in the pajamas he must have been wearing when Kimball had called to say they needed his help ASAP. Now the pajama sleeves were rolled up and blue surgical gloves covered his hands, spattered in blood from tending to Saul's wound. He stepped back from the table, pulled the gloves off, and tossed them in a trash can.

"Is he going to be all right?" Kieran asked from the stool in the corner where he was perched, watching over the procedure intently. It wasn't that he was actually concerned for Saul. It's just that he didn't want Saul slowing him down.

Dr. Belland nodded as he washed up in a utility sink. "It looked a lot worse than it was. A bleeder, but it'll heal fine. You'll want to stay off it for a few days."

"Can't," Saul protested, pushing up into a sitting position. "Where are my pants?"

"Here," Dr. Belland said, extracting a pair of khakis and a button-down from a tub stored beneath a nearby table. "Take these. Yours are ruined. They'll be a little big, but it's better than what you had." Saul took the pants and began gingerly stepping into the legs. He wobbled, and Dr. Belland reached out to grab his arm, steadying him.

"You got anything in there for me?" Kieran said, pointing to the bloodstains Saul had left all over him.

Dr. Belland inclined his head toward the tub. "Knock yourself out."

Kieran dug through the bin while Dr. Belland scribbled on a prescription pad, then ripped the page off and held it out to Saul. "You may not want to rest, but you'll want to get this filled at any rate, unless you want to risk an infection. It's for antibiotics. You'll need them. And one for a painkiller. In the meantime..."

Kieran had removed his bloody clothes and was putting on the spares, when Dr. Belland had him lean over so he could reach into a cabinet behind him. He did, and Dr. Belland rifled through some bottles, then turned back to Saul, holding out two large pills and two smaller ones. "Take one of each now and again in another six hours. That should hold you till you can get that filled," he said, nodding at the slip of paper in Saul's hand.

"Thanks, Doc," Saul said, popping the first two in his mouth. He slipped the extra pills in his pocket as Kieran wondered exactly how long it would take for the medication to kick in and how loopy it would make Saul once it did.

"Thank me by getting out of here," Dr. Belland said. "Grace won't be up until seven, but I want you long gone by then, you hear? She thinks I'm done with this stuff. If she finds out, I'll never hear the end of her complaining."

"Bet she isn't complaining about the extra cash we send your way for your services."

Dr. Belland's stare bored into Saul. "Just be gone." He glanced at Saul's leg one more time. "And that's gonna slow you down. You lost some blood. It's gonna take a toll."

"I got it, Doc. Better go back to Grace."

Dr. Belland shook his head. "Fine. But lock it up when you leave. I don't want any stupid teenagers getting in and making off with my painkillers." Saul nodded, and the doctor exited through the front of the shed.

Saul's gaze swiveled to Kieran. A mirthful smirk exploded on his face, and he guffawed. Kieran knew why. He had to look like an idiot, now dressed in a slightly baggy pair of white-washed jeans, a gray t-shirt with an "I Love NYC" logo printed on it and a light brown jacket. But it was the best of the lot.

"You've been awfully quiet," Saul said, and slid off the metal table, the lingering smirk disappearing as he landed and winced.

Kieran swallowed his annoyance and folded his arms across his chest. "You should have let me go meet her. I could have had this done already."

"No way was I letting you out of my sight. You're not doing this without me."

"Look, I know you don't want to trust me, but you're going to have to, or this won't work. I didn't have to be here for this. Every second counts and it's been over an hour. What if she's been spooked by the wait?" Kieran said.

"The delay will have made her all the more desperate to

talk to you, see you, to figure out what's going on. Which is the point, right?"

"Yeah, right," Kieran answered, making sure to laden his words with sarcasm.

A knock sounded at the door. It eased open, and Kimball stepped inside.

"So?" Saul asked.

"It's done. We're good to go. Matty's out in the SUV."

"Good," Saul said. "Go ahead with it, then. Get in touch," he told Kieran.

Kieran looked at Kimball. "Where is it?" he asked, and held out his open hand.

Kimball lumbered over to him and slapped a cell phone in his palm. "Six-four-six-seven," he said, then pivoted and walked out the door.

Kieran tapped the security code into the phone, bringing up the home screen. He opened the text app.

"For your sake, kid," Saul said, "I hope you're right about this."

For my sake, I hope I am too, Kieran thought as he typed away.

35

"1913?" Rune asked, taking the nickel from Evie and turning it over in his palm. The aged silvery coin glinted as he turned it. Even from that distance, she could read the imprint of the year it was minted on its face.

Evie nodded solemnly. "It's a Liberty Head Nickel. It belongs to one of the players—Mr. Forrester. He told me about it once." Her focus moved from the coin to Rune, his reddish hair sticking out from behind his right ear as he studied the five-cent piece intently, his brow furrowed. He looked up at her, his gaze piercing.

"It's worth a lot, isn't it?"

Her eyes drilled into him. "A few million, I think."

"You aren't serious."

"It's rare. There were only five or six ever made. Forrester told me."

Rune shook his head in disbelief. "What in the world is a person doing, walking around with this on him?"

"I know. It's crazy, but these people, they don't live in the reality we do. The others did the same sort of thing—with diamonds, or bearer bonds—I doubt Forrester really even thought about it. And besides, unless someone knew its value, it just looks like he's carrying a regular nickel."

"But what if he lost it, or accidentally spent it?"

"No, the last time I saw it, when he showed it to me, he put it in a little protective case. I don't know what happened to that, though."

"So, how did Kieran get it?"

How did Kieran get it? A slow, sick feeling bubbled up in her, even as she tried to come up with a rational reason. "Maybe Forrester gave it to him?"

Rune eyed her skeptically, one eyebrow arched. "What—for safekeeping?"

"Yeah, I know. It's not likely."

"No. If Jamison's chasing it, which seems to be the only explanation right now, then Kieran didn't come by it legitimately. I'd bet whatever this nickel's worth that Kieran stole it from—who'd you say it belonged to?"

"Forrester."

"Yeah, Forrester. Could Kieran have pulled that off in a room full of people? Stolen it, I mean?"

Evie paused, considering his suggestion. "Maybe," she finally said. "If Forrester kept it on him instead of in the safe, or if he gave it to Jamison and he held onto it, I guess it's possible. Kieran *was* bumping into people all night. I thought he was drinking too much, but maybe it was just for show. You think he could have lifted it that way?"

Rune shrugged. "It would explain a lot. But what I don't understand is why Jamison didn't call the cops? If this game is legit, if it's above board and someone stole something there, why wouldn't he report it? That's what most people would do, right?"

"You would think." Evie's sick feeling intensified. Calling

the police is exactly what an honest game host would have done. So what did it mean that Jamison hadn't? What kind of person had she been working for?

Rune rubbed his temple. "I don't care what he's told you and the hotel about that game, something's not right. And that's the reason he doesn't want the police poking around in it. That's why he's coming after you himself. He knows Kieran gave the coin to you, and he can't ask for help from the police."

"Maybe I should just meet him. Explain that I knew nothing about this, turn over the nickel, and be done with it." Even as she said it, she knew it was a terrible idea.

"Except the question is, even if he believed you, would he let it go at that point? Or have things gone too far?"

"What do you mean, 'too far'?" Surely he wasn't saying what it *sounded* like he was saying. "You're not suggesting he would need to get rid of me or something, are you?" When Rune raised his eyebrows invitingly in response, she wagged her head. "No. That's nuts. You've seen too many movies."

"Really, Evie?" Rune pressed, grasping her forearm gently, as if trying to draw her into his way of seeing things. "He's already had somebody come after you—an *armed* somebody. And according to Kieran, Jamison sent someone after him too. Beat him, even. There's a lot of money at stake. Millions. People have killed for less."

Something about that rang true, though she didn't want to believe it. Her shoulders sagged. "So, what do we do?"

"I don't think you can give the nickel up. It's your only leverage, and the only thing holding them off. I think we've got to go straight to the police. It's the only way to make sure you'll be okay."

Deep concern welled in his eyes as he spoke. His fingers still clenched her arm, but not in a manner that was severe. Instead there was something kind in it, although urgent.

Warmth radiated from the place on her skin where he touched her, and a pang of regret rippled through her. She truly had misjudged him badly over the last few months.

Whereas she had always second-guessed Kieran's motives and flirtatious behavior, she knew there was nothing to second-guess here. There was an undeniable I-am-what-I-am quality about Rune. No pretense. No games. He was bravely honest about his intentions, why he had stayed away from her, why he hadn't wanted to, and why he regretted it now. And here he was in this moment, with her, seeing this through for no reason other than he wanted her to be safe. And while Kieran had certainly sparked flickers of attraction in her, he had *only* done that, while Rune—she melted a bit inside as she realized—Rune was kindling embers of affection.

He looked up from the nickel, his eyes meeting hers. Her breath caught, as she took in his handsome face, his stubbly trimmed beard, and his eyes brimming with unspoken intensity. Wrong-footed by her own unexpected reaction, she glanced away sharply, severing their connection. She was wondering exactly how red her face must have been, when her stare landed on a notepad to the right of the keyboard in front of her. Fear drove her stomach into a dive as she registered the first few letters of a word—*Jam.* The rest of it was hidden by a mug of stale, cold coffee.

She shot an arm out, sliding the cup off the note and snatching it up so that she held it between them.

Jamison 2125557277

Her jaw dropped, matched by Rune's. At the same moment, both their heads snapped to the door behind them, which Glick had shut on his way out. Rune jumped out of his chair, moved to the door, and cracked it open.

Evie stood and peered over his shoulder. Despite what Glick had said about needing to leave to assist in the lobby, he was still there in the security office, standing down the hall in the first of the two offices Evie and Rune had passed on their way in. Though partially obscured by that office's half-closed door, he was visibly engaged in a conversation on his cell.

"He's on the phone," Rune whispered, as Glick looked up and saw them staring at him. The security officer's expression froze, but his lips kept moving. He looked so guilty, so exposed, that Evie had no doubt he was talking to Jamison.

Rune closed the door and leaned his back against it. "We've got to go. Now," he said, grabbing her arm. "You ready?"

Together they charged through the doorway, racing for the exit. Glick stepped out into the hallway as they reached the office he had been using. He extended a hand, motioning for them to stop. "Hey, hold up. Where are you—"

"We're leaving, Evan," Evie said, following Rune as he ignored Glick, sidestepping around him.

Glick grabbed Evie's right wrist as she went by him. "Sorry, I can't let you—"

Rune lunged for Glick, but before he connected, Evie had already twisted her palm up and toward her, breaking Glick's hold. Simultaneously, she clamped her left hand just beneath his wrist and rotated her hips to the left, twisting his arm unnaturally and sending him off-balance and stumbling into the wall. They were out the security office exit and running down the hallway before he had even righted himself, the door slamming shut behind them.

They pounded through the many turns until reaching the exterior exit to the alley. Evie slammed into the latch bar across the door's middle and flung it open, revealing the still-dark skies of the very early morning. They barreled out, sprinting for the end of the alley where it opened up onto the street.

"Hey, you okay?" Rune gasped, drawing in heavy breaths.

Evie nodded, breathing too hard to speak.

"You learn that...in Texas...too?" he said, as they careened onto Fifth Avenue, taking a left and heading north.

She took a big gulp of air. "Self-defense course," she said. "Mark insisted on it...before we moved here."

"Smart guy," Rune replied, as they ran headlong down the sidewalk, neck and neck.

"Yeah," she said, her breath ragged. "You have no idea."

~

"WHERE ARE THEY?" Jamison bellowed as he plowed into the security offices, barreling past Glick who had opened the door for him and was still standing there, holding the handle.

"They just ran out—"

"They what?" Jamison snapped, turning so that Richards, following closely on his heels, nearly crashed into him. Pressure was pounding in his ears. "You let them go?"

"There were two of them, what was I supposed to do?"

"Which way did they go? How long ago?"

"Like, less than two minutes. They went out the back alley entrance."

Jamison, resisting the urge to throttle Glick, glared at him. "Show me," he said.

Jogging at a pace that left him breathless, Glick guided them through the halls until reaching the door that led into the alley. Jamison shoved by him and careened through it, meeting only silence and the smell of the dumpsters as he skidded to a stop on the asphalt.

"Where did they go?" he demanded, spinning around to face Glick, his body rigid, his heart pummeling his chest.

"I didn't follow them, but I saw on the monitor," Glick sputtered nervously. He pointed to the camera mounted above the door. “It’s aimed down the alley, where it meets the sidewalk. They turned left on Fifth.”

Jamison and Richards took off running, hanging a left at the end of the alley and disappearing as they sped off, sprinting up the Fifth Avenue sidewalk.

36

Evie and Rune ran up Fifth Avenue, periodically checking behind them as they went. So far it didn't look like anyone was following them. They kept going until finally, heaving and out of breath, they reached the New York Public Library at Fifth and Fortieth and turned left down Fortieth Street.

"Come on, here," Evie said, jogging alongside the library toward Bryant Park, the open green space that took up most of the block behind the public building. Halfway there she stopped at a construction dumpster parked at the curb and leaned against the back of it, using it to shield her from Fifth Avenue. The gun in her waistband had shifted during their sprint, and she adjusted it, tucking it back down. Her chest ached as she tried to catch her breath, a stitch seizing her side.

Rune fell in beside her, panting. He leaned over, bracing his hands on his knees. After several seconds of heavy gasping, he peeked around the dumpster back toward where they had come from.

"I don't see anybody," he said.

"We got lucky," she said, sucking in air. "If we hadn't seen that note..."

The cell phone Kieran had given Evie buzzed in her pocket. She dug it out and read the notification that flashed on the screen. Shock waves rolled over her as she recognized the number—it was Eleanor's. Nausea crested as she read the text and grabbed Rune's arm to steady herself.

You know who this is. Do not contact the police.

Evie's knees wobbled as though they were made of rubber, and she squatted to the ground, her nerves on fire. Rune slid down next to her, and she read the text again as he peered over her shoulder.

I repeat, do not contact the police. We have Gabby. You know I'm telling the truth because I'm texting you from your nanny's phone. If you contact the police or anyone else for help, we will dump Gabby where you will never find her. Do you understand?

Evie's hand shook as it held the cell. "Jamison. He's gotten Eleanor's phone somehow—and he's threatening Gabby..."

Rune reached out, wrapping his fingers around hers. "Evie—"

"What is happening?" Evie cried. "This is insane. How did he even get this number? This isn't my cell!" Her head started to swim, a faint blackness hovering at the edges of her vision. "Kieran," she whispered. "Something's happened to—"

The phone buzzed again as another message came in from the same number. It was a photo of Gabby, in her footie pajamas, lying facedown with something tied around her head. Evie cried out and Rune wrapped an arm around her, holding her steady.

Do you understand?

"Evie, I think he wants an answer. You'd better respond," Rune said urgently.

She forced her shaking fingers to type. *Yes, I understand.*

Good.

She typed, *Is Gabby alright? Where is Eleanor? Where is Kieran?*

Three horrible dots appeared, lingering, lingering...Then the text came.

> *Gabby and Eleanor are both fine and will stay that way if you do what I say. Kieran's been dealt with. We got your number from his cell. He isn't your concern anymore. Head over to Queens. I'll text the address. Be there by 6:15. After that I'll send more directions.*

Evie fingers flew over the virtual keyboard. *Where is Gabby? Eleanor?*

No answer followed. She sent the same questions again. Still, nothing.

"He won't respond. He's not responding!" A black vacuum of horror threatened to consume her.

"Evie," Rune said tenderly, placing a steadying hand on her back as she bowed her head, the hand holding Kieran's cell dropping to her side. "It's gonna be okay."

"They're threatening my daughter, Rune. My daughter! And what about Eleanor? And it sounds like they," she swallowed thickly, "hurt Kieran."

"I know. But," he exhaled softly, "they said they won't hurt them. I don't see why they would. It wouldn't help them at all."

"I have to do something," she said, rocking back and forth, then jumping up and turning in a circle before zeroing in on him. "He said he had Gabby but didn't say what's happened to Eleanor. Does he have her too?" Her eyes grew wet as the words tumbled out of her. "Or has he done something to her, like he probably did to Kieran? Rune, I have to call somebody! I have to go check the apartment, or have the police—"

"You can't, Evie," he said gently. "I know that you want to, but it'll do more harm than good if they're watching your place, and they could be. I mean, for all we know, they're still in your apartment, holding Gabby and Eleanor there."

"We could call the police."

"I really don't think you can," he said, his expression pained. "You don't want to risk Jamison seeing either you or the police at your place. He doesn't have a reason to hurt Gabby and Eleanor now, but you don't want to set him off. If he's willing to have someone shoot a cop, if he got scared—"

"He might hurt them." She sucked in a full measure of the tepid early morning air through her nose, looked down at the sidewalk then back up. "I know you're right! But, ahhh!" She screamed, turning helplessly in place, grabbing the sides of her head. "I have to do something! What about the coin? Should I threaten to get rid of it?" She wrung her hands as if flinging off excess water. "I can't think straight. My brain's buzzing!"

"I think that might make things worse," Rune said. "Threatening to chuck the coin may just make him more desperate. If he believes he's about to lose millions of dollars—"

The cell phone buzzed again. It was another text message from Eleanor's phone. An address, and nothing else.

"How far is that?" Evie asked, but Rune was already pulling it up in Google Maps.

"It's in Long Island City. Not far by the time we walk to a station and hop on a train. Maybe fifteen minutes when they're all running? But at this time of day...I don't know. The schedule should pick up soon, but it's, what," he glanced at the clock on the phone, "just now five thirty? They might not be running as often. We might get there and have to wait."

She turned his hand so she could see the map better. "That address is on my line. The 7 train. It's direct from Grand Central to Vernon Boulevard. No stops." Her finger traced the purple line indicating that the train service ran from Grand Central Station, under the East River, then popped out after reaching Queens. She traced her finger back over the line to Grand Central, then followed it a bit further west to the next station.

"But the Bryant Park station is closer to us," she said, pointing on the map to the Fifth Avenue-Bryant Park subway station located on the north side of the block they were now standing on. "There would be an extra stop, but we'd get to the train faster. But, you're right, the 7 is only running, like, every ten minutes now, and we could get there and have to wait for it."

"Well, let's start in that direction. If we end up missing the train, we'll grab a cab. Or call an Uber. Whatever. The traffic leaving the city isn't that bad at this hour. A cab wouldn't take that much longer than the train."

She nodded, her legs trembling beneath her. But the dizziness had cleared. They were going to do this. They were going to save Gabby and Eleanor.

"Come on," he said, extending his hand to her. "We'll get them back. And then we'll go to the police. Okay?"

Evie clasped her hand around his, and he tugged, urging her to move. The warmth and weight of his grip was comforting and spurred her on, her steps quickening to follow after him. They had just reached the corner, when through the cross traffic, Evie caught a flash of something hurtling rapidly up the sidewalk, a block away.

Jamison was racing straight for them.

37

Kieran sat in the second row of the Traverse while Saul drove, as if chauffeuring him around. Saul had insisted on driving, despite his bad leg, and based on his grunting and cursing, it was hurting pretty badly. Kieran could sense the tension coming off Saul like ripples from a stone thrown in water, and he suspected the man's patience was nearly out.

At 5:40 a.m., traffic was beginning to pick up as commuters came into Manhattan from the other boroughs, trying to beat the rush that would begin clogging the island's arteries in the next half hour or so. This slowed them a bit, but they were still making good time. Saul and Kieran followed behind Matty and Kimball, who were now driving another car, a sedan they had picked up from Saul's garage on the way to Long Island City.

"You're sure about this warehouse?" Kieran said, sliding Eleanor's cell phone into his pocket. He was uncomfortable with the fact that he hadn't had a chance to scope the place beforehand. Unknowns were wild cards that could land you in a lot of trouble.

"My buddy bought it to flip," Saul said. "It's been deserted for years. He's putting together the cash to gut it and renovate, so no one's in it now. It's a few blocks from the parking garage. Matty can stay there with the girl till you make the exchange in the warehouse." He gave a jerk of his head toward the rear of the SUV. "I still don't like this. Taking her was risky."

"Yeah, well, we needed leverage. It's the only way to keep Evie from bringing the cops back in."

"Unless she calls them anyway."

"No. No way. She won't risk Gabby's safety." Kieran looked over his shoulder into the cargo compartment of the SUV. Gabby lay there in her little footie pajamas, with an old T-shirt wrapped around her eyes. Kieran's earbuds filled her tiny ears, piping in classical music over Bluetooth from his cell. Her hands were tied behind her. *Was she sleeping or simply following the instructions they had given her to stay still and not say a word?*

"I don't like messin' with kids," Saul said.

Kieran's stomach tightened. "And you think I do? This isn't what I wanted, but it'll be enough to secure Evie's cooperation. And when it's done, we'll turn the kid loose and somebody will get her back to Evie. Easy peasy."

"You think she's got a clue?" Saul asked.

"Who, Evie? No," Kieran said, shaking his head. "Right now she's thinking the guy she had a crush on is dead and that it's all Jamison's fault. To her, he's a thief, kidnapper, and murderer, and that's who she'll point the cops to once this is all over."

Saul hunched in his seat, leaning one arm on the center console. "It won't hold up. Jamison'll have other alibis. Other people will have seen him. There will be other calls he's made —her story will get torn apart. They'll know you're involved."

"Maybe, maybe not. He's got people working for him, right? That could explain a lot. But the story will definitely cause enough confusion to give me time to disappear." Kieran let out a hiss of breath. "Even if they eventually figure out that 'Kieran Carr' was involved, by then 'Kieran Carr' will have fallen off the face of the earth, I'll be someone else, and no one will ever know you had anything to do with this."

"You better be right about that," Saul grunted.

"I am," Kieran said confidently. Because, as always, he had a plan.

Saul snorted. "Well, I'd ask you if you were willing to bet your life on that—but, seeing as you already have..."

GABBY LAY very still in the back of the car, moving only when the bumps in the road rocked her. The music was very, very loud. Loud, fancy music, like the kind in the movie when Cinderella went to the ball. Not so loud that it hurt. Just loud enough to make it very hard to think. Loud enough that she couldn't understand what the bad man in the seat in front of her was saying. She could tell he was there because she could hear him talking, even though the music in the earbuds made him sound all mushy.

Her tummy hurt. She wanted to go home. But they said she couldn't go home yet and told her to stop asking.

She didn't know what the bad men looked like. She couldn't see the ones in the car because her eyes were covered and she was keeping them closed, just like they told her to. And she didn't see the man that took her out of the apartment either, because he had been wearing a mask. He had carried her out in his arms, just like mommy did when Gabby got really, really tired after walking around the zoo all day.

She loved the zoo. Mommy took her there sometimes on Saturdays, and they would watch the bears and the penguins and the lions, and get cotton candy and Cokes. She wished she was there now, holding Mommy's hand at the zoo and drinking a Coke.

Her face was getting hot and she wanted to cry. But she

knew she couldn't cry, so she sniffed it back. She had tried crying and screaming when they first took her from the apartment. Then the man in the mask told her that if she didn't stop, Eleanor and Mommy would get hurt. So, she stopped, and did exactly what the man had said. She had to obey, because she didn't want anything bad to happen to Mommy or Eleanor.

She had been in the car for a long time. It felt like at least a whole *PAW Patrol*. Maybe more. The bad man had said that they were taking her to see Mommy, but she didn't believe him because she knew that bad people tell lies. Mommy had always told her not to believe what strangers said, because they might be someone trying to take her. Mommy said that if she ever met a bad person, she should get away as fast as she could.

Super fast, Mommy? Should I run super fast?

Super fast, baby. Faster than fast.

And that's what she would do. She would run away faster than fast. Because just like Ryder in *PAW Patrol*, she had a problem and she had a plan. Step one of the plan: Pray. And she had been praying. Praying for Mommy and Eleanor and for God to let her get away and run faster than fast.

Step two of the plan: Lie there quietly, not saying a word, listening to the loud, fancy music, and doing exactly what the bad men said.

Except for one thing.

38

Evie pushed herself, keeping up with Rune, whipping her head back to check the distance between them and Jamison, who she now saw wasn't alone. Another man was alongside him, also barreling toward her and Rune.

They had sprinted up Fifth Avenue, planning to make a left on Forty-Second and then run down the block to the subway station at Bryant Park, but halfway there, Rune yanked on her arm.

"Change of plans," he said, dragging her to the right and pulling her into the middle of Fifth Avenue, dodging cars as they ran pell-mell across the road, heading east on Forty-First Street instead.

"What are you doing?" Evie yelled over the honking of angry drivers, as she and Rune darted between cars to reach the sidewalk on the opposite side. "I thought we were headed to the station at Bryant Park."

Rune shook his head. "Not with them chasing us. It's too small. They'll find us in there. It's after five thirty now. Grand Central Terminal will be open. We might be able to get lost in the crowds there and then catch the 7 without him seeing us."

She nodded, working to turn on even more speed. As she flew by a signpost, she jerked her hip and rotated to avoid ramming into it as her mind raced.

Why is Jamison here chasing us when he's supposed to be meeting us in Long Island City? Where's Gabby? Should we just stop and confront him?

But as she sped after Rune, she had no answers for any of these questions except the last one. Because one look at Jamison's posture and the ferocious way in which he was pursuing them told her that letting him catch up to them would be a very bad idea. Her gut said to keep going, and so she did. Rune, who was charging ahead of her, must have felt the same because he never slowed.

After another block, with Jamison and his companion still close behind, they cut left at Park Avenue, headed toward Grand Central Terminal. Commuters had begun filtering into Manhattan from the other boroughs, and the increasing traffic gave Evie and Rune something to work with. They cut between cars like a frenzied game of Frogger, glaring beams from car headlights slicing the weakening darkness as the pair ran through them, using the vehicles as a makeshift barrier separating them and the approaching Jamison.

They reached the terminal's impressive main entrance on Forty-Second Street running full tilt. The Beaux-Arts architectural wonder towered above them with its imposing limestone arches and *Glory of Commerce* sculpture at its pinnacle. They burst through the outer doors, then through a second set of interior ones, as Evie took the lead.

"Come on," she said, grabbing his arm and dashing across Vanderbilt Hall. She skipped the most direct route to the subway, instead skidding to a stop in the cavernous Main Concourse, beneath the golden celestial mural decorating its cerulean blue ceiling.

"Why'd you skip the passage to the subway?" he asked, his chest heaving.

"I thought we might shake him in here," she explained. But it was obviously a no-go. The terminal was crowded, but not crowded enough to provide sufficient cover. "This way," she barked over the drone of announcements being made over the loudspeaker that reverberated off the hall's creamy, imitation Caen stone walls. Snagging hold of Rune's sleeve, she yanked him forward sharply, picking up speed as they crossed the pink, Tennessee marble floor.

The next quick right took them down a short passageway. At the end of it was a set of escalators and stairs leading down to the subway platforms for the 4, 5, 6, 7, and S trains. More people were gathered here, and they pushed through them to the stairs, taking several steps at a time. Just as they reached the bottom, they heard Jamison shouting, and turned to see him, his face and shoulders visible above the other descending travelers.

"Evie! Stop, Evie!" Jamison bellowed, shoving his way down the stairs after them.

"Come on! Come on!" Rune shouted, elbowing past another commuter and jumping the turnstile.

Evie followed suit, yelling, "This way!" as she went, cutting through the open common area from which the passageways to the various subway lines branched off. They followed the signs marking the way to the platform for the 7 train, pink tiles turning to white, Rune nearly tripping over the backpack of one man leaning up against a column, checking his phone. Evie grabbed Rune's arm, helping him recover, then guided him as they tore down more steps, rounded corners and raced through the pathways so familiar to her after making the same commute for years.

They burrowed deeper and deeper into the bowels of the station until finally chugging down the last set of stairs and hurtling onto the platform for the 7 train. A set of tracks ran along either side of the platform, with signs suspended over each displaying a purple circle with a white "7" at its center. One was Queens-bound, headed east; the other, west, farther into Manhattan. The train they wanted, the Queens-bound one, wasn't there.

Please, please, Lord, Evie prayed silently as she peered down the track and saw nothing but darkness. No headlights of an approaching train. Nothing. Her eyes flashed to Rune.

"It's not here. It's not here!" she yelled in panic.

Rune locked into her gaze, his face twisted in worry, his troubled visage clearly communicating that he wanted to say something, to do something, to make it better. He bit his lip, his head swiveling back to the stairs they had just come from.

Jamison wasn't there yet.

"Maybe we lost him. We took those tunnels really fast."

Evie's nervous stomach told her different. "Rune—"

"Come on," he said, once again holding his hand out to her. She grasped it, and he pulled her farther along the narrow platform, speed walking away from the stairs. All around them people sat, stood, paced...waiting for the same train, but not desperately. Not terrified that everyone they cared about was about to be taken from them.

Ahead of them, near the end of the platform was another set of stairs. Rune nodded at them. "We'll go back up if we have to, try to lose them again if we run out of platform before the train gets here. Maybe hail a taxi up top—"

An unnatural breeze slowly built in pressure, catching tendrils of Evie's hair, now loosed from her bun, blowing them around her face. The pair spun as the lights of the Queens-bound 7 train bore down on them. In seconds it thundered past where they stood, then, with an ear-splitting screech, quickly came to rest. The doors opened.

Evie and Rune darted inside the nearest compartment,

silver-sided with hard brown plastic seats. The car was only half full, but neither sat, instead grabbing on to a metal pole in the center aisle, their eyes glued to the staircase that had brought them to the platform, watching for any sign of Jamison. In half a minute, the doors would shut, and they would be safe.

Ten seconds passed...

Fifteen...

"This is a Queens-bound 7 local train," announced a prerecorded female voice. "The next stop is Vernon Boulevard, Jackson Avenue."

Twenty seconds.

A male voice replaced the female one. "Stand clear of the closing doors, please."

They looked at each other.

Twenty-five seconds.

A "ding-dong" bell sounded, first at a high pitch, then a lower one. "Stand clear of the closing doors, please," the voice repeated as the doors began to slide together smoothly.

And then Jamison emerged, flying down the stairs and landing so hard at bottom that he nearly fell. He grabbed the railing, steadying himself as his companion sailed past him, racing along the platform, scanning erratically, attempting to look in every direction at once.

Evie's heart dove, weakness claiming her. Through the grimy glass she watched Jamison hustle determinedly down the side of the train, scanning the faces in every car. She gripped the pole, clasping one hand over Rune's, until finally Jamison reached their car, more than halfway down the train, and spotted them inside. He slapped his palms against the window, and Evie jumped, letting go of the pole and backing up to the seats on the opposite side of the car. Raw anger twisted Jamison's features as he screamed her name, still pounding on the window as the train pulled away from the platform.

39

Saul had parked the Traverse in a dark corner of a multi-level garage about a five-minute drive from the abandoned warehouse where Kieran would be meeting with Evie. The garage was decades old, with rusty metal spots on its supports and chipped chartreuse paint that, in places, revealed at least two other shades from years gone by. By the looks and sour smell of it, the garage was due for another sprucing if it was going to keep up with the revitalization happening in much of Long Island City. Saul had backed into a secluded space on the fourth floor, preventing all but the car next to it from having a view into its rear compartment. And given that the windows were heavily tinted, even if someone tried to peek inside from the adjacent space, they wouldn't be able to discern what was currently stowed in the back unless they actually pressed their face to the glass.

Kieran moved up to the passenger seat next to Saul as they waited for Matty to join them. He was walking up through the garage to meet them, while Kimball remained in the sedan parked on the street. Kieran checked his watch, wondering how much longer it would be before Matty got there. If this plan was going to work, they couldn't waste any time. Matty would be taking over babysitting duty while Saul, Kimball, and Kieran recovered the coin from Evie. Once Matty got word that they had succeeded, he would drop the girl somewhere farther out from the city, where she would be found.

"If he heads east on the LIE, there's a stripmall just inside Syosset that would work," Kieran commented, pointing to a spot right off the Long Island Expressway on the map he had pulled up on his phone. He kept his voice low, not wanting Gabby to overhear through the earbuds. "That's what—an hour away? It's far enough out that it shouldn't be a problem for us. Matty can turn her loose there, and somebody'll notify the cops. They'll get her back to her mom."

Saul's face wrinkled in distaste. "Dropping kids off in parking lots? I don't have a good feeling about this."

Kieran forced himself not to groan. "I'm telling you, you're golden, Saul. You said the plate on this car can't be traced to you. Matty has sunglasses and a ball cap, so even if someone or some camera gets a look at the SUV, they won't be able to tell who it is. It won't come back on you. You've got nothing to worry about. All cons get complicated at some point. This one's no different. We just have to work through it."

"It wouldn't have had to get complicated if you had just delivered my share of the one and a half million you scammed from Meyer like you were supposed to, instead of gambling it away," Saul said.

"Don't you think I know that? I've beaten myself up plenty over that fact. The con you came up with for Meyer was a good one, and it was an easy three-quarters of a million for each of us."

"That con was a work of art."

"Yeah, it was. More so than the crud that hangs in 'The Carr Gallery.'" Kieran made air quotes as he spoke of the gallery in Brooklyn that served as his legitimate business front. "Look, I'm aware I screwed up. I appreciate the trust you put in me, calling me in when you needed a point man. And I *did* do my job."

"To a degree."

"You needed someone to smooth-talk Dallas Meyer, and I did that. 'Martin Lane,'" he said, tapping his chest, "the CEO of 'FutureTech,' was the perfect cover. And I sold him one hundred percent on the fake, next-gen identity protection software your friends worked up for us. Meyer couldn't get me a cashier's check fast enough. *I did my job.*" Kieran's body tensed. He was a professional, and he didn't like being accused of being anything less.

"And then you stole my share."

"I borrowed it. And now I'm giving it back, with interest. Your three-quarters of a million is about to be two million. So, can we stop this whole 'I stole from you' business? You're going to more than double your take. I'd say that's worth whatever trouble you've had to go through. I don't know why you're complaining. I'm the one who'll have to walk away from here and start over as someone else."

"Don't try and sell me that. You have plenty of other identities for plenty of other cons to cheat plenty of other rich idiots." Saul shifted in his seat, leaning back and taking the pressure off his injured leg.

"You going to make it?" Kieran said, unable to keep a note of sarcasm from bleeding through.

"I'm fine," Saul replied, glaring at him. "When she shows up at the warehouse—if she shows up—you really think she'll do it? Just hand that coin over to you?"

"Absolutely. But it won't come to that. She doesn't even know she has it. I'll get it from her before she realizes what's going on. Then I'll tell her to go, you'll tell Matty to drop the kid off, and we'll be four million richer while she tells the cops it's all Jamison's fault."

"And she just walks away, right?" Saul asked.

"It's the best way. No bloodshed, and she helps point the finger at Jamison for as long as possible."

"And once we have the coin? How are you planning on splitting that up?"

"There's an underground market for this sort of thing. I made inquiries weeks ago. I've already got a buyer in China, actually. He's just waiting on confirmation that I have it. Four point one million." Kieran rubbed his hands together greedily.

"Four point one? You're sure."

Kieran nodded. "I'm sure."

"You're not stepping a foot out of this city until I have my cash in hand. Not to do that deal. Not for nothin'."

Kieran snorted. "No. I figured you wouldn't be up for that. When I let the buyer know we've secured the coin, he'll send a man over to make the exchange. Shouldn't be more than two days."

Saul shot him a suspicious stare. "I have a feeling there's a catch in there somewhere."

Kieran shook his head. "No catch, Saul. This part *is* simple. We sell that coin, and you'll instantly be two million dollars richer."

To their immediate left, the metal door to the stairwell swung open, clanging as it hit the wall, the sound echoing in the vast cavern of the garage, bouncing around the hard surfaces of the concrete structure. Matty walked through the doorway and headed straight for them.

"Here's your boy," Kieran said, opening his door. "Time to move."

40

The train sped through the tunnel toward the Vernon Boulevard stop, Evie's heart still thundering in her chest. The other passengers, however, had quickly moved on from Jamison's outburst, blithely returning to their phones, books, and earbuds. She rubbed her palms, slick with sweat, against her pants and glanced up at the arrival monitor. They had five minutes before reaching the station. Evie pressed further into her seat as Rune knelt in front of her, bringing his face level with hers.

"You okay?"

A warm, wet tear leaked from her eye. Evie wiped it away with the back of her hand, then took a deep breath to steady herself. "Yeah, but...Rune, if Jamison was just chasing us—who are we meeting in Long Island City?"

She looked at him, searching his eyes for an answer that was better than the only one that made sense now.

His expression was grim. "I think you know."

"No." She shook her head obstinately against the growing certainty in her belly.

"Evie, come on," Rune sighed. "The nickel? He hid that thing in your pocket. *On purpose.* You saw—"

"There has to be a reason. There has to be." *There has to be.* She couldn't have gotten it so terribly wrong. Kieran had befriended her, laughed with her...

"No," she said, jamming her hands in her lap. "He wouldn't do that. He...he wouldn't take my daughter and threaten to hurt her." She sniffed, thinking that her words sounded hollow even to her. But maybe if she said them enough times, it would be true. Maybe then, she wouldn't feel so stupid.

"Then what? Evie, seriously, what do you think is happening here?"

She tossed out the one explanation she could come up with. "What if it *is* Jamison behind it all, and it was just an unlucky coincidence that we crossed paths? Maybe he's sending us to meet his people in Long Island City." The car jerked as it barreled down the track, jarring Evie forward and nearly sending Rune to the floor. He grabbed onto the pole again for stability.

"Evie, don't you think it's odd that Jamison would want us to go all the way to Queens to meet him if he's sitting in Midtown? It would be one thing if Jamison was already in Queens—if he took Gabby and was still in the area. Then it might make sense that he would want to meet us there. But that's obviously not the case."

She shrunk in her seat. "I don't know."

He exhaled, his eyes full of sympathetic sadness. "Why are you fighting this so hard? Why can't you accept the obvious? You like this guy that much, that you're willing to ignore the only explanation that fits?"

Heat flushed through her. "No! No, it's not that. I just...I just can't be *that* wrong about judging him, about judging his...feelings, or whatever, toward me. Because if I am, do you see how gullible that makes me? What an idiot that makes me?"

Rune wagged his head. "Evie, no. If this *is* Kieran, then he planned this. It was a well-thought-out plan designed to use you, at least on some level. He intentionally misled you. Anybody could fall for that."

She bit her lip, rubbing a hand over her hair, allowing several moments to pass before answering. "If you're right, and Kieran is involved—then what does that mean? Have we been running from the wrong person this whole time?"

Rune dropped into the seat next to her, their arms touching. The connection was comforting, and she allowed herself to lean on him as he spoke. "Evie, I don't think we could have done anything differently. Even if it is Kieran who is pulling the strings, you saw Jamison at that door." He tipped his head at the place where Jamison had railed his fists against the glass. "He may not be the person who's taken Gabby, but Jamison's working some kind of angle in this thing, and I don't see how we can trust him. I mean, he did send someone after you on the street..." He paused. "Unless that was Kieran...or someone else..."

As Rune's words trailed off, his shoulders drooped. He inhaled heavily, closing his eyes as if centering himself, then turned calmly to Evie, resting a hand on her arm. "The one thing we do know is that, whoever we're heading toward on this train—whether it's Kieran or someone else—the fact is, that as far as we can tell, they've got Gabby. They're dangerous, and they've shown that they are willing to do whatever it takes to get this coin—including shooting a cop. In the end, we don't have a choice but to follow through to get Gabby and Eleanor back."

Evie's gaze flicked up to the monitor. Only a couple of minutes remained before the train arrived at Vernon Boulevard station. "So, I meet him. And then what? Does he just walk away and give Gabby back to me? Let us get on with our lives? How can he be sure that I won't run straight to the police and tell them what's happened? Because that's what I'll do." She reached into her pocket, gripping the nickel. "What if he has no intention of letting me go?"

Rune didn't answer.

Evie pushed. "Why leave a witness? If he's set this entire thing up to look like Jamison is responsible, why would he want me around?"

"Maybe that's it. He's banking on you being around to point to Jamison. That you'll be left to tell the world that Jamison was the one behind everything."

"Or he'll pin my murder on Jamison and really seal the deal." She threw her hands up. "We can't call the police because they said not to, and we don't want to spook them and have them end up hurting Gabby and Eleanor, but I don't see how we can do this alone. I feel like there's no way this can work out."

Another pre-recorded announcement verified that the next stop was Vernon Boulevard. The monitor confirmed that there was one more minute of travel time.

"Maybe we're looking at this all wrong," Rune said.

"What do you mean?"

"If we hadn't run into Jamison on Fifth, we wouldn't know that something more is happening here, right?"

She nodded slowly, wondering where he was going with this.

"We could have missed this train. Or it could have been late."

"Okay," she said, feeling her brow wrinkle as she eyed him.

"And I might not have been on the street when I was earlier, for that matter. I might not have been there to stop that guy coming for you."

"You're saying...what, exactly?"

"I'm saying that as lost as we feel at this moment, as bad as it looks, you shouldn't give up hope. I don't believe we're in this all alone. Do you?"

"It sure feels like it."

"Right now you need to go with what you *know*, not what you feel. Feelings can lie," he said.

"I'm not sure how that helps us."

"If we hadn't run into Jamison, we would still be thinking that he was the bad guy in all this."

"He is the bad guy," she said.

"Maybe. But not the worst guy."

"This is Vernon Boulevard/Jackson Avenue. The next stop is Hunters Point Avenue," the recorded voice announced to the car.

Rune rocked out of his chair and grabbed the pole as the train slowed. "We may have to rethink our strategy. If that *is* Kieran on the other end of that phone, then given how he's acting and what he's said up to now, it seems like he still believes you don't know about the coin. He hasn't mentioned it once that I can think of."

She searched her memory. "No, he hasn't."

"He hid it on you without your knowing. It was thin, small, light—practically disappeared in that jacket pocket. He hasn't told you it's there. I don't think he had any intention of ever telling you."

"And?"

A hint of a hopeful smile curved his mouth. "And that gives us an advantage."

41

Saul stepped off the parking garage elevator before Kieran, groaning as he put weight on his just-sutured leg. Kieran, directly behind him in the elevator, cursed. "Forgot my phone," he griped, as he held his finger on the "Close Door" button.

"Wait—" Saul said, stepping quickly toward him, his leg catching and his face twisting in pain.

"I'll be right back."

"No—" Saul's words were cutoff as the door sealed shut. Kieran continued pressing his finger on the button, ensuring Saul wouldn't be able to open the door by recalling the elevator. In less than a second, it was already rising, on its way to the fourth level where the Traverse was parked.

The door opened with a whirring and soft thump as it retracted. Kieran walked out and heard a loud beep-beep coming from somewhere else in the structure—the opposite end or maybe one floor down from the sound of it—triggered by a driver locking his vehicle remotely. Wherever they were, Kieran couldn't see them from this position, which was a good thing. But that wouldn't last long. At 5:50 in the morning, soon other drivers would be rolling through the garage, either leaving it or looking for a space. They would be walking through it, too, on their way in and out, some going right by here to get to or from the elevator. He had to move fast.

He twisted back to the elevator, and just before the door closed, stooped and placed his balled-up jacket on the threshold between the frame and the door, preventing the door from shutting. As the door made repeated attempts to close, Kieran strode to the SUV, a short twenty feet away. He knocked on the driver's door with the knuckle of his forefinger. Through the darkened glass, he detected a spastic flurry of movement.

The door popped open. "What the heck, man!" bellowed Matty. "You scared—"

"You didn't see me coming?" Kieran interrupted. "You're supposed to be keeping watch. What—were you sleeping?"

"Uh," his slow response and guilty look betrayed him. "Nah. No, just fiddling with the radio."

Kieran opened the door the rest of the way. "Well, come on out here. Quick. We gotta talk."

"Where's Saul?"

"Downstairs. His leg's killing him. Didn't want to come up. Come on," he said, tugging on Matty's arm. "Plans have changed a bit, and I have to explain."

Matty's face fell. "Why don't you just get in—"

"The girl doesn't need to hear this, and I had to turn off her music when I left. Look, I don't have time for this, Matty," Kieran said, grabbing his arm and pulling him out. "Just come on."

"Okay, fine," Matty relented, following Kieran as he led him around to the back of the SUV. Kieran peered into the window of the cargo area, pressing his nose up against the glass. Gabby was still blindfolded and bound. She hadn't moved. He looked up as Matty came around the corner of the vehicle.

"So, what?" Matty said, a hint of annoyance in his tone. "Am

I not waiting here anymore?" The alarm bell from the elevator was going off and Matty swiveled sharply toward the noise. "Why is that going off—"

His question was cut short by the swift flash of a knife. Matty's hands shot up, clutching at his throat where the blade had sliced across it, and he dropped to his knees.

Kieran leaned in close, whispering, "You guys should have searched me again *after* we visited the bar. All kinds of dangerous stuff in there." He straightened up and watched coldly as, over the span of seconds, the life finished draining from Matty's eyes and he collapsed facedown on the dirty concrete floor.

Kieran dragged Matty's body another foot so that it was completely hidden behind the SUV, then bent over it to fish out his phone and gun. Once finished, he shoved Matty's corpse beneath the bumper, pushing and tucking, until he was certain it wouldn't be seen by anyone passing by. Then he strode out from behind the Traverse, calmly retrieved his balled-up jacket from the elevator, and stepped inside as the alarm ceased and the door slipped shut.

~

THREE FLOORS DOWN, the elevator opened to a crimson-faced Saul showering Kieran with curses as he stepped out. The tirade continued as Kieran pushed past him toward the parking deck exit, Saul hobbling behind him and grumbling.

"Do not do that again! And what were you think—"

"I was thinking I needed my cell phone," Kieran snapped angrily, charging through the heavy metal door that led to the sidewalk. It slammed open against the concrete wall of the vestibule as he swiveled to face Saul, limping through after him, struggling to keep up. "What's your problem?"

"My problem is that I don't trust you," Saul spat, passing Kieran, who was standing in place.

"Well, I don't trust you," Kieran barked at Saul's back. He clenched his fists, then quickly strode to come alongside Saul as he walked down the sidewalk. "You sending Kimball and Matty after me earlier tonight was proof that you don't exactly have my best interests at heart. But you don't see *me* throwing temper tantrums, do you? Throwing my weight around like some kind of middle school bully?"

Saul's eyes narrowed dangerously. "You don't have any weight in this thing *to* throw around."

Kieran's eyebrows shot up. "Really? 'Cause I'm thinking that four million dollars weighs a whole lot."

Kieran took several steps forward before realizing Saul had stopped walking. He turned back to him, and for a few moments they stood there, facing off. Vehicles rambled by them in both directions, their headlights filtering through the expiring night, making way for dawn and the onslaught that would soon be headed for the Queens-Midtown Tunnel. Finally, Saul reached up and poked Kieran in the chest, igniting a red-hot spark beneath Kieran's skin where Saul's finger hit him.

"That four million does not give you leverage," Saul seethed. "That four million is your last hope. Because if you fail to get me that four million, the only *weight* you're gonna have is the one tied around your neck, keeping your bloated corpse at the bottom of the East River."

The spark had fanned out from the spot on Kieran's chest into flames that licked through his center. He snorted. "See? *That's* what I'm talking about. Think about it, Saul. Why would I be planning to cheat you out of your half of that four million? I mean, I didn't even have to tell you how much I was getting for it. If I was planning on cheating you, I could have just told you it was two million, right? I didn't have to tell you about all four.

But I did. Because I admit I messed up and that I owe you. And this is me, making good on that debt. So, relax already."

Saul was rigid, his gaze raking over Kieran as if physically digging into him. "You do this thing, you get me that two million, and we are *done*. But until then, you do what I say and you do not leave me behind again. Got it?" He brushed by Kieran, his limp pronounced as he resumed walking toward Kimball, still sitting in the sedan parked just a couple of spaces away.

"Yeah, I got it," Kieran hissed under his breath, quelling the angry heat within him by contemplating his plan and how good it was going to feel to execute it.

42

Gabby took a deep breath and listened. The car was awfully quiet. The music in the earbuds wasn't playing anymore, but she had stayed still, pretending to be asleep, doing what they told her to do so the men didn't get mad. The last thing she had heard was a while ago—voices, and then a door slam, then someone behind the car, bumping against it. After that, it had just been quiet.

She was trying extra hard to be quiet herself, because if they knew what she had been doing, they would be really mad. But she needed to get out and warn Mommy and Eleanor and find a policeman. Mommy always said that if she ever was scared or lost or anyone tried to take her, she should find a policeman, and they would make her safe.

She needed to get away. So, even though the man had told her to be still, she had been working and working at the scratchy string tied around her wrists—something one of the men had called "twine." Another man had said they needed something called a "zip tie," because the twine wouldn't work. She had pretended really good that it *did* work, even though he was right, because they hadn't made it very tight, and now the string was getting looser and looser as she picked at it.

After several minutes, Gabby stopped working and listened again. Not only was it super quiet, but she *felt* alone. The same way she felt alone when she was in her bed at night, eyes squeezed shut and trying to hear Eleanor watching the TV down the hall. She could tell when she was the only person in the room. And it felt like that now.

What if they've left me? Then I could get away and run to the police so, so fast.

She tugged a little harder on the string than before, rubbing her hands back and forth, until she could really feel the piece of string moving. She rolled on her side, to be able to get at it better, and tried to pull her fingers through, but it wasn't loose enough yet. She worked some more, the string hurting her wrists as she tugged and tugged. She made her hand as tiny as she could and tried again to pull it through—oh, it burned—and then, suddenly, it popped out. She yanked off the shirt wrapped around her head, and blinked.

She rose slowly, bracing against the back seat until she was just high enough to peek over the top of it. The car was empty. There was no one in it. She was all by herself.

Gabby crept from side to side, the rustle of her pajamas the only sound as she checked to see if anyone was standing outside the car. No one was there.

The bad men were gone!

Her heart beat faster as she started to climb over the back seat. But then she saw a car driving down the row toward her, and she dropped down as it went by, hoping that they wouldn't see her.

What if it was more bad men?

She peeked out the window, making sure the car had gone, then ripped the earbuds from her ears and threw them on the floor.

She pulled the string from her other wrist, then climbed over the back seat and yanked on the rear door handle. The door opened, and she pushed out, dropping with a thump onto the ground.

Gabby knew where she was. This was a parking garage, like the one Mommy sometimes parked in when they went to the big, giant mall. That one was huge and full of cars and confusing because it went round and round. Her tummy felt sick. If this one was like that garage, she might never find her way out.

Wait—that's an l-vator!

It was right there, right next to the bad men's car. Her heart lifting, she ran to the l-vator and pressed the down button.

43

Evie and Rune bolted from the subway as soon as the doors opened at the Vernon Boulevard-Jackson Avenue station. Her eyes shot back and forth, searching for any sign of Jamison.

Were they safe? Did Jamison know they were coming here—and was he on the street now, waiting? Was that even possible, could he have caught a cab and beat them there?

No. It wasn't likely, but it didn't stop Evie from being terrified that he had somehow managed it. But the street was clear—no Jamison or his companion, or anyone that seemed interested in them.

The address they had been given was up Vernon Boulevard, just a couple of blocks from the subway. She had agreed with Rune that it was best not get there by the direct route. Instead, they would take the long way, in case someone they couldn't see was following or watching them. It would also give them extra time to think through their plan. So, rather than walking north on Vernon Boulevard, straight to their destination, they crossed the intersection, heading west on Fiftieth Avenue. They would go around the block, then come at the address from the back side.

They had only gone a few yards down the sidewalk when Evie gasped, her heart wrenching. The 108th Precinct of the New York City Police Department was right beside them, a three-story multi-colored brick building with patrol cars out front. A lone police officer leaned against the top railing of the entryway stairs. He stood before the large front doors, which were flanked by huge, ornately adorned vintage wrought iron lamps. The precinct called to Evie like a siren song, exerting almost a physical pull on her.

She caught Rune's eye as they walked. "They're right here, Rune. I don't know...should we—"

"No," he said firmly, grasping her hand and leading her on. "Don't look back, don't draw attention."

"But what if we're wrong? *They're right here.*" She pictured herself running to the officer on the stairs, explaining everything—

"And what if Kieran, or whoever it is, sees them coming? Or what if the police won't let us meet up with them and Gabby suffers because of it? It's too risky."

They continued on, until the precinct and patrol cars were well behind them. Evie heaved a sigh, fighting the fear that they had just allowed their best hope to pass them by. "I know you're right. I just don't like it." She inhaled a heavy breath, the catch in her lungs betraying how hard she was working to keep it together. "This feels so out of control," she said. "Like I'm being tossed around by fate without any say whatsoever. I can't fix it or stop it or..."

Rune nodded. "I get that. But you can do this." Nodding, Evie brushed a tear from her cheek and tightened her grip on Rune's hand. Then, unbidden, he began praying quietly—for Gabby's and Eleanor's safety, for wisdom, for courage, for protection.

His words washed over Evie, settling her anxious heart and grounding her once again. Profound gratitude welled inside her. This man, a mere stranger hours ago, was, at this moment, one of the most cherished people in her life. Turning right one last time, they rounded the sidewalk onto Forty-Ninth Street, headed toward their final destination at the end of the block.

SAUL, Kimball, and Kieran approached the warehouse on Vernon Boulevard from the north, getting a decent look at the structure's front before turning right onto the side street beside it. The windows of all three stories of the old building were boarded up. Its painted brown brick was splattered with a wide array of graffiti, including a bizarre alien with razor sharp teeth, a frightening clown, illegible bubbled letters outlined in white, and lanky red numbers which were likely part of a code that meant nothing to the uninformed passerby. Trash had settled along the building's base—bottles, wrappers, and dirty pages of newspapers and flyers. Some had collected at the threshold of the front double doors, which were chained and padlocked together.

The sedan continued down the side of the building, then turned into the alley that ran behind it. Three dumpsters, presumably used by the other shops on the block, were spaced along its length, overflowing to the point that it seemed they had probably been missed during the previous collection or two. Near the first of the dumpsters was a plain metal door that served as the rear entrance to the warehouse.

Kimball parked just a few yards from the door, several feet to the left of the dumpster. The putrid smell from the receptacle hit hard as they got out of the car, a stomach-churning punch powered by the decay of whatever refuse was packed inside.

"It's after six," Kimball noted as Saul stepped to the door, which was secured by a padlock clipped through a latch bolted to the frame.

"We're fine," Saul said, and spun the tumblers on the padlock into the correct number sequence and yanked down, popping it open. He handed the lock to Kimball, flipped the latch, then dug a keyring holding a dozen or so keys out of his pocket. He flicked through them and selected a silver one, then inserted it into the keyhole and twisted the knob.

"Awfully convenient that you have the keys on you," Kieran remarked.

"I've always got the key. I'm part owner of the place, remember? And I like to handle business here sometimes," he said, stepping inside. "It's good to have a place like this when you need it."

Kimball stood by the door, one arm braced against the upper edge of it, waiting for Kieran to follow Saul. Kieran swept his hand in front of him.

"After you," he said, motioning Kimball through.

"Uh-uh," Kimball refused, shaking his head. "You first."

Kieran rolled his eyes. "Suit yourself," he said, and went in behind Saul. Kimball followed, closing the door after him.

"Wait, hold on," Saul called out to Kimball. He held out the key that he had worked off his keyring. "Hide this behind the dumpster. Put it under a can or something on the ground."

Kimball nodded and walked back outside.

"What's the point of that?" Kieran asked.

Saul glared at him. "The point is that I don't want someone other than this girl wandering in here and complicating things. You'll tell her where the key is when you reach out."

Kimball returned, shutting and locking the door. "The key's under an orange soda can at the back left corner of the dumpster."

"Got that?" Saul asked, cutting his eyes at Kieran.

"Yeah, I'll tell her," Kieran droned in response.

As sunrise was drawing near, it was darker inside the building than it was outside. The only illumination came from a few windows high on the second level where it seemed single boards had been strategically removed to allow light from the sun and street lamps to filter in. The room they had entered was cavernous, taking up most of the first floor, and was littered with the detritus of the building's former functions. According to Saul's description on the ride over, that included serving as a jam cannery in the 1960s, then an automobile parts warehouse until its closure about ten years ago. The space was two stories high, with a grated catwalk around the entire perimeter at the second floor level, presumably intended to enable monitoring of the line workers when the building was a cannery.

Upright shelving, pieces of dismantled shelving, cardboard boxes, and remnants of crates were scattered throughout the dank room. Inches of dust and grime covered almost every surface. Water pooled here and there, where it hadn't drained into one of the many circular or trench drains installed in the concrete floor. The water indicated that there were probably holes in the roof, or perhaps broken windows somewhere. To their immediate left, in one of the more well-lit sections of the room beneath one of the exposed windows, was a makeshift mattress of old, dusty blankets spread over newspapers. A collection of crates was arranged like furniture around the blankets, as if someone had attempted living there at one point in the past, but was gone now.

"So, where's the best place to do this?" Kieran asked.

Saul's chest expanded as he inhaled, then sank as he blew out an exaggerated breath. "Kimball, go on up to the roof. Watch things from up there—make sure she's alone, there's no cops, etcetera, etcetera."

"Got it," Kimball replied, stepping further into the shadowy room. "Elevator? Stairs?"

"Stairs," Saul said, pointing to a door in the far right corner. "No power. No elevator."

Kimball headed for the stairwell, his footsteps echoing loudly in the huge space.

"You're sure nobody will stumble onto us in here?" Kieran asked, swiveling his head as he took stock of their surroundings, a bit of a frown shaping his mouth.

"It's still early, and the shops around here won't open for another couple hours. Whatever goes down here won't come to the attention of anyone outside. I say you do it right here," he said, gesturing to where they were standing. "It's pretty dim. It'll be hard for her to make out much, and there's plenty for me to hide behind and stay out of sight." He tipped his head in the direction of some of the crates. "She won't even know I'm here, but I can keep my eye on you. You get to keep the Jamison-con going, and I get to stay out of it. Everybody's happy."

Kieran nodded. "Yeah, this should work." He pulled out his cell. "Guess it's go time, then," he said, then typed out a text and sent it.

44

The address texted to Evie was for a Dunkin' Donuts. When Rune had first mapped it, she had thought that couldn't be right, it was just too strange. But when they neared it, that was exactly what they had found. The donut shop sat on the corner of the street that it shared with a bicycle store and a twenty-four-hour grocery with rows and rows of colorful bouquets on racks outside its door.

The surreal nature of it all struck Evie anew as she opened the door and was greeted by an electronic bell, glaring overhead lights, and the fragrant aroma of richly roasted coffee. This was the place of everyday things, of routine and day-starting comfort, not a place where life-threatening intrigue unfolded. Not the place where one plotted and scrambled and prayed to get one's daughter back.

The sugary smell of fried batter and sticky icing drifted across her path as she spotted Rune in a booth against the wall. He motioned her over and she went, sliding in beside him on the same hard seat, facing the door.

"I don't think they're here," he said. "I don't think anyone is watching us." She had agreed that they should come in separately, just in case anyone was watching the door, or was inside waiting for them. So, they had split up after turning the corner on Forty-Ninth Street.

"Are you sure?" she asked. "How do you know?"

He nodded toward the customers standing in line at the counter. One was dressed in office attire, probably grabbing something quick before hopping on the 7 train into Manhattan. There was a woman in yoga leggings and a teen in a hoodie and sweatpants. "They've just been strolling in and right out," Rune said, as the besuited man finished paying and left. "No one's sticking around, except him," Rune said, tipping his head toward an older, silver-haired man in a booth near the front windows. His cane was propped next to him as he pored over the *New York Times* and nursed a cup of something. "And he doesn't look the type."

"Okay," she said, and leaned back. The scent of food and coffee made her realize how bone-tired she was, just as it had at the Midnight Diner hours ago.

Had it really been only hours since then?

It felt like days. Time was no longer functioning properly. Logic and reality seemed suspended. She should be on the train, nearly home, heading in to make breakfast for her sweet, kind, energetic daughter. Her child. Her life. Her whole world. With excruciating clarity she felt just how much she wanted to hold Gabby, to pull her in close and snuggle on the couch, watching cartoons on TV and leaving their empty dishes streaked with pancake syrup on the coffee table. Both of them safe and sound.

She checked her phone. It was 6:10 a.m. They were early. "I don't get it," she said, fidgeting in her seat. "Why have us come here first? Why not just meet us?"

"I think it was so that they could control the timing better, or maybe get a look at us, make sure you weren't bringing anyone along. We'll still have to make sure we get wherever we're going next without them seeing me."

"How?"

"I don't know. We'll figure it out." He forced a thin smile, reached out, and covered her hand with his. "It'll be okay."

She searched his green eyes to see whether or not he actually believed that, because she didn't know what to believe. Claws of fear, unlike anything she had felt since Mark had died, tightened in a chokehold around her heart.

"I can't lose her, Rune. I can't lose like that again."

"I know," he echoed, his eyes mirroring her pain.

It moved her that he could feel for her, sympathize that acutely, when they barely knew each other. When they were hardly more than acquaintances. She laid her other hand on top of his, clutching on until her knuckles began turning white.

"Just focus on what we have to do," he insisted, and pulled away, scooting out of the seat. "I'm gonna go see if they have what we need. Sit tight, okay?"

She watched him approach one of the clerks behind the counter. While they spoke, she tried to do what he had asked and focus solely on the task before them. Summoning her resolve, she steeled herself, pushing aside imaginings of loss and tragedy. In their stead, uncompelled, came the ringing thought: *I can do all things through Christ who strengthens me.*

It startled her. This was the thought that had rotated through her brain for months after Mark's death. Round and round and round. Anchoring her when her world had fallen apart, when she was spiraling, when she couldn't breathe.

When officers from the NYPD had knocked on her door, and told her that her husband was dead.

I can do all things through Christ who strengthens me.

When family and friends eventually went home after the funeral, and it was only the two of them, Gabby and her, in that cruelly quiet apartment.

I can do all things through Christ who strengthens me.

When Gabby asked questions about when Daddy was coming home. When fears of raising a child alone and the loss of dreams kept her from sleeping.

I can do all things through Christ who strengthens—

Kieran's cell buzzed where Evie had laid it on the table. She snatched it up, pressing on the screen to reveal the latest text message.

Come now. Around the back. The door's in the alley behind the building.

"Is it him?" Rune asked, sliding into the booth beside Evie. She nodded and held the phone up for him to see. It buzzed again as another text came through. This one provided a new address. Rune quickly looked it up on Google Maps. It was also on Vernon Boulevard, just a few blocks directly north of where they currently sat.

Coming, Evie typed in return, then locked eyes with Rune. "Did they have it?"

Rune nodded. "Let's get you ready."

~

EVIE WATCHED from inside the coffee shop as Rune pushed the door open, the bell ringing again as he charged through, side-stepping a woman in a skirt and heels headed inside. The traffic light was with him, and he hustled north across the intersection, then turned left. Suddenly, he stopped mid-stride beside the building on the corner, and waited.

Why wasn't he moving? He was supposed to go on without her.

After two minutes, Evie followed him out as planned. But instead of walking straight up Vernon Boulevard, after crossing the intersection she went to him.

"What's wrong? You weren't supposed to wait for me. What if they see you?" she asked worriedly.

"Anyone looking for you to come up Vernon can't see us behind this building," he said. Then he grasped her arm, looking at her so intently, concern blazing in his features, that for a second she thought he might gather her up his arms. "I don't like this," he said. "This splitting up—me going the back way, leaving you alone."

Evie's shoulders dropped and she shook her head. "I don't know what else we can do. They can't see you coming. They just can't." She tried to sound brave, but the truth was she dreaded the separation, however short, because he was steadying and strong and between the two of them they had gotten this far.

"If they're watching the alley, they'll see me anyway. I don't know if it's worth it."

"If they're watching the alley, then at least they won't know you're there until the last minute."

He watched her for a few more seconds, pressing his lips together tightly, as if holding something back, then spoke. "Stay in sight of the traffic, so there are lots of witnesses. They won't do anything with people watching. When you get to the alley, I'll be there already, okay? Walk slowly. Give me time to get there," he said, backpedaling away from her.

"Thank you," she said, her voice heavy with emotion.

He nodded. "We're gonna get them back," he said confidently, then turned and jogged down the side street as she began walking up Vernon Boulevard alone.

45

Gabby ran down the sidewalk as fast as she could, the fabric of her pajama footies making a scruffy, scratchy sound as she went. It was so dark and scary. She could hear the beat-beat of her heart in her chest as she ran, looking back sometimes to see if anyone was chasing her. She wasn't supposed to be out alone on the street like this, Mommy said. It was dangerous with all the cars. A lot of cars had driven past her—she was afraid they might have been the bad men—but none of them had stopped. One man on a bicycle rode right by her on the sidewalk going the other way, then started calling to her. She just kept running. Mommy had always told her not to talk to strangers. Hopefully she could find a policeman before any more strangers tried to talk to her.

Gabby felt like she had been running forever and ever. She passed closed stores, a bus stop, and lots of buildings. But there was no police officer. Then, it started to get harder to breathe. She just couldn't fill her lungs up all the way.

Her tummy started to hurt because she knew what that meant. It was like when she played soccer in the spring, 'specially when they had just lawn-mowed the grass. It was her asthma getting her again. And she didn't have her inhaler or her neb-lyzer or Eleanor. Or Mommy.

Her chest was so tight. She was tired and couldn't breathe and was afraid for Eleanor and Mommy. She wanted to cry, but instead she bit her lip. She couldn't cry right now. It would make the asthma worse. She had to be brave and do what Mommy would want her to do.

The rule was that whenever the asthma happened she was supposed to sit, breathe slowly, and calm down. Or else the asthma could get really, really bad. One time when it got really, really bad, she had to go to the hospital. There had been a lot of tests and medicine and even a shot, and she never wanted to do that again. So, even though she wanted to keep running, she had to sit down.

But there wasn't anywhere *to* sit down. There wasn't a bench here or a bus stop or anything. She clenched her fists, turning in a circle—and saw it, a doorway just ahead that dipped into the building a little bit, making a sort of hiding place. It was dark there. Maybe no one would see her. Then she could sit and catch her breath and hide until she could run again.

Gabby darted to the doorway and scooted down against the wall till she was sitting on the ground, her legs drawn up to her chest. She put her head on her knees, closed her eyes, and tried as hard as she could to breathe.

46

Officer Steven Briggs looked over at his partner, Officer Demetrius Marvin, as Marvin yawned again and pulled their patrol car to a slow stop at the light. Marvin had just turned fifty-eight, and it seemed to Briggs that the last hours of each shift were more draining for him than they used to be. They were reaching the end of a long eleven-to-seven today, and his partner had been yawning for thirty minutes. But, even if he was tired, Briggs knew Marvin would never admit it, especially to him, since he was nearly twenty years younger.

"Gettin' sleepy old man?" Briggs asked, tossing his partner a sly smile from the passenger seat.

"Not even," Marvin replied, straightening up noticeably. "You're seeing things."

"Yeah, you—"

"Hey," Marvin said, interrupting him, his eyes on the rearview mirror. "Man on a bike, coming up to your window."

Briggs turned just as a man riding a bicycle on the sidewalk rolled up to his window and braked. The man's clothes were worn, dirty, and hung loosely on his gaunt frame. He leaned over and rapped on Briggs's window. Briggs lowered it, immediately catching the scent of alcohol.

"Yes, sir? What can we—"

"There's a little girl back there," he said, jerking a thumb behind him as he straddled the bike. One of the handlebar grips was missing, and the front tire looked flat. "She's running down the sidewalk, man, all alone in her PJ's, headed toward the river. Something ain't right, man. I mean, she's little. Real little."

Briggs rotated even more in his seat, looking over his shoulder in the direction the man was pointing. "Where?"

"Way back there, man. 'Bout three blocks back or somethin', and like, I don't know, two blocks that way," he said, thumbing to the right. "She's all alone. It ain't right." He shook his head, his face sour.

The light changed to green, and the vehicle in front of the patrol car drove through the intersection. Officer Marvin activated his hazards and put the car in park.

"You got a name?" Briggs asked.

The man sniffed, considered this request, then spoke. "BB."

"All right, BB, well, how old is this girl?" Marvin asked, leaning over the center console toward the window.

BB fidgeted on the bicycle. "I dunno. Four, five, maybe?"

"And she's just running, all by herself?" Briggs asked.

BB nodded enthusiastically. "That's what I'm saying, man. Weird, right?"

"And you let her go like that? You didn't stop her?" Briggs asked, his jaw tightening.

"Hey, man," BB said, raising his hands in surrender. "You think I'm stupid? I ain't gettin' nowhere near a little five-year-old girl that don't belong to me. Next thing you know I'm gettin' picked up for some kinda kidnappin' or somethin'. Ain't no way. I told you about her, didn't I? Didn't have to do that."

Officer Marvin raised a hand. "Yeah, okay, BB. You're right.

Thanks for letting us know. What about a last name? A number where we can reach you if we need to talk again?"

"Nope. No phone."

"Uh-huh," Briggs said, pursuing his lips. "What about an address?"

"No, man. I'm at Grace Mission some nights when they got enough room. But I'm tellin' you, you better be gettin' after her if you want to find her 'cause she was runnin' pretty fast. She'll be gone." Then BB pushed off, pedaling down the street and picking up speed.

Marvin wagged his head. "Funny how witnesses always seem to take off right after we start asking about getting in touch," he said sagely, disengaging the hazards and pulling forward.

Briggs turned to look behind him, where BB said he had seen the girl. His stomach knotted at the thought of a five-year-old on those streets alone. "You think there's something to this?"

"I guess we'll find out," Marvin said, nodding at the radio. "Call it in."

47

Kimball stood against the low, waist-high wall encircling the roof of the warehouse. Given that the building was only three stories, the rooftop didn't offer much of a bird's eye view. But, if he positioned himself in the northeast corner and leaned out a bit, he could at least see down a block or two, which would allow him to watch the woman heading up from Dunkin', as well as see whether anyone else was tagging along with her. The sun was finally coming up, so that helped. A pair of binoculars would have been useful in the situation, but as the whole thing was a last minute, fly-by-the-seat-of-your-pants disaster, he didn't have any.

It was ridiculous and unforgivable. Kieran had created this mess because he had been greedy, gambling the boss's money away, cheating Saul out of what was his. Stealing from his own partner. What's more, Kieran was stupid if he thought he could simply hand over an unexpected windfall of two million and all would be forgiven. That Saul would let bygones be bygones, and he would forget all about exacting justice on the kid for robbing him of his take from the Meyer con—a con that Saul himself had set up.

Kieran should have known better. Anyone in this business knew that an example *always* had to be made when thieves stole from thieves. Kimball tapped the embers from his cigarette over the edge of the wall, watching as they floated down in space, burning out before reaching the next floor. If Kieran didn't know that already, he would soon. He had no problem with Saul's plan to let the kid run this job, get the money, and then bury Kieran. *Literally*. This time next week, Kieran would be lining the bottom of a trash heap at the dump, and his tale would further bolster Saul's reputation as someone not to be messed with.

A squeak sounded behind him, and Kimball turned to see Kieran pushing through the stairwell door, its hinges rusty and in much need of some grease.

"Not very stealthy," Kimball muttered, stepping on the last of his cigarette, putting it out on the tar-and-gravel roof, the rocks crunching beneath his shoe.

"Not trying to be," Kieran countered, walking over. "Saul sent me up to check on you. Make sure you could see what you need to." He nodded at the roof's edge. "Any sign of her yet?"

Kimball looked back down the street, focusing once more in the direction of the Dunkin' Donuts. "Nah. Did you give her the address?"

"Of course I did. You sure you didn't miss her?"

Kimball scowled. "I'm sure."

Kieran stepped next to Kimball, sliding into the narrow space behind him along the wall. "Well, then, it shouldn't be long," Kieran said.

As if Kieran had planned it, at that moment Kimball spotted a slight figure, clad in dark clothes, emerging from a sidewalk scaffolding tunnel constructed from metal pipes and green boards just two blocks away. In the weak light of the approaching sunrise it was impossible to make out the face from that far away. But the timing was right.

"I think that's her," Kieran said, pointing.

"Yeah, okay. If that is her, it looks like she's alone. You can go back down. I don't need you up here," Kimball told him, now laser-focused on the street and the approaching figure. "I'll call Saul when I see her duck into the alley. And let him know that the next time he wants an update, he should just text me. The less I have to see your—"

Pain ripped Kimball in two as a violent intake of breath cut his words short, followed by a guttural growl, the sound of a wounded animal, roaring from his lips. "You...you..." he stuttered, dropping to his knees as Kieran stepped away from him, out of reach of Kimball's limply swinging arms, clawing for a piece of him.

"You really should do a better job of watching your six," Kieran said callously, his face screwed up in disapproval as Kimball sputtered.

Pain was all Kimball knew as he sunk onto the gravel. He managed to swing a hand around and felt the knife Kieran had plunged into him protruding from the left side of his back, several inches below his shoulder. Kieran pushed Kimball the rest of the way over, till he was flat on the ground, then yanked the knife out. He wiped it on Kimball's shirt, depositing an angry red stain. Blood poured from the wound.

"I'm just gonna leave you up here, out of the way," Kieran said, as he disarmed Kimball. He removed the magazine from Kimball's pistol and slipped it in his pocket, then tossed the gun to the far side of the roof. "I already borrowed Matty's so I don't need yours." His eyes raked over Kimball. "If it's any consolation, it shouldn't be long. Seems like I might have hit a major artery."

Kimball rolled on one side, pulled his arm under him, and tried to push up. But after only an inch, it gave out. He dropped flat again, this time faceup, the gravel around him drenched in crimson as he stared into Kieran's unsympathetic eyes. Panic gripped him, his heart turning to jelly. "You...you said no blood trail," he whispered hoarsely. "Said...wouldn't be...smart."

"I did say that, didn't I?" Kieran replied, opening the door to the stairwell. He stepped through, calling out as it closed behind him, his hollow voice floating back to Kimball, as all sound began to fade from his ears. "Well, that's the thing about con artists. We lie."

48

Officer Briggs scanned the right side of the street, while Marvin drove their patrol car down the right-hand lane of Forty-Fifth Road, watching the left side. After talking to BB, they had started making their way through the area in a grid-like search, which would hopefully prevent them from missing the little girl if, in fact, there was a little girl to be found.

"Anything?" Briggs asked.

Marvin braked as the SUV in front of them came to a stop before starting up again. "Nah. Not unless you count that guy crawling home singing 'Piano Man' at the top of his lungs."

"Maybe she went off on a cross street," Briggs proposed as the car advanced.

"If she even exists. Maybe BB was full of it," Marvin countered.

Briggs shook his head. "It'd be a strange thing for him to make up. Why draw attention to himself for no reason? More likely he at least actually *thought* he saw a girl run past him. He could be on something, hallucinating...stranger things have happened."

"Okay, well, we can check the cross streets next and then, traffic's picking up on the roads, maybe someone will—"

"Marvin! There—look over in the doorway!" Briggs exclaimed, pointing to a brick building on their right. Several garage-sized roll-up doors were spaced along its length with a few standard entry doors beside them. Tucked into the alcove of one of those was a child, balled up on the ground.

Marvin cut on the vehicle's light bar as Briggs hopped out. His pulse jack-hammered as he sprinted to the alcove. It was a girl, curled up like a cat taking a nap. She could not have been more than four or five, just as BB had said. She wore peach-colored footie pajamas and had dark, mussed hair that spilled over her face and shoulders. The once-white soles of the footies were a grimy, tattered gray. Briggs's chest seized as he knelt down beside the girl, fearing the worst. He gingerly shook her and held his breath.

The girl's eyes fluttered open, wide and afraid. Briggs expelled a whoosh of relief, as her fear dissolved into a grin that stretched across her soft, sweet face. She threw her arms around his neck. "I knew it," she said, clinging tightly to him. "I knew I'd find you. Mommy said to find a policeman, and I told God I needed a policeman, and he sent you."

Briggs scooped the girl up and hustled to the patrol car.

"Is she all right?" Marvin asked, his face contorted severely as Briggs opened the rear passenger door.

"I think so," Briggs said, as he set the girl in the seat. He brushed back her hair, tangled with knots and flyaways. Her angelic smile was missing a single front tooth. "Are you okay, honey? Are you hurt?"

She shook her head. "No. I'm not hurt. My asthma's making it hard to breathe a little, but I'm not hurt."

Briggs glanced at Marvin, ready to tell him to call for the paramedics, but he was already on the radio, requesting an ambulance. Briggs turned back to Gabby. "What's your name, sweetheart?"

"Gabby. Gabby Diaz."

"Hi, Gabby Diaz. I'm Officer Briggs. And this," he pointed to Marvin, "is Officer Marvin. Can you tell me what happened? You said your mommy told you to find a policeman?"

She nodded. "Mommy said if anything bad ever happened, I should find a police officer for help because I can trust them."

"Your mommy sounds very smart. Do you know where she is?"

Gabby frowned. "No. But the bad men said that if I did anything wrong, they would hurt Mommy and Eleanor, and so I was good until I could run away fast."

Briggs shot a glance at Marvin. His partner's expression told him they were thinking the same thing. "You ran away from some bad men? Is that how you ended up in the doorway?"

"I was trying to stop my asthma. I don't have my inhaler or anything. And it worked," she said, her countenance brightening. "I'm breathing better."

Briggs patted her leg. "That's good, Gabby. Really good. You're smart just like your mommy."

Gabby smiled wider at this.

"Can you tell me about the bad men, Gabby?" Briggs asked.

He listened as she explained how one of the bad men had woken her up and taken her out of her apartment without Eleanor, and that he had put her in a car. "We kept going and going for so long."

Briggs asked Gabby for her address, and she proudly rattled it off. Marvin quickly conveyed this information over the radio with instructions to immediately look for Eleanor. Briggs continued questioning Gabby, making sure to keep his voice gentle despite the urgency of the situation.

"Gabby, did you hear the bad men talking? Do you know why they took you?"

Gabby wagged her head. "They made me listen to music," she said, covering her ears. "It was really, really loud." Her lip began to tremble. "Can you help my mommy and Eleanor? I don't want the bad men to get them."

Briggs's heart melted. He wrapped an arm around her. "I promise we will do everything we can to help them. Okay, Gabby?"

She nodded and sucked in a quivering breath.

"You said you ran really fast. Do you know where you started running from?"

"No," she answered, pouting.

"What about turns? Did you make lots of turns or just a few turns?"

"I didn't make any turns. I just rode down the l-vator and went out to the street and started running."

"You ran straight down this street?" Briggs asked.

"Yes, sir," she said.

"And the elevator, what kind of building was it in?"

"A big, big building with lots of cars inside."

Briggs's gaze flashed to Marvin. "You thinking what I'm thinking?"

"Parking garage at the end of the road."

"Radio for child services to meet us there," Briggs said, as he buckled Gabby in. "Hang tight, Gabby," he told her, squeezing her shoulder. "We're gonna take a little ride."

49

This is not what he had planned.

He lay on his side staring across the filthy floor of the dilapidated warehouse, unable to move. His eyes still worked, though his vision seemed to be growing dimmer by the second. He had tried to speak, but it was impossible. There was no strength to move his jaw. Only hissing noises escaped his lips.

He was buried beneath a mountain of refuse—cardboard and rotting pallets and the blankets probably used by some vagrant for warmth. His marginal line of sight through this covering was narrow and impeded by an obstacle course of discarded things. What was more, because he could not lift his head, could not even turn it, *this* was the sad view that would be his last. Ratty papers, empty boxes, and cigarette butts, left behind like the garbage it was. Just like he would be soon.

This was not how this was supposed to go. He was supposed to come out on top tonight. Ahead of the game. Four million dollars ahead. It would have been enough to make changes. Enough to breathe new life into his situation. But this would not happen now. Nothing else would happen now, and that reality gripped his insides. Panic, dread, and disappointment coursed through him, same as the blood that was leaving his veins.

Had things gone according to plan, he would have kept everything. He would not have had to share it with anyone, least of all with the man that now watched him from the concealed location behind the boxes on the left, where he waited for Evie Diaz to show up. Where he waited to take the coin from her and, probably, her life. If it had been up to him, if he were the one still standing, that's not the way it would go. If it were up to him, she would have walked away after handing the coin over—back to her daughter, back to her life. Now, he doubted she would get the chance.

A brown mouse scurried across his darkening peripheral vision, against the wall near his feet. He could see it, frantic and twitchy, scrabbling to its destination, as if desperate to get out of sight before something saw it, before something came for it. The rodent moved quickly, and then was gone, darting under a door through the slim space above the threshold.

He should have been more like the mouse. More paranoid, more aware. But he had thought he had everything under control. That the whole thing was in the bag. He had been too confident. And now it would cost him everything.

Just like it would cost Evie Diaz.

50

At 6:25 in the morning, Evie stood before the rear door to the warehouse holding the key she had found beneath the soda can at the corner of the dumpster, exactly where the text said it would be. She inserted it into the lock on the doorknob and turned it. A quiet click announced that it had worked. She pivoted toward Rune, who had been waiting for her in the alley when she arrived, still breathing roughly after running several blocks in only minutes. She tensed. He wouldn't like what she was going to say.

"What?" Rune asked, his face falling as he studied her, apparently recognizing something was off.

"I think you should stay out here." She said it softly, but firmly, leaving no room for debate. She didn't want to argue.

Rune shook his head. "No. No way. That's not a good idea."

"It is. He isn't expecting the both of us. He told me to get rid of you, right? If you come in now, it might spook him, or them, or whatever. I can't risk it. They've got Gabby and Eleanor. I just can't."

His features contracted sharply. "It's too dangerous."

"It has to be this way. You have to understand."

Rune brought both hands up, vigorously rubbing them against his slight beard before dropping them by his side. He glared at her, not angrily, but in desperation, his gaze pleading for another viable option to present itself. For a few fleeting seconds, a tense silence filled the space between them, until impatient honking from somewhere on the streets beyond cut through it. Rune exhaled bitterly. "It isn't right."

Evie squeezed his hand gently, quickly letting go. "It's the only way. I'll go in and you wait here. If you hear anything, you can come in—at that point I'll *need* you to come in, okay? But let me try this first."

"No."

"I already thought through this. I put the sim card back in my phone. I'll call you and keep the line open. Then you can hear what's going on."

A severe frown creased his lips.

She dialed him, then slipped the phone back in her pocket after he answered, the call still active.

He grabbed her arm. "One scream, one *anything,* and I'm coming in."

She nodded. "Thank you. Thank you for everything."

He eyed her wistfully. "I'll be right here."

After taking a deep breath to steady her nerves, Evie clasped the doorknob and turned it. The hinges whined as she pushed the door open and stepped through into the darkness. She shut the door behind her, the sound ushering in a forbidding sense of aloneness. There were no lights on, and by the derelict look of the place, she judged that it probably had not had power for a very long time. The weak light filtering in from outside was only enough to get a general feel of the space, but not much more, leaving the corners and edges full of shadows and who knew what else.

The enormous room seemed to absorb nearly the entire footprint of the building. The exception to this was positioned along the wall to her right where several doors led to what looked like private offices. Each contained a large window overlooking the main floor. She couldn't discern much in the farthest reaches, given the lack of illumination, other than the metal utility stairs at the end of the row of doors, tucked into the far right corner. The stairs went up one flight, turned at a landing, then continued to the second level which offered two choices: connection to the catwalk that looped the circumference of the room, or another flight of stairs continuing out of sight to the floors above.

"Hello?" Evie called out. The word was short, choked off by the fear and anguish scratching at her insides that insisted on having her daughter back *now*. Her legs threatened to tremble, and she fought them, as she fought the voice in her brain screaming at her, telling her that she was going to lose Gabby, just like she had lost Mark. Gathering her resolve, she tried again.

"Where are you? I'm here!" she yelled. "I followed your directions. I want my daughter!"

The cell phone Kieran had given her buzzed. It was a text from the number supposedly being used by Jamison.

Lock the door.

Her eyes flashed to the door, a ripple of tension cascading through her. If she locked it, Rune wouldn't be able to get inside if she needed him. She would truly be alone in this.

A second text came.

Lock it now. For her sake.

There was no other way. Evie stepped to the door and turned the lock on the knob. Her heart sank as it clicked, and she wondered what Rune must be thinking right now, standing on the other side, probably with his ear pushed hard against it. As she let go, the shuffle of quickening footsteps sounded directly behind her. She started to turn around, but before she could, something cool pressed against the back of her neck as a hand gripped her left upper arm.

"Don't move. Don't turn. Just stand still." The voice was rough with an unnatural, calculated air. The speaker was obviously striving to make it unrecognizable. Her pulse drummed in her head.

"Where is she?" Evie whispered. "Where's Gabby? And Eleanor?"

"You'll get them when this is over. Just be patient." The words were a grating rasp.

"I want to know where my daughter is."

"Not far. Hold the key out in your hand, close your eyes, and keep them closed."

Evie did as she was told, extending and unfurling her hand so that the key lay in the center of her palm. She felt it plucked from her, then, as he maintained his grip on her shoulder, he guided her several steps farther into the space and stopped. He tightened his hold, keeping her in place. She complied, her body tensing as she tried to master the myriad of thoughts racing through her brain.

Hot breath blew across the hairs of her neck. "Now, hold still."

Evie forced herself to remain statute-like, despite the tremors wanting to break like waves over her. She could not lose it. Panic was her enemy. Panic would render her completely ineffective, and she could not be ineffective if this was going to work. And it had to work. It was all they had.

His hand slipped around the left side of her waist, his fingers searching for the lip of the small, shallow jacket pocket, which really served as nothing more than decoration. They found it, then groped inside its thin, hemmed opening, stretching down into its mere two-inch depth until reaching the bottom seam. His fingers darted back and forth across the width of the pocket, calmly at first, then frantically.

"Where is it?" he snapped, the hand clasping her shoulder digging harder into Evie's skin as all traces of the confidence that had previously cloaked his words vanished.

"Where is what?" she asked.

He shoved her forward, still clenching her shoulder, then yanked her back to him by it. He dug into the left pocket again so violently that it tore, the sound of ripping threads meeting Evie's ears as he abandoned that one and tried the one opposite with his other hand. Once more, he came up with nothing.

"What happened to it?" he seethed.

"I found it," she said, keeping her voice as steady as she could.

He sucked in slowly. "What did you find?"

"The coin."

"And where is it?" he hissed.

"Where are Gabby and Eleanor?" she said, matching his steely tone.

"That's not how this works."

"You give them to me. Then you get the coin."

He increased the pressure of the gun barrel against her neck until it hurt, promising a bruise. "I get the coin, then you get Gabby."

"You are such a liar, Kieran Carr."

At the mention of his name, he instantly released her. She sprinted out of his reach, then turned to face him.

51

Officer Briggs remained turned in his seat, watching Gabby as Marvin drove up to the parking garage. His heart winced just looking at the girl. She was so small, huddled there in the back seat, hugging herself. A surge of heat flushed through him as he thought about the "bad men" who had taken her.

Gabby had done really well answering their questions. She had even been able to tell them her mother's workplace and her cell number, but calls to the cell had simply gone to voicemail. They would keep trying, but so far, Evie Diaz hadn't returned the calls. Briggs hadn't heard back yet about what the hotel had to say about Evie Diaz's whereabouts.

Gabby's eyes widened as they pulled into the parking structure.

"Do you recognize this place?" Briggs asked gently.

Gabby nodded. "This is where the bad men took me."

Marvin parked in a space by the elevator on the first floor, labeled with a "No Parking" sign and rows of diagonal white lines painted through it. He hopped out and began scanning the packed rows, while Officer Briggs moved to the rear door, opened it, and squatted down on Gabby's level.

"Hey, Gabby," Briggs said, releasing her seat belt with a pop. "Can you get up on your knees there and take a look?"

Gabby complied, turning to look out the rear window. Her dark, long hair fell around her like a curtain, making her seem even smaller.

"Does this look like the place you ran from?"

Her brow furrowed and, in sober concentration, she pursed her lips and swiveled her head back and forth. She turned to Officer Briggs and nodded, then raised her chubby forefinger and pointed at the pedestrian entrance. "That's the door. The one I ran out of." Her finger moved a little to the left. "And that's the l-vator I rode on."

"That's good, Gabby. Really good."

Gabby grinned, clearly pleased by his praise. "Mommy says I'm a good helper."

"You are. You really are." Briggs's gaze flicked to Officer Marvin, who had returned to the car. "Anything?" Briggs asked.

Marvin shook his head. "Nothing out of the ordinary on this level."

"Backup?" Briggs inquired.

"In five to ten?" Marvin replied, his tone questioning the accuracy of his own estimate. "Child services, too."

Briggs's stare flashed to Gabby. He smiled and she followed suit. "So, Gabby, do you know what floor you were on when you got on the elevator?"

The corners of Gabby's mouth drooped slightly. "No. I just got on and pressed 'one' like we do at home."

"Of course you did. That's what you're supposed to do." Briggs shifted from one knee to the other. "Do you think you could recognize the car you got out of if we find it?"

Gabbed nodded vigorously. "Yes, sir."

Briggs smiled, patting her leg reassuringly. “Okay, then. Let’s see if we can do that.”

52

Waves of nausea broke over Evie. She had not wanted to believe it, even though she knew it was probably true. But now she stared into Kieran Carr's face and couldn't deny it any longer. She had been wrong. So very, very wrong.

"You knew," Kieran said, his features bearing both surprise and regret. He stood with his legs spread in a V-stance, a gun in his right hand, hanging at his side.

Evie took several more steps backward, widening the distance between them until more than a dozen feet separated them. He raised the barrel of the gun slightly and twitched it, as if reminding her it was pointless to run, in case that was what she was thinking.

"I figured it out," she finally said.

"I wish you hadn't." A bitter smile curved his mouth.

"You wanted me to think it was Jamison behind everything."

"That was the plan."

"And then what? I tell everyone that Jamison is the one that hunted me down, shot a cop, kidnapped my daughter, and who knows what else?"

"Like I said, that was the plan."

"You are such a liar."

He inhaled deeply. "I don't know why you keep saying that."

"Because it's true." She straightened her shoulders, wanting to appear strong, despite the lightheadedness setting in.

"Yes. Maybe about some things. But not about this. You were supposed to give me the coin. Then I would tell you where Gabby is, and you would find Eleanor safe at your place, tied up in the closet. Everything would have been fine."

"More lies," she insisted severely.

He groaned and cocked his head. "Where's the coin, Evie? I'll search you if I have to."

She took another step backward. He wasn't touching her again. "You say you were framing Jamison for this. If that's true, then I was never going to leave here alive. Because *if* Jamison is the one who is supposed to have done all this, he couldn't possibly have let me live after meeting him. If he *had* done this, and he let me live, then he would know I would go to the authorities and tell them everything, and then his life would be ruined. He would never do that. If this *had* been Jamison, there's no way he would have been able to let me walk out of here and back to my daughter. He would have had to kill me. So, you would have had to kill me to make it look like it was Jamison. The only way your con works is if I'm dead."

He shifted his stance, leaning on his right leg, and tilted his head, appraising her. Faint beams of sunrise were filtering in through the few unboarded windows, sweeping the shades of night from the room. Rather than lessening the forsaken feel of the place, it heightened it, better revealing the extent of its dank, squalid state. Even more disturbing, the addition of this small measure of natural light cast Kieran's visage in a pale glow that highlighted something sinister behind his eyes. A shiver vibrated down Evie's spine.

"No," he said, dismissing her conclusion out of hand. "That

wasn't the only way." He took a step toward her. She matched it by taking another step back. "Just now I came up behind you so that you *wouldn't* see me. I would have stayed there—kept you from seeing me—and you could have left here never realizing it was me, and not some hired man of Jamison's. Yes, I would have *told* you I was going to kill you. I would have completely convinced you that I was his hired man planning to kill you on Jamison's orders. And then," he sighed sadly, "I would have let you escape. I wouldn't need to actually kill you as long as you *believed* I was going to. That makes the plan work without having to kill you. Then you getting away would have seemed fortuitous, not questionable. You would have found Eleanor and Gabby safe and sound where I left them, you would have blamed Jamison, and all would be right with the world as I walked away with millions."

He shook his head. "I've been doing this a long time. This con thing, Evie. And I'm really good at it. I liked you. I didn't want to involve you at all. But I always have to have a contingency plan in place, and using you to carry off the coin was my contingency plan, my plan Z. Yes, I prepared for it, made allowances for it—sorry about the flirting, by the way, but it was necessary to make this scheme work if I ended up needing it, which I did," he said, tossing her a thin smile, "and tonight when I had no other way to get out of the hotel with the coin, I executed it. But killing you? No. That was not part of the plan. Like I said, I like you."

She glared at him. "And now?"

He exhaled, remorse seeping from his lungs along with his breath. "Well, now I can't con you, and I can't use you to con everyone else." The sick feeling in her stomach ramped up. She knew where he was going with this. His expression became more rigid, and his shoulders dropped. "Give me the coin, Evie."

She steeled herself for what was coming. "No," she said.

"Give me the coin, and I'll make sure Gabby is returned safely. You're right, I can't let you go now, but I can make her safe. It's your only play. I'm sorry, truly. But it's your only play."

"No, it's not," she said. Reaching inside the waistline of her pants, she felt the masking tape Rune had gotten from the clerk at Dunkin' Donuts. Digging under it, she extracted the coin stuck to it and pitched it away—high and to the right—in an arc that was unmistakably destined to end dangerously close to one of the large circular drains in the concrete floor that carried water, and anything else that landed in it, to the pipes beneath the building.

Horror flashed across Kieran's face for half a second, his eyes wide in disbelief.

Then he dove.

53

Officer Briggs sat in the rear of the patrol car beside Gabby as they drove through the garage, floor after floor. She knelt on the seat, looking out the rear window while Briggs steadied her frame with his hand on her back. Their journey around levels one, two, and three had produced nothing, as Gabby was adamant that she didn't see the vehicle she had escaped from. Only two floors remained. The patrol car completed its slow roll around the pillar at the next corner, turned on the landing, then started up the long stretch through level four of the parking garage.

"Okay, Gabby, so, here we go again. Look at all the cars and see if any of them look like the right one," Briggs encouraged.

She nodded vigorously, her lips set firmly in determination. "I'll tell, I promise." Her head swiveled. "Where's the l-vator? It was right by the l-vator."

"It's coming up. Just watch all the cars as we go by," Briggs instructed.

He kept his tone light, though he was getting concerned about the time. It was 6:30 a.m., and the traffic in the garage was getting heavier. Already a small line of vehicles had formed behind the slow-moving patrol car. More traffic meant more people, which meant more risk. He was considering whether they should close the garage off, when Gabby shouted.

"There!" she exclaimed, as they neared the elevator on the northwest corner of the fourth floor. "That big, black truck. That's it!"

He followed her finger to a black Chevy Traverse, parked engine-out in the last spot in the row, right beside the elevator. "That's great, Gabby, that's great. Are you sure?" Briggs asked.

"Yes, sir. I'm sure. See, it's right by the l-vator."

On the driver's side of the Traverse was the concrete wall of the elevator shaft. On the passenger side, a beige Honda. Officer Marvin stopped directly in front of the Traverse, then looked over his shoulder through the partition separating him from the back seat.

"What d'ya think?" he asked Briggs, jerking his head toward the SUV. "Wait for backup?"

Briggs grunted. "Backup's late."

"Shouldn't be more than another minute or two."

"Yeah, I heard the radio," Briggs said, but knew that, despite what the dispatcher had told them a few minutes ago, it could take a lot longer for help to arrive. "But we're here *now,* and there's an actual vehicle to go with her story."

"I'm not telling stories. It's true," Gabby said, her lip pouting.

"No, honey. I don't mean that," Briggs replied, passing a hand over her tousled hair. "Gabby, was anyone else in the car with you? Was anyone around the car when you left?"

She shook her head. "Nobody was there. It was just me. Everybody was gone."

Briggs exhaled. "I'm checking it out." He gestured to the next level with a sharp nod. "Take the car on around, out of the way, and stay with her. But stay where you can keep an eye on things."

Marvin's eyes narrowed as he considered Briggs's proposition. From somewhere behind them, a horn honked. "You sure?"

"I'm sure," Briggs said.

After promising Gabby that he would be right back, Briggs slid out and watched as Officer Marvin drove up and around the ramp, stopping about ten yards in, allowing for a direct line of vision between them. As Marvin motioned the train of vehicles to drive past him, Briggs stood by the row of cars opposite the row that held the Traverse, waiting for the cars to clear. When the last one moved through, he slowly crossed the twenty feet to the Traverse, his hand hovering over his holstered weapon. "Anyone in there?" he called out, tapping the passenger side of the front bumper hard with his foot. There was no response.

The windshield wasn't tinted quite as dark as the other windows, and from his view through it, the cabin appeared to be empty, though there was no way to see the cargo space or the floorboards from his current vantage point. Still keeping one hand poised over his weapon, Briggs stepped back again, putting several feet between him and the SUV. He crouched down to peer beneath the vehicle, and sucked in a breath.

A body, folded and stuffed under the rear bumper like a ventriloquist dummy in a suitcase, lay unmoving in a dark red puddle.

54

The coin hit the floor, catching an edge and rolling like a car on two wheels toward the slotted, gaping maw of the drain. Kieran's dive was a running lunge, low and aimed to head the coin off before it disappeared into the depths of the plumbing. In mid-slide he swapped his gun into his other hand, leaving his right one free to stretch out, fingers wildly scrabbling for the five-cent piece.

He landed in front of the drain, using his body as a barrier between it and the coin. Just before it reached the first circle of the drain's grate, his fingers clenched around the coin, saving it from dropping into the belly of the building. His eyes squeezed shut in relief, shades of victory stealing across his features as the click of the weapon sounded.

Several yards away, Evie extended Layla's gun before her, pointing it squarely at Kieran's chest. Her right pants leg was askew at the bottom, bunched up from where she had pulled it from the makeshift holster she had fashioned from Rune's belt and strapped to her ankle.

Kieran's eyebrows rose. "Now, that's a surprise."

Evie fought to keep her voice from shaking. "Put the gun on the floor and slide it to me."

"You're not going to shoot me, Evie."

He was so confident. Even now. Even when she held him at gunpoint. It incensed her. "Do it," she ordered.

He did, and the weapon clattered as it skidded across the concrete, collided with her foot, and came to a stop. Reaching down, but never letting her barrel stray from Kieran, she picked it up and tucked it into the back of her waistband, the metal cool on her skin. She pulled her cell out, still live on the call to Rune. "You get that?...Yes, Kieran. I've got him...Just stay on the line." She slipped it back in her pocket.

"We both know you're not going to shoot me when I'm unarmed," Kieran said boldly. "I have the nickel now. So, I'm going to get up and walk out with it, and you're going to let me, because you're no murderer and whoever's on the other end of that call—your getaway driver, I'm guessing—isn't one either."

She jabbed the gun at him. "Where are Gabby and Eleanor?" Evie growled the words, focusing on Kieran through narrowed eyes. She squared off against him, willing him to get the message that she was prepared to do whatever it took to recover her daughter and her friend.

In one fluid movement, Kieran rose up and advanced a single step toward her. Evie squeezed the trigger. The deafening shot reverberated through the vast space as the bullet struck the floor to the left of Kieran's shoes. Bits of concrete shrapnel flew into Kieran's legs as he jumped back. Frantic pounding and muted yelling rang out from the door behind them.

The hefty confidence that had lined Kieran's features moments before was gone. He regarded her with wide eyes, as around him swirled an excess of dust released by the bullet and his mad dash, spotlighted by narrow golden beams of sunlight. "You shot at me," he said, a bit of shock bleeding through his words.

Evie ignored him, slightly tilting her head toward the pocket that held her phone. "I'm fine, Rune!" she yelled, hoping the receiver would pick her voice up. The pounding on the door ceased. Weak relief flooded her. Rune must have heard.

She steadied herself. "Where are Gabby and Eleanor?" she demanded once more of Kieran, holding the gun in front of her, pointing it at his chest again. A rushing sound filled her ears as she strove to keep her hands still.

Kieran cocked his head as if measuring her with his stare. A smile threatened to crown, but he visibly worked to suppress it, so that only his lip curled. "You missed me from twelve feet away. I'm not sure you could hit me if you wanted to." The undertone of swagger had returned to his voice.

"I don't miss. That was a warning shot. I want my daughter, Kieran." Evie could feel fire creeping up her neck and into her face. Did he realize how scared and desperate she was? How much did those eyes see? And how had she ever been drawn to them?

"The problem here, Evie, is that I know you won't shoot me."

"You're right, I don't want to," she said, her tone heavy with weariness and regret. "But you shouldn't underestimate what a mother will do for her child."

"Not murder. Not you."

"It's not murder if it's self-defense."

"I'm unarmed."

"I don't know that. I don't know anything," she said, and something like concern flickered across his face. "I don't know where Gabby is, if she's in immediate danger, if she has air to breathe..."

"She's not in immediate danger. But she will be if they don't eventually hear from me. If I don't report back to them within the hour that I've got the nickel, they'll take her away and you'll never see her again. Not to mention what will happen to Eleanor."

"You don't have the nickel."

His visage wrinkled in skeptical amusement as he lifted the coin he saved from the drain, pinched between his forefinger and thumb, as if reminding her of what had just happened. He shook his head, dismissing her comment, then all went dark in his expression as he studied the face of the coin.

Its inscription recorded that it was minted in 2009.

His gaze jerked to her, then back to the useless modern nickel clutched in his hand, before he spat, "What did you do? Where is it?"

A thrill whooshed through her at his enraged disbelief. "You're not getting it. Not until I get Gabby and Eleanor. Then I'll tell you where it is."

"You're lying. If I give them to you, I have nothing to bargain with. You'll turn me in."

Evie eyed him callously. "And if you don't give them to me, I can call the cops right now and turn you in."

His lip twisted. "And Gabby will be dead."

The blood in her veins turned to ice. He wasn't going to back down. Even in this moment, when she had him—when he was at her mercy—he would not relent. But he had to. He *had* to.

"Kieran, I'm giving you one last chance. I don't care about the coin. I don't care about the money. I don't even care about making sure you end up in jail for this, as much as I want that." Though she knew it gave him power, she could not keep the sound of hopeless longing out of her voice. "I just want my daughter and Eleanor. You tell me where they are, you tell your people to let them go, and I'll have Rune go get them. When he calls and tells me that they're with him and that they're okay, I'll give you the nickel and I'll let you walk out of here."

Kieran watched her silently, his chest moving rhythmically as he breathed, his stare like granite.

"Kieran, do you want the deal or not?"

He swiveled his head in slow, dramatic passes. "Once you have them, there'll be no reason for you to let me go."

"I'm not saying I won't call the police, but I won't stop you from leaving. I won't interfere. You'll have a chance. I'm betting that you want to avoid prison at all costs. I'm betting you'll take a chance on trusting me to keep my part of the bargain before you'll let yourself be taken out of here in handcuffs."

His eyes scanned her face. Her rigid stance. The stable weapon in her hand.

"It's your only play, Kieran. If you want to avoid prison."

He shifted his weight, a tight grimace pulling at his cheeks as he seemed to mull this over. Finally, his shoulders relaxed incrementally. "Fine. She—Gabby—is in a parking garage five blocks away at the end of Forty-Fifth Road. In a black Chevy Traverse. Fourth floor by the elevator."

"She's alone?" Evie gasped, stricken.

"For now. But my people are standing by to whisk her away again if I need them to."

Without removing her focus or the gun from Kieran, Evie yanked out her cell phone. "Did you get that? She's in a parking garage, fourth floor, by the elevator. Black Chevy Traverse. End of Forty-Fifth Road. Hurry, okay?" she begged desperately, pausing while he asked about her. "I'm fine, go, go! And he's got people working with him. Don't call the cops, Rune. I don't want to risk panicking his people if they're watching. Get to her first, and then call me." She slid the phone back in her pocket and wrapped a second hand around the gun's grip.

"What about Eleanor?" she asked.

"She's not there," Kieran muttered. "She's still at your place, tied up in the closet."

Evie's mouth dropped. "She's seventy-six years old."

"She's resting in an air-conditioned space. She'll be all right."

The depth of his apathy was beyond belief. It made her physically ill, and she swallowed to suppress the nausea rising within her. "How could I be such a bad judge of character? I...I liked you, Kieran. I can't believe I was so wrong."

Though his face was tense, a slight smirk bled through. He shrugged. "Don't beat yourself up. It's just part of my job. And I'm very good at my job," he told her, then heaved a sigh. "So, now what?"

She held the gun on him. "Now, we wait."

OFFICER BRIGGS STOOD by the Traverse with the two additional officers who had finally arrived as backup. Their patrol car was parked perpendicular to the Traverse, pulled up tightly against the front bumper, creating a shield of sorts. They huddled with Briggs on the driver's side of the SUV, beside the concrete wall of the elevator shaft. As they waited for further instructions to come over the radio, Briggs spared a glance for Marvin, sitting with Gabby in their vehicle, parked up the ramp leading to the next level. He hoped she was okay. Last he checked, she was watching cartoons on Marvin's cell.

Finding an actual corpse had changed the situation entirely, converting the call from one about a suspected kidnapping and child endangerment into an active murder case with perpetrators at large. The crime scene unit and detectives that would ultimately handle the case would arrive eventually, but for now, they were it.

The biggest problem at the moment was deciding how to proceed. Should they block off the area, or wait to see if anyone came back for Gabby? The more time that went by, the greater the chances that this would turn into a circus. Although the body was completely hidden from view, vehicles passing by still slowed at the spectacle as they maneuvered around the stopped patrol car. And they had already had to shoo away a few curious pedestrians trying to get a closer look at what was happening. Whatever they were going to do here, they needed to do fast before the integrity of the scene was compromised. Finally, Briggs's radio squawked as his commanding officer relayed orders as the others listened in.

"...Yes, sir. I understand," Briggs said. "Copy that." Briggs disconnected the communication and turned his focus to the other officers. "Did you get all that?

They both nodded, and Briggs swiveled to the officer on his left, a stocky female with shoulder-length hair secured in a low ponytail. "Since child services just showed up downstairs, head there and hand Gabby over to them, then position your cruiser down the street so you can block off the garage entrance if need be. I'll walk Gabby over to you, just give me a second."

As the female officer returned to her vehicle, Briggs tapped the other officer on the arm. "Right," he said. "You're with me."

The slim, umber-skinned officer had a face so youthful he could have been only days out of the academy. He kept pace with Briggs as he walked around the corner and up the incline to where Officer Marvin and Gabby waited. Marvin lowered his window as they approached.

"So," Briggs said, leaning on the car's roof, "let me give you the rundown of how this is gonna go."

55

Rune pounded the pavement, barreling through the increasing traffic and sea of pedestrians packing the early morning commute. A city bus turned left in front of him as he darted across the street, the groaning metal beast nearly clipping him. The driver laid hard on his horn, but Rune was gone, sprinting away in his desperate race to reach Gabby.

Though still a quarter to seven, the air was already humid and heavy. Beads of sweat trickled from his hairline as Rune sucked in thick breaths, his mind racing along with his feet.

Gabby. He had to get to her. She was all that mattered to Evie.

Evie. A rock dug into the pit of his stomach. He hadn't wanted to leave her. The thought of her there, alone with Kieran and whoever else was in that warehouse with her, was like a rope tethering him to the place he had just left. It ensnared him—pulling on him, demanding that he turn around and help her. That he make her safe. But he couldn't. Right now, the best way to help Evie was to find her daughter.

He hated that she had refused to let him call the police. He understood that she was too afraid of what might happen if Kieran's accomplices got wind of any police involvement, but at this point it felt too dangerous *not* to call. But she wouldn't have it. Not until Gabby was safe. *Of course, she wouldn't. She's a mother. It's what a mother would do.* Even if it meant putting herself at greater risk.

Determination welled up in him again, adding fuel to his fire. He would find Gabby. He would call Evie with the news, and she would call the police. It would be all right.

His chest heaved as he tore down the path to the garage at the end of Forty-Fifth Road, four blocks ahead. Commercial buildings lined either side of the street, lots of wholesalers and warehouses, with roll-up doors allowing easy loading access. On the opposite side of the street was a small park populated with cyclists and joggers getting their exercise in before the withering heat of the day. He passed it all without slowing, speeding toward the end of the road, where soon, very soon he hoped, the parking garage would come into view.

Rune's heart battered his rib cage, his sprint forcing it into overdrive. He reached the next intersection, and though the light was against him, he dashed across anyway, incurring another ear-splitting barrage of honks. He landed on the sidewalk, accidentally ramming his shoulder into a man too busy looking at his phone to mind his sidestep, but kept going without slowing down.

He wanted to save all three of them. Gabby, Evie, and Eleanor. He wanted to be worthy of the trust Evie had put in him. He would not let her down. Pushing himself harder, he sped on—and then he saw it, just a block and a half away. A vertical sign, white plastic with green letters that read "Public Parking," suspended over the garage's entrance. The sight of it was a steroid to his purpose, and he ran even faster, hope and trepidation gripping him ever more tightly.

OTHERWORLDLY. It was the word that came to her as she waited, holding Kieran at bay with a loaded weapon pointed in his face. As the word flashed in her mind, she immediately thought the description too fanciful, too science fiction, too...something for the situation. But what other word was there? Because this reality in which she found herself—what she was doing here, in this place—was not of her world. It was not of her Central Park Saturdays, cartoon movies and popcorn, and Mommy & Me playdates. Not of her exhausted, single mother, ride-the-train-from-Queens-into-the-city-to-make-ends-meet existence. It was a dream—a nightmare—and she shook with the fear that if she didn't get Gabby back, it was one from which she would never wake.

They stood silently, facing off, waiting for the phone call from Rune that would confirm he had Gabby with him, safe and sound. Minutes went by, nothing passing between them but tension and Kieran's murderous stare.

"You weren't drunk earlier, were you?" she finally asked, severing the silence. "That was part of this, right?"

Something in his expression shifted, vague interest emerging. "Yeah, I wasn't."

"How did you know Jamison would have the coin on him tonight?"

"I knew it would be there. It's common knowledge among the players that Forrester brings that nickel to every game. I was planning to take it off of him. It would have been a little harder, but I got lucky and he needed to turn it over to Jamison after all his losses. Made it a lot easier with Jamison moving around the way he does. But, it would have worked either way. I'm a pretty good pickpocket. First skill I ever learned."

"What if Jamison had put it in the safe?"

Kieran sniffed. "Well, that would have changed things." His

face hardened again as he eyed her meaningfully. "I'll share it with you, Evie. The take from the sale of the coin. It's worth four million dollars. I'll split it with you, eighty-twenty. That's—"

"No," she said, cutting him short. She had no desire to hear this. She had no interest in his blood money. And she didn't believe he meant it anyway. Even if she went along with it to save Gabby, she had no doubt he would turn on her, and then who knew what would happen to her daughter.

"All right, seventy-five, twenty-five. Come on, Evie, that's one million dollars. You could use a million dollars."

"I don't want your money."

He took a step toward her, and she jabbed the gun at him, taking two steps backward and nearly tripping on a pile of boxes and other trash stacked haphazardly behind her, before righting herself. "Don't. I mean it."

He held his hands up in surrender. "Sorry. But, look, just think about this for a minute. You may not want the money, but you *need* it, don't you? For your new place? To keep Eleanor nearby? Otherwise you'll have to move, and that means a new nanny—new everything—and bye-bye to all the memories with Mark. And little Gabby will lose Eleanor just like she lost Daddy."

His words shattered her. It pierced her heart to have these things—her struggles, her worries, the precious shards of her life—flung at her like darts. He should not have these weapons to use against her. But she had willingly handed them to him, sharing these bits of her life with him before, during and after the games. In conversations with him about his own family back in Oklahoma. The family he was supporting with his earnings from his art gallery. A father that had suffered a stroke. A mother selling off pieces of her farm, working tirelessly to keep the place afloat—wait, she thought, realization striking. He knew she was from Texas. That her parents owned a cattle ranch. She had thought it a coincidence they came from similar backgrounds. Now, she knew better.

"It was all a lie, wasn't it? Your family, the farm in Oklahoma."

A sheepish, guilty grin cleaved his face. "Yeah, well, I needed you to feel a connection to me."

A possibility occurred to her, shedding light on the situation as if a hundred-watt bulb had been flicked on in her brain. "Is your name even Kieran? Or Carr?"

"Now, Evie, I can't go telling you all my secrets, can I? Not if I'm going to have any chance of evading the police once you let me out of here like you promised."

She glared at him. "That's only if I get—"

Her voice seized in her throat as something latched onto her right ankle, gripping hard. Reflexively, she jerked her foot away and turned to look behind her. A hand, bloody and striped with grime, strained to reach her from beneath the mountain of debris she had stumbled on moments ago. She screamed as she panned up from the hand and realized it belonged to a man, almost completely obscured by the pile, but for his arm and blood-streaked face. His entire countenance was twisted in pain and panic, his eyes begging for some kind of salvation.

A mass with the force of a train collided with Evie from behind, sending the gun outstretched in her hand clattering off somewhere to the far right. She hit the ground mercilessly, her head whacking the concrete. Momentarily stunned, she could do nothing as Kieran retrieved his gun from her waistband. Then her mind fired up again, and she scrabbled at his shirt, pulling him down and kneeing him in the groin, causing him to drop the gun. He rolled off her, bellowing as she scrambled up, her eyes searching for the weapons.

Where are they?

Evie's heart threatened to burst out of her chest as she frantically scanned the room in the dim light. Moving slowly, Kieran pushed himself up on one knee, breathing raggedly. At the same time, their gazes found his gun, which had landed a few yards to his right. Then hope drained from Evie as she spotted Layla's gun lying several yards beyond Kieran's. He was closer to both. And to the front door.

Black pools of loathing swam in his eyes as he focused on the guns, then on Evie.

He doesn't have the coin. He can't kill me yet.

Evie broke toward the stairs in the back corner, dashing across the thirty-yard stretch and charging up the steps. She flew up the first flight, then rounded the landing headed for the next, the sound of Kieran's slow, measured footfalls on the concrete rising up from below.

56

Rune hurtled into the parking garage, careening through the wide vehicle entrance. He skidded to a stop in the lane as a car pulled in right behind him, eliciting another round of angry honking directed his way. He ignored it, scanning the area for the elevator, which he quickly spotted on the wall to his right, next to the stairwell.

Elevator or stairs?

Evie had said the Traverse was parked just past the elevator on the fourth floor. He ran to the wall and slammed a hand across the call button. The lingering odor of exhaust fumes assaulted his nostrils as he waited, his insides revving like an engine. The digital floor indicator mounted above the elevator ticked from three to two then one. A bell pinged and the door slid open, revealing a car full of people. They stepped past him one by one, until the elevator was finally empty. He dove inside, hit "4," then held the "Close Door" button down, forcing the door shut over the emphatic calls to hold it from a man racing to catch a ride.

THERE WAS NOWHERE ELSE to go.

The third floor of the warehouse was wide open, just like the first floor, except for an old desk and some shelving. It offered no refuge, not even a door she might barricade herself behind. Below her, Evie could hear Kieran's rhythmic progression up the metal stairs.

Step.

Step.

Step.

His gait, slow and steady, sent ominous reverberations throughout the space. He was clearly not in a rush. She thought she understood why. She was trapped without a gun. He was certain he would prevail.

Her only choice was to continue up.

There's always a door at the top of the stairs that leads to the roof, she reasoned hopefully as she climbed. Maybe she could block it somehow and hold him off.

If the stairs actually do lead to the roof.

Evie charged across the last landing, her spirit soaring when she spotted a door at the top of the stairs. She raced up the last steps and threw herself against the push bar at the door's middle, flying through the opening out onto the gravel roof. Sunlight, bright and warm after the half-light of the dank warehouse's interior, crashed into her. The noise from the street, full of cars and people and buses and life at this hour, blared, including the fading bars of a techno-pop song rolling past with whatever car radio it was booming from. And to the east, a receding orange-and-pink glow highlighted the silhouette of the skyline, preparing to resolve into the blue hazy sky that marked these summer days.

She whipped around and slammed the door shut. There was no lock, no latch, no deadbolt to secure it. Evie pressed against it, frantically scanning the rooftop in search of something, anything, she could use as a wedge. But from this position her view of the roof was limited, and there was nothing within sight that would work. If she could move, she could check on the other side of the concrete housing that enclosed the stairwell, but then she would have to let go of the door.

His steps resounded, closer and closer. He was nearly there. She braced herself, the humid breeze blowing wisps of her loosened hair across her face as she dug her shoes into the gravel, bent at the knee, and leveraged all her weight against the door.

It wasn't enough.

He rammed into it and it swung outward, sending Evie sprawling away like a pinball struck by a paddle in a machine. She fell, skidding facedown across the fine rocks, their edges grinding against her palms, some sticking to her, some actually embedding in her skin before she came to rest on the other side of the stairwell housing. Pressing her bleeding hands onto the rooftop, she pushed up—and screamed.

Six feet over lay a dead man, his eyes staring at her, unseeing, as her shriek ripped the air.

RUNE THOUGHT he would jump out of his skin as he waited for the elevator to reach the fourth floor. When the doors finally opened, his whole body hummed as he shoved himself through the narrow opening and burst into the garage.

There it was—a black Chevy Traverse, parked in the first spot past the elevators. His heart skipped a beat. It was really there. His gaze raked over the SUV for any signs of life or threats, but he saw nothing.

He ran at it, and suddenly screams erupted around him. "Don't move! Don't move! Put your hands in the air!"

Rushed, heavy footsteps swept toward Rune, and his face was crammed sideways against the concrete wall as multiple police officers swarmed him. They pulled his wrists behind his back and handcuffed him before spinning him around.

"Who are you?" one of the officers demanded. "What's your connection to this vehicle?"

"I'm looking for a little girl—Gabby Diaz—she's inside—"

"You know Gabby Diaz? Is this *your* SUV?" the officer bellowed.

Hope surged through Rune. If they knew who Gabby was, did that mean they had already found her? "Do you have her? Is she safe?" he asked.

"Briggs," another of the officers said, holding up Rune's identification. "Name's Bruno Agnellini."

"Yeah, I'm a friend of her mother's. I came to get Gabby. Where is she?"

"She's safe," Briggs barked. "Now, answer me—is this your truck?"

"No, it's not mine! Someone took Gabby. They told us she was here, so I came for her—"

"Okay, take him down to my cruiser," Briggs interrupted, "and I'll come hear him out. We've got to clear the area in case anyone else comes back for—"

"No!" Rune shouted, dragging his feet as the officer grasping him starting pulling him away. "You have to listen to me right now! I wasn't part of this. Not like that. Her mother's in danger. You've got to help!"

Officer Briggs motioned with one hand for the officer to stop, then eyeballed Rune intently. "Explain."

~

GLASSY, blank eyes, devoid of any of the life that had once resided there, stared uncomprehendingly at Evie. She shot up to her feet, clutching her chest and backing away from the body. Her gaze vacillated between it and Kieran, horror paralyzing her.

"Kieran...two people?" She couldn't breathe. She couldn't process it.

Two people. He's killed at least two people.

And there could be more. Probably were. What if he was lying about the parking garage and Gabby? What if Eleanor wasn't all right like he had said? Her thoughts raced in a swirl of electric panic, her heart stampeding against her ribs.

Kieran stepped toward her. "Give it to me."

She trembled, her brain racing as she worked to speak and, at the same time, tried to manufacture a way out. If she could just stall him...

"I don't have it," she said, trying her hardest to sound confident.

He squinted at her in calculating fashion. "Now who's the liar?"

She swallowed, shifting her stance.

"Yeah," he said, bobbing his head knowingly. "You've got it. You wouldn't leave it just lying around somewhere." His stare traveled down her frame and back up again. Extending the gun before him, he walked to her until they were only inches apart. "Hold still."

She felt the hot breath of his words on her skin. She closed her eyes, closing out him, closing out all of it, as he ran a finger along the front of her waistband, then stopped at the slight bulge near her hip.

Evie's eyelids flicked open. A victorious grin split Kieran's face as he gently reached in and pulled the second piece of tape out. He withdrew it slowly, carefully, dangling the yellowish strip in the space between them. A nickel, stamped with the year "1913," was stuck to its center.

He plucked the nickel off and slipped it into his pocket. With an undeniable hint of swagger, he stepped back from her, the crunch of gravel underlining every footfall, till they were separated by several yards.

He raised the barrel of the gun.

We were so close. Wetness gathered at the edges of her eyes. Gabby and Eleanor flashed in her mind, and she prayed they were alive and safe. She thought of Rune, relieved that he wasn't there, that he wasn't the one at the wrong end of a gun. And Mark. *I'm sorry,* she whispered in her heart, an avalanche of regret smothering her. *I did my best.*

The breeze picked up, fluttering strands of hair about her face. She waited for the inevitable to come, readied herself—but seconds went by and Kieran didn't pull the trigger. Maybe there was hope. She decided to try one more time.

"Kieran, please. Just let me go. Just leave, take my phone, and go. I won't be able to call or do anything to stop you."

He wagged his head. "Can't Evie. Wish I could, but I can't. This is the only way I can still keep the ruse up and make it look like Jamison's responsible. Like he killed you and everyone else. It should hold up long enough to put some distance between me and this city."

"Ru—" she cut the word short, stopping before giving away Rune's name. "My friend knows. He knows you're here. Killing me won't change that now. Just let me go."

"Your friend—the driver, right? He can't prove it was me. Not for sure. He didn't see me. He'll talk, but by the time they get it all straightened out, I'll be long gone. Believe me, when I leave, everything will point to the idea that Jamison forced you to tell your driver friend I was here, and that Jamison's the real mastermind behind the whole thing. As for your friend, I can take care of him later if I need to, but, honestly, as evidence goes, I don't think he will be much of a problem. You, on the other hand..." He sighed regretfully. "I can't see my way around it."

She was drowning. She was drowning and her head was

slipping beneath the surface for the last time. "I have a daughter, Kieran."

"Yeah. That's too bad. You're smart, Evie, I'll give you that. You nearly had me. I mean, the gun-on-the-ankle thing? Totally inspired. It's lucky for me that Saul was too stubborn to die fast, or it would still be you holding the gun on me."

"Please."

"I'm sorry, truly." He lifted the gun, leveling it at her chest. "At least you'll see your husband again."

Suddenly the sound of heavy, quick footsteps radiated from the open stairwell behind him. Kieran's head jerked toward it as several police officers, one after the other, rushed through the doorway, weapons drawn, barking at Kieran to drop his weapon and get down.

Kieran dropped his gun as if it were hot metal. They were instantly upon him, kicking the gun away and forcing him to the ground, his face buried in gravel as they handcuffed his wrists. One of the officers moved to Evie.

"You all right?" he asked her, his gaze intense as she wobbled.

A wave of dizziness rocked her, and she teetered, then bent forward, resting her hands on her knees. The officer placed a hand on her back as she took ragged breaths, then looked up at him through her mussed sable hair.

"How...how did you know to come?" she asked.

His eyes were kind and full of concern. "Are you all right?" he repeated. "Are you hurt?"

She shook her head. "I'm not hurt. But my daughter..." She waved a hand at Kieran, then the corpse. "They've taken her! You've got to help me."

Another officer walked over to them, speaking into her radio as she approached. She focused on Evie. "Are you Evie Diaz?"

Evie nodded.

"I'm Sergeant Barnes. Ma'am, your daughter is safe."

Supreme lightness overtook Evie, weakening her legs and making her head spin. Gabby was safe.

My daughter is safe!

Giddiness bubbled up, and Evie let out a part-laugh, part-sob as she stumbled slightly and Sergeant Barnes caught her arm. "We need to get you checked out," she said.

"Wait, no, no!" Evie exclaimed, shaking her arm loose. "My friend, Rune Agnellini—he went after Gabby. And Eleanor—she's my nanny—we have to help them—"

Sergeant Barnes held up her hand. "Mr. Agnellini is fine. He's with your daughter now. He also mentioned your nanny, Eleanor Johnson, and—"

"Eleanor, yes, he said they left her in a closet in my apartment! She's over seventy—someone needs to get over there—"

"We already have. Ms. Johnson seems to be fine too, though she's being checked out at the hospital to be sure. Let's just get you downstairs—"

"No, I need to get to Gabby. Right now!"

Sergeant Barnes smiled patiently over the squawk of her radio. "That's what I meant, ma'am. Let's get you downstairs, and we'll take you to her."

She was going to see Gabby. Warmth filled Evie, strengthening her as she moved toward the stairwell, followed by Sergeant Barnes. She stepped past Kieran, who was still lying facedown on the ground, then abruptly halted, turning around to Barnes.

"I almost forgot," Evie said. "You need to check his pockets for a nickel..."

57

The police station was only a few blocks away, the very one Evie and Rune had passed after exiting the subway at Vernon Boulevard. With sirens and lights parting the traffic, it took less than two minutes to get there, but to Evie it felt like they would never arrive. In the rear of the patrol car, as they raced toward her daughter, all Evie could think of was Gabby. Gabby and her sweet face, her sweet hands, her sweet smell. She said nothing out loud, but inside, over and over, she thanked God for returning her child to her unharmed. For giving this most precious gift back to her again.

And then they were there, and Evie was running up the entrance steps, following the officer down the hall to a room where Gabby sat with a child services officer, holding a fluffy teddy bear and sucking on a bright red lollipop. Gabby grinned, pushed herself from her chair and ran to her. Evie scooped her up, tears flowing, burying her face in Gabby's long, messy hair and squeezing her more tightly than she could ever remember doing.

Evie heard something behind them and looked up. Rune

stood in the corner, moisture collecting at the edges of his eyes. Evie freed one hand from Gabby and motioned him over. When he hesitated, she wagged her hand even more vigorously, until finally he came to them. She grabbed his shoulder, pulling him into their embrace, hanging on and not letting go.

58

TWO WEEKS LATER

For the third time in two weeks, Evie found herself sitting in one of the chairs opposite the desk of the Queens County prosecutor, in his modest eighth-story office. Stacks of legal file folders and stapled documents were piled high on nearly every available surface, including much of the floor. The trash can overflowed with crumpled papers and at least five discarded Diet Coke cans, suggesting to Evie that he had a bit of an addiction. Hefty, leather-bound legal tomes filled the bookcase behind her, although the thick dust on the lip of the shelf betrayed that they were rarely moved and likely just there for show.

Evie glanced beside her and, not for the first time, gratitude swelled within. Violet Reed, her dear college friend and a prosecutor herself in California, sat in the second of the guest chairs. Violet had moved up her trip to the city for Evie's birthday by a few weeks, to help Evie navigate some of the legal fallout from this nightmare—visits to the police precinct, interviews with the hotel's lawyers, and meetings like this one.

Contrary to how Evie felt, Violet seemed more than comfortable in these surroundings. She had settled into the chair, her posture relaxed, as the prosecutor gave them the latest update. Violet even looked like she belonged in a lawyer's office, with her pressed camel-colored slacks, short-sleeved cream silk blouse and gold stud earrings, all of which offered a sharp contrast to her full, raven waves, several shades darker than Evie's hair.

Evie's gaze drifted out the window. It had poured the day before and all during the night, but now, through the stumpy windows along one wall, she could see the sun shining out from behind the remaining clouds. The landscape of the city was steamy, a haze rising up from the baking streets, thanks to an uncomfortable, and unwelcome, late-season heat wave. Beyond the glass, the urban jungle bleated away, the muted din pushing its way into the room. It played like a background score beneath the lengthy explanation currently being delivered by Assistant District Attorney Lucas Daniels. Evie forced herself to focus on what he was saying, as he straightened his owlish glasses, centering them on the bridge of his nose.

"...and as a result, in addition to the charges filed against Kieran Neal—a.k.a. Kieran Carr—of two counts of murder in the second degree, he has also been charged with one count of attempted murder given that Saul Kozlowski survived, aggravated assault for his actions regarding you at the warehouse, kidnapping and assault related to Eleanor Johnson and Gabby, plus the lesser charges we've mentioned before. And that's just the beginning. Charges have also been filed by the Manhattan District Attorney for first degree grand larceny for the theft of the coin and a charge arising out of his connection to the attempted murder of Officer Layla Driver, so they've got a hold on him as well. And that only covers the events surrounding your particular ordeal. We expect there will be more.

"Mr. Kozlowski is cooperating, giving us a lot of information in exchange for consideration in sentencing. Apparently, he and Mr. Neal recently worked together to swindle a second-rate record producer by the name of Dallas Meyer out of one and a half million dollars by convincing him to invest in some non-existent identity-theft computer program. But Neal lost the money in Jamison's poker game before he gave Kozlowski his share. Neal owed him and, according to Kozlowski, that's what started this whole thing. In another day or so we'll have charges filed against them both on that front too. Frankly, given the way our investigation into Mr. Neal's activities is going, I believe multiple jurisdictions will be charging him with a very long list of additional crimes well beyond the ones that involved you."

"Can you expand on that?" Violet asked. Evie cast her a sideways glance and saw that Violet's deep blue eyes were holding Daniels's gaze confidently.

"Unfortunately, Ms. Reed, not at the moment. We can't provide any details about our ongoing investigation into those matters, as I'm sure you can understand, being an attorney yourself."

Violet smiled charismatically at Daniels, a slight crook in her eyebrow. "How about a little professional courtesy? One prosecutor to another?"

Boy, she is good, Evie thought.

He snorted softly, visibly pressing back a smile. "Sorry. But I *can* tell you more regarding James Jamison's status—and yes, that is his real name. So far, we haven't uncovered any evidence that would make his actions concerning you—specifically his attempts to track you down that night—in any way actually a crime. He insists he was simply attempting to locate you before you made off with the coin, as he believed you were a party to the theft. He claims he had no intention of harming you."

Evie tensed, feeling a frown take over her face. "It sure didn't feel that way," she muttered, folding her arms across her chest, the sheer summer sweater she wore draping her like a cocoon.

"No, I'm sure not. Which brings me to the charges we *are* filing. It seems the reason that Mr. Jamison chased you and Mr. Neal down himself instead of contacting the police was because he did not want anyone poking around his game too much because he was running it illegally."

Evie sat up straighter. "What? No, he wasn't. The hotel vetted it." She knew they had. The Wexsor would never have allowed an illegal game.

"He was smart enough to keep the illegal aspects hidden from the hotel."

"Are you saying he took a rake? A percentage of the pot? Because I was in and out of the games, and I never saw anything like that happen. The hotel would never have allowed it to be held there if there was any hint of impropriety."

"No. He wasn't taking a rake. Not as such. It was more of a 'pay to play' situation. Most players—not all of them, though—would have to pay a fee to be invited to the table. He would collect it separately, beforehand, so that the other players who weren't aware of the arrangement wouldn't find out. There were a few big fish, ones with very deep pockets, or certain famous individuals, that Jamison allowed to play without charging them a fee. He needed them to draw in the paying players—the ones who were happy to shell out for the notoriety of being included in such an exclusive game and for the chance to win big."

"But I saw him being paid tips after the games. Those are legal, right?" A lump grew in Evie's throat as she remembered all the tips she had accepted over the last two years.

"Yes, the tips are fine as long as they actually were tips and not some kind of required payment in disguise. But that money you saw change hands would've only been a drop in the bucket, likely done to put a good face on the enterprise. The real profit was in the fees. He was pulling in over five million a year."

"Jamison's being charged, then?" Violet interjected.

Daniels nodded. "That happened yesterday. We've kept it quiet, but there's a press release going out today. You'll hear more about it, but there are organized crime ties as well. Jamison's game was being backed by one of the players who was also taking a sizable cut of the fees—someone we've been looking at for a while in connection with other potential racketeering activities."

Evie suspected she knew who he was referring to. "Is it Art DeVries?" she guessed. "I mean, I don't know anything, but something just always seemed off about him."

Daniels looked impressed, the corner of his mouth turning up. "I can't elaborate further at this point, but the name will be released soon. Though it doesn't sound like you'll be surprised."

"And what about Mr. Forrester?" Evie asked. "Was he involved?"

"That one I *can* answer. No. We're fairly certain he wasn't involved in either the scheme with Neal or as a pay-to-play player. He's been on the 'Top Fifty Moneymakers in Manhattan' list for the last decade. That qualified him to be one of the deep pockets I mentioned, a draw for the other players, so Jamison was just glad to have him there, no fee required. As far as we can tell, Forrester knew nothing about the payments to play."

"Will Evie have to testify?" Violet asked, leaning forward in her chair. "I know it's early in the process, but if you can put her mind at ease at all, that would be appreciated."

Testify. Every time the word came up, it sent cold waves of nausea through Evie.

Daniels rocked his head back and forth. "Well, like you said, it's early in the process. However, based on my initial communications with Neal's attorney, I think he'll plea bargain. If he does, he won't have a trial, and you won't need to testify against him. Then there's Kozlowski, but we're already working with him, so there won't be a trial in that case either. I'm not sure about Jamison, yet. If he doesn't agree to a deal, then even though you don't know anything about the payments, we might need you to testify regarding the generalities of the games he hosted, his routine, etcetera. We'll know more in a couple of weeks. I'll be in touch as soon as we get some clarity on that."

"Thank you," Violet said, and Daniels tipped his head toward her in acknowledgment.

Evie's stomach knotted. *This thing is going to drag on forever,* she thought. "So, what do I do in the meantime?" she asked him, truly hoping he could offer a suggestion that would help her move on, at least as much as was possible with the case ongoing.

"In the meantime," Daniels said, leaning forward on his elbows, planted on one of the mounds of paper on his desk, "you go home, hug that daughter of yours, and get on with your life."

59

Dinner in Evie's apartment that night was a jovial affair. Together, Evie and Gabby boiled water and tossed in spaghetti, later throwing hot, slippery noodles against the wall far more than necessary to determine whether they were done or not. They concocted the signature "Diaz Family Special Sauce," which came mostly from a jar, but was doctored with seasoned ground sirloin and spicy sweet sausage, mushrooms, and fresh garlic. Eleanor contributed a salad while Violet, who was not a cook at all, did an excellent job of cutting the double mocha chocolate cake she bought from Sugar Dreams Bakery a couple of blocks over.

Wilson was the first to arrive. Evie's heart soared as she flung her arms around her friend in a huge hug as they stood in the doorway. After the ordeal with Carr, she had taken two weeks off work to be with Gabby, and this was the first time she had seen the doorman since. He squeezed back, chortling. When she finally stepped away, feeling a grin stretching her face tight, she saw that Rune was standing behind Wilson in the hall. Evie locked eyes with him, a rush of affection surging through her as Gabby pushed past her and jumped in Wilson's arms.

"Gabby-girl!" Wilson bellowed, picking Gabby up and carrying her into the apartment, leaving Rune and Evie alone in the hallway. A radiant smile broke out on Rune's face, matching the one lighting up Evie's.

"Hey, you," he said, pulling two beautiful bouquets from behind his back, one with a dozen tiny pink sweetheart roses, the other a long-stemmed yellow, red, and pink rose mix. "The little ones are for Gabby," he explained.

"She'll love them. Pink's her favorite." Evie extended her hand to him, and he grasped it, sending a warm tingle across her skin as she led him inside.

~

THEY WERE HALFWAY THROUGH DINNER, Evie laughing as Rune tried to teach Gabby how to balance a spoon on the tip of her nose, when a knock sounded at the door. The adults grew quiet, while Gabby continued squealing as the spoon slid from her face and clattered onto the wood floor.

Wilson leveled a knowing look at Evie. "You better get that," he said, and winked. That confused her enough, until she realized he was winking at Eleanor, which confused her even more.

Evie squinted at him. "What's going on?"

Wilson shrugged. "How should I know? It's your door."

Feeling like she was missing something, Evie crossed from the dining area into the living room and peered through the peephole. Her breath caught in her throat as she recognized the caller.

"Mr. Forrester," she said as she opened the door, unable to keep the surprise out of her tone.

"Hello, Evie."

"Would you...like to come in?" she asked, stepping to the

side a bit to allow him to enter, trying to imagine what in the world would cause this man to turn up at her home. "We're just having dinner," she explained, gesturing toward the next room as a gale of laughter erupted from that direction. "I'm sorry, but was I supposed to know you were coming? I don't remember Mr. Daniels saying anything about it—"

"No, no. This is completely unannounced. Please forgive the intrusion, but I felt it couldn't wait any longer." He glanced at the couch to his left. "Would you mind if we sat for a moment?"

They did, and he fidgeted for a few seconds, tugging at his collar before starting in. "First off, I want to tell you how sorry I am for what happened to you—"

"No, Mr. Forrester, it's not—"

"Please, Evie, just let me get this out. And call me Henry, all right?"

His face was flushed, and the rigid way he was holding himself told her that this wasn't easy for him. She nodded. "Okay—Henry."

He swallowed and started again. "I truly am so sorry for what happened to you. It's my fault the coin was at the game in the first place. It was stupid of me to bring it. It was just convenient because it was small and...well, it doesn't matter. The thing is, I thought it was safe because I knew I wouldn't lose it in the game. It would be simple enough for me to buy it back from Jamison if I ever borrowed against it and lost—which I did once before. But I should have realized the problems that having it there could have created. I should have been smarter than that, and I wasn't, and I'm sorry."

"Okay, thank you."

"If I had known, if I had had any inkling of the lengths which Jamison would go to in order to retrieve the coin—if I had realized he would handle it how he did—I would have gone straight to the police the minute he confessed that it had been stolen."

"Why didn't you?" she asked, wondering whether two people might still be alive if he had.

"Jamison begged me not to. He told me his reputation as a host would be ruined if it got out that, not only did someone steal something as valuable as the coin during a game, but that he had to get the police involved to make it right. He said he would never be able to run a game again. I liked Jamison. I wanted to give him a chance to take care of it. Plus, I didn't exactly want it known that I've been gambling as much as I have. And honestly, I was embarrassed. That nickel is a family heirloom. My grandfather stumbled onto it in an estate sale seventy years ago. If I'd been responsible for losing it..." His words faltered, and he ran a worried hand across his forehead, as if realizing once more how close he had come to that.

She leaned in sympathetically. "But you didn't lose it."

"Thanks to you."

"I didn't do anything heroic when it came to that nickel. I would have handed it over in a heartbeat if it would have saved Gabby and Eleanor."

His features blanched. "And that's something else...your poor daughter. And Mrs. Johnson." He sighed. "I'd like to apologize to them also, and to Mr. Agnellini before I go, if I could."

"You can, but this really wasn't your fault. This was down to Kieran Carr and Jamison and the rest of them. We don't blame you."

"That makes one of us," he said, offering a sad smile. "Which brings me to the other reason why I'm here. I want to do something to make up for what's happened."

"You really don't need to do that," Evie said, and she meant it. She had no desire to benefit from any of it.

"I know. But I want to. It'll help me sleep better at night, and you wouldn't want to deprive me of that would you?"

She narrowed her eyes. "I suppose not."

"Good. I've been making inquiries, talking to some people

about how I might best repay you. And I hope you don't mind, but I went down to the hotel, asked around, and spoke with Wilson—"

"Ah," Evie said. Now Wilson's winking made sense. "That's what that was about," she muttered.

"Excuse me?"

"Nothing. Sorry," she said, shaking her head.

"Wilson had an idea. He mentioned your apartment situation and that Mrs. Johnson was probably going to have to move in with family elsewhere, leaving you without a caregiver for Gabby."

"Mmm-hmm." She was definitely going to have to have a talk with Wilson.

"Evie, you're aware that I'm a real estate developer, right?"

From what she understood, "real estate mogul" was a more fitting label, but she wasn't going to argue. "Sure."

"Well, I've got a building right next door in Sunnyside that I bought last year, and we've just finished converting it into condominiums. It's older, but completely updated now. I want you and Gabby and Mrs. Johnson to take one of the three-bedroom units. It's all ready to go. It's just waiting for you to say yes. I've already talked to Mrs. Johnson, and she says she would be thrilled to move in if you would have her—"

"Have her? I've been trying to get her to agree to that for the last few months, but she wouldn't let me pay—"

"Now neither of you have to pay, so she seems perfectly fine with the notion."

Evie had to work to keep her jaw from dropping. Was he actually saying what she *thought* he was saying? "Mr. Forrester, I couldn't. That's too much."

He steamrolled over her objections. "The elementary school is excellent. And it'll cut your commute to the city by half. I know it's not Flushing, but it's only a fifteen-minute train ride from here. You won't have to sever any ties. Wilson explained how upset you've been about this looming out there in your future, and now it doesn't have to be. Please let me do this for you."

Every nerve ending in Evie's body flashed warm. *Was this man really offering her everything she needed to make their world right again? But even if he was, she couldn't accept. Not this much.* "I can't...I can't just take it without paying."

Forrester scooted forward on the seat, then turned to Evie, his hands folded in his lap. Sighing, he ducked his head down an inch until it was level with hers, caught her eye, and held it meaningfully. "How about this? You take the condo. It's yours. And you pay monthly whatever your rent is on this place. Only it won't be rent, it'll be payments on a loan, and if you ever need to move, you can sell the place and keep the proceeds."

When Forrester was finished, he gave Evie a hopeful smile, and she was forcibly transported back to when she was a young girl. It was the same pleading expression her father used to deliver when he wanted to help her with something, but she stubbornly insisted on doing it herself. Even when she truly did need the assistance, but pride kept her from accepting it.

Is that what I'm doing now?

For the first time since Forrester had brought it up, she seriously considered his offer. If she paid for the place, then she wasn't getting it for free. They could stay. She could keep Mark's dream alive for his daughter. The fact was, she was running out of reasons to say no.

"That's insane," she said.

"That's my final offer. And no interest, either. I mean it. And I get to pick the purchase price, which I promise you will be *well* below market value."

Evie wanted to laugh, to scream—something—but instead, she simply said, "I don't know what to say."

He squeezed her hand. "Say you'll take it, and lift some of the burden off this guilty man's shoulders."

60

By the third week in September, fall had finally arrived in full force, the temperatures dropping pleasantly with a crisp breeze that tickled Evie's nose. At 4:45 in the morning, though an indigo sky still blanketed the city, the abundant glare from street lamps and store windows brightly lit the route up Fifth Avenue from the Wexsor to Grand Central Station.

Rune walked beside Evie, her hand in his, their fingers interlaced. She glanced down, reveling in the warmth of his touch, then cast a sidelong glance at him. He was beaming at her. She looked away, feeling her face flush with heat.

This trip was ridiculously out of the way for him. His place was only two quick subway rides from a station just south of the hotel—a station much closer than Grand Central. But Rune insisted on walking the extra twenty minutes uptown with her, then catching a different train back downtown.

"So," he said, squeezing her hand, "Layla texted me. She started back on desk duty tonight."

Evie's heart soared at the news. Layla's injury had weighed heavily on her. "Oh, Rune, that's great!"

He nodded. "Another month and they think she'll be able to get back out there."

"Did you tell her we want to get together for dinner?"

Rune chuckled. "She says we better be prepared to pay."

"Definitely."

They walked past the bakery on the corner, and Evie inhaled deeply. Though it didn't open for another hour or so, as it did every morning, the tantalizing scent of warm croissants and muffins somehow managed to spill onto the street despite the locked door. It was her second most favorite thing about the walk home.

"And speaking of dinner," he continued, bumping into her playfully, "you ready for tomorrow night?"

She straightened her shoulders, tossed him an exaggerated look of determination, and counted off on her fingers. "Brynn, Britta, Brianna, and Bristol."

"Nicely done," he said, tipping his head toward her.

"Remembering your sisters' names is the least of my worries. I want your mother to like me."

"Are you kidding? She's been praying for me to bring someone home every day for the last ten years. As long as you don't walk in and start insulting her cooking, she'll love you. She left me a very enthusiastic voicemail telling me how much she can't wait to meet you."

"Oh—voicemail!" Evie exclaimed, pulling down on his arm to stop him in his tracks. "I completely forgot—I got a message earlier tonight. I got the final interview at the Bankcroft!"

His face erupted in a wide grin as he swung his arms out, nearly slapping another pedestrian who side-stepped him at the last second to avoid a collision. "What! How could you forget to tell me?"

"Sorry, sorry," she said, laughing. "I checked it right before that catering disaster with the Kristopher reception, then got sidetracked dealing with that—"

He plunged in, sweeping her into a tight hug and burying his face in her neck. "I told you. I told you that you were a shoo-in for that job."

"I haven't gotten it yet," she protested.

"You will." He leaned back and studied her. "Manager of the Hotel Bankcroft," he said with a refined air. "You'll be great."

"If it happens, it will be great. And it's early daytime hours, too. I'd be home by four. Eleanor could pick Gabby up from school, and I'd get the whole evening with her."

He clasped her hand as they started walking again. "I'm proud of you. It's a big step."

Evie nodded, sucking in a breath. "It's time. I've held on too tightly for too long. But change comes anyway, whether you want it to or not, right? And I have a feeling that if I don't step out, I'm going to miss out on whatever God has for me next." A twinge of disappointment fluttered in her gut. "The only thing is, if I work days, I'll be working opposite you, with you still driving nights for the Wexsor."

"Nah, I'll just switch it up. School's only three days a week. I can drive after class is over, and on the days I don't have school, and take a Saturday here and there. I'm tired of sleeping during the day anyhow. I don't like the whole reverse schedule thing."

"I'm not sure it's that easy. Gerald won't want—"

"Gerald's been asking me to move to days for two months. It's easier for him to find drivers wanting to work nights than days for some reason."

She stopped, leveling her gaze at him. "If that's true, why haven't you switched already?"

His twinkling eyes narrowed, and he shook his head in mock exasperation. "Seriously?"

"Seriously," she said, though she thought she might know the answer.

"Well," he said, drawing the word out, "I had this hopeless crush on the night manager."

She laughed again, moved in close, and kissed him, threading her fingers through the ginger hair at the base of his neck. Hope and the promise of something new, as fresh as the promise of autumn, washed over her, and for the first time in so very, very long, she felt change coming and wasn't afraid.

AFTERWORD

If you're wondering, the 1913 Liberty Head Nickel is a real thing. According to the Smithsonian Institution, five such nickels exist and there is quite a bit of mystery surrounding how they came to be. The belief is that they were minted sometime in early 1913 and eventually made their way into outside hands.[1] Each of the coins has an interesting history and all are presently accounted for.[2] In 2018 one of the nickels sold for $4.5 million.[3]

For the purposes of my story I invented a sixth coin, which Henry Forrester's grandfather purchased for a mere fifteen dollars in 1948. Bored on a Saturday, he happened upon an estate auction in his Brooklyn neighborhood and fell in love with an old cedar chest he wanted to buy for his wife. The chest was auctioned to Forrester along with its contents, mostly old clothing. In the bottom of the chest Forrester found a worn apron, in the pocket of which was an envelope containing the nickel and a 1922 letter from a husband instructing his wife to hold on to this "special" piece from his coin collection while he went out west looking for work. Not thinking much of the simple nickel, Forrester stuck the coin in a drawer, where it sat for over a decade before his son stumbled onto it. The son (Henry's father), already interested in stamp collecting and the like, soon discovered the truth about its rarity and potential value.

The coin went into a safe where it remained for decades, except when the Forresters produced it on several occasions to secure multiple loans for the family's fledgling real estate business. Eventually that business grew into an empire, due in large part to the early loans obtained by leveraging the nickel. Upon his death, Henry Forrester's grandfather willed the coin to his son. Upon his death, Henry Forrester's father willed the coin to Henry. And Henry took it to a poker game...

(1)https://www.si.edu/search/images?edan_q=1913%2Bliberty%2Bhead

(2)https://auctions.stacksbowers.com/lots/view/3-BINKT/1913-liberty-head-nickel-proof-66-pcgs-cac

(3)https://www.newsweek.com/eliasberg-1913-liberty-head-someone-has-just-paid-45-million-nickel-1076417

TO THE READERS

I hope you enjoyed A Criminal Game. If you did, please leave a review on Amazon, Goodreads, Bookbub, and whatever other social media platforms you enjoy. You can also like and share my pages on Facebook and Twitter at: @dlwoodonline. Reviews and word of mouth are what keep a book alive, and I would be extremely grateful for yours.

Would you like a free, award-winning short story? Please visit my website at www.dlwoodonline.com to subscribe to my newsletter, which will keep you updated once a month on my work, new releases, promotions and other free goodies. You'll also be alerted to opportunities to become a part of my Advance Review Team for future novels. The short story is my free gift to you for subscribing.

Finally, check out my other CleanCaptivingFiction™, including *The Unintended Series*. This award-winning, thrilling suspense series, laced with romance and faith, has over 2 million pages read on Kindle Unlimited. The stories follow Chloe McConnaughey, an unsuspecting travel photojournalist, thrust into harrowing and mysterious circumstances ripe with murder, mayhem, and more. And by more, I mean a handsome man or two that seem too good to be true—and just might be. Here's an excerpt, just to get you started.

CHAPTER ONE

"He's done it again," groaned Chloe McConnaughey, her cell held to her ear by her shoulder as she pulled one final pair of shorts out of her dresser. "Tate knew that I had to leave by 3:30 at the latest. I sent him a text. I know he got it," she said, crossing her bedroom to the duffel bag sitting on her four-poster bed and tossing in the shorts.

Her best friend's voice rang sympathetically out of the phone. "There's another flight out tomorrow," offered Izzie Morales hesitantly.

Chloe zipped up the bag. "I know," she said sadly. "But, that isn't the point. As usual, it's all about Tate. It doesn't matter to him that I'm supposed to be landing on St. Gideon in six hours. What does an assignment in the Caribbean matter when your estranged brother decides it's time to finally get together?"

"Estranged is a bit of a stretch, don't you think?" Izzie asked.

"It's been three months. No texts. No calls. Nothing," Chloe replied, turning to sit on the bed.

"You know Tate. He gets like this. He doesn't mean anything by it. He just got . . . distracted," Izzie offered.

"For three months?"

Izzie changed gears. "Well, it's only 3:00—maybe he'll show."

"And we'll have, what, like thirty minutes before I have to go?" Chloe grunted in frustration. "What's the point?"

"Come on," Izzie said, "The point is, maybe this gets repaired."

Chloe sighed. "I know. I know," she said resignedly. "That's why I'm waiting it out." She paused. "He said he had news he didn't want to share over the phone. Seriously, what kind of news can't you share over the phone?"

"Maybe it's so good that he just has to tell you in person," Izzie suggested hopefully.

"Or maybe it's—'I've been fired again, and I need a place to crash.'"

"Think positively," Izzie encouraged, and Chloe heard a faint tap-tapping in the receiver. She pictured her friend on the other side of Atlanta, drumming a perfectly manicured, red-tipped finger on a nearby surface, her long, pitch-colored hair hanging in straight, silky swaths on either side of her face.

"He'll probably pull up any minute, dying to see you," Izzie urged. "And if he's late, you can reschedule your flight for tomorrow. Perk of having your boss as your best friend. I'll authorize the magazine to pay for the ticket change. Unavoidable family emergency, right?"

Chloe sighed again, picked up the duffel bag and started down the hall of her two-bedroom rental. "I just wish it wasn't this hard." The distance between them hadn't been her choice and she hated it. "Ten to one he calls to say he's had a change of plans, too busy with work, can't make it."

"He won't," replied Izzie.

With a thud, Chloe dropped the bag onto the kitchen floor by the door to the garage, trading it for half a glass of merlot perched on the counter. She took a small sip. "Don't underestimate him. His over-achievement extends to every part of his life, including his ability to disappoint."

"Ouch." Izzie paused. "You know, Chlo, it's just the job."

"I have a job. And somehow I manage to answer my calls."

"But your schedule's a little more your own, right? Pressure-wise I think he's got a little bit more to worry about."

Chloe rolled her eyes. "Nice try. But he manages tech security at an investment firm, not the White House. It's the same thing every time. He's totally consumed."

"Well, speaking as your editor, being a *little* consumed by your job is not always a bad thing."

"Ha-ha."

"What's important is that he's trying to reconnect now."

Chloe brushed at a dust bunny clinging to her white tee shirt, flicking it to the floor. "What if he really has lost this job? It took him two years after the lawsuit to find this one."

"Look, maybe it's a promotion. Maybe he got a bonus, and he's finally setting you up. Hey, maybe he's already bought you that mansion in Ansley Park . . ."

"I don't *need* him to set me up—I'm not eight years old anymore. I'm fine now. I wish he'd just drop the 'big-brother-takes-care-of-wounded-little-sister' thing. He's the wounded one."

"You know, if you don't lighten up a bit, it may be another three months before he comes back to see you."

"One more day and he wouldn't have caught me at all."

Izzie groaned jealously. "It's not fair that you get to go and I have to stay. It's supposed to be thirty-nine and rainy in Atlanta for, like, the next month."

"So come along."

"If only. You know I can't. Zach's got his school play next weekend. And Dan would kill me if I left him with Anna for more than a couple days right now." A squeal sounded on Izzie's end. "Uggggh. I think Anna just bit Zach again. I've gotta go. Don't forget to call me tomorrow and let me know how it went with big brother."

"Bigger by just three minutes," she quickly pointed out. "And I'll try to text you between massages in the beach-side cabana."

Izzie groaned again, drowning out another squeal in the background. "You're sick."

"It's a gift," Chloe retorted impishly before hanging up.

Chloe stared down at the duffel and, next to it, the special backpack holding her photography equipment. She double-checked the *Terra Traveler* I.D. tags on both and found all her information still legible and secure. "Now what?" she muttered.

Her stomach rumbled, reminding her that, with all the packing and preparation for leaving the house for two weeks, she had forgotten to eat. Rummaging through the fridge, she found a two-day old container of Chinese take-out. Tate absolutely hated Chinese food. She loved it. Her mouth curved at the edges as she shut the refrigerator door. *And that's the least of our differences.*

Leaning against the counter, she cracked open the container and used her chopsticks to pluck julienne carrots out of her sweet and sour chicken. *Too bad Jonah's not here,* she thought, dropping the orange slivers distastefully into the sink. *Crazy dog eats anything. Would've scarfed them down in half a second.* But the golden retriever that was her only roommate was bunking at the kennel now. She missed him already. She felt bad about leaving him for two whole weeks. Usually her trips as a travel journalist for *Terra Traveler* were much shorter, but she'd tacked on some vacation time to this one in order to do some work on her personal book project. She wished she had someone she could leave him with, but Izzie was her only close friend, and she had her hands full with her kids.

Jonah would definitely be easier than those two, she thought with a smile. He definitely had been the easiest and most dependable roommate she'd ever had—and the only male that had never let her down. A loyal friend through a bad patch of three lousy boyfriends. The last of them consumed twelve months of her life before taking her "ring-shopping," only to announce the next day that he was leaving her for his ex. It had taken six months, dozens of amateur therapy sessions with Izzie and exceeding the limit on her VISA more than once to get over that one. After that she'd sworn off men for the foreseeable future, except for Jonah of course, which, actually, he seemed quite pleased about.

She shoveled in the last few bites of fried rice, then tossed the box into the trash. *Come to think of it,* she considered as she headed for the living room, *Tate'll be the first man to step inside this house in almost a year.* She wasn't sure whether that was empowering or pathetic.

"Not going there," she told herself, forcing her train of thought instead to the sunny beaches of St. Gideon. The all-expenses paid jaunts were the only real perks of her job as a staff journalist with *Terra Traveler,* an online travel magazine based out of Atlanta. They were also the only reason she'd stayed on for the last four years despite her abysmal pay. Photography, her real passion, had never even paid the grocery bill, much less the rent. Often times the trips offered some truly unique spots to shoot in. Odd little places like the "World's Largest Tree House," tucked away in the Smoky Mountains, or the home of the largest outdoor collection of ice sculptures in a tiny town in Iceland. And sometimes she caught a real gem, like this trip to the Caribbean. Sun, sand, and separation from everything stressful. For two whole weeks.

The thought of being stress-free reminded her that at this particular moment, she wasn't. Frustration flared as she thought of Tate's text just an hour before:

Flying in tonite. Ur place @ 2. Big news. See u then.

Typical Tate. No advance warning. No, *"I'm sorry I haven't returned a single call in three months"* or *"Surprise, I haven't fallen off the face of the earth. Wanna get together?"* Just a demand.

A familiar knot of resentment tightened in her chest as she took her wine into the living room, turned up Adele on the stereo and plopped onto a slipcovered couch facing the fire. Several dog-eared books were stacked near the armrest, and she pushed them aside to make room as she sank into the loosely stuffed cushions. She drew her favorite quilt around her, a mismatched pink and beige patchwork that melded perfectly with the hodgepodge of antique and shabby chic furnishings that filled the room.

What do you say to a brother who by all appearances has intentionally ignored you for months? It's one thing for two friends to become engrossed in their own lives and lose track of each other for a while. It's something else altogether when your twin brother doesn't return your calls. He hadn't been ill, although that had been her first thought. After the first few weeks she got a text from him saying, *sorry, so busy, talk to u ltr.* So she had called his office just to make sure he was still going in. He was. He didn't take her call that day either.

She tried to remember how many times she'd heard "big news" from Tate before, but quickly realized she'd lost count years ago. A pang of pity slipped in beside the frustration, wearing away at its edges.

She set her goblet down on the end table beside a framed picture of Tate. In many respects it might as well have been a mirror. They shared the same large amber eyes and tawny hair, though she let her loose curls grow to just below her narrow shoulders. Their oval faces and fair skin could've been photocopied they were so similar. But he was taller and stockier, significantly out-sizing her petite, five foot four frame. She ran a finger along the faint, half-inch scar just below her chin that also differentiated them. He'd given her that in a particularly fierce game of keep-away when they were six. Later, disappointed that she had an identifying mark he didn't, he had unsuccessfully tried duplicating the scar by giving himself a nasty paper cut. In her teenage years she'd detested the thin, raised line, but now she rubbed it fondly, feeling that in some small, strange way it linked her to him.

He had broken her heart more than a little, the way he'd shut her out since taking the position at Inverse Financial nearly a year ago. He'd always been the type to throw himself completely into what he was doing, but this time he'd taken his devotion to a new high, allowing it to alienate everyone and everything in his life.

It hadn't always been that way. At least not with her. They'd grown up close, always each other's best friend and champion. Each other's only champion, really. It was how they survived the day after their eighth birthday when their father, a small-time attorney, ran off to North Carolina with the office copy lady. That was when Tate had snuck into their mother's bedroom, found a half-used box of Kleenex and brought it to Chloe as she hid behind the winter clothes in her closet. *I'll always take care of you, Chlo. Don't cry. I'm big enough to take care of both of us.* He'd said it with so much conviction that she'd believed him.

Together they'd gotten through the day nine months after that when the divorce settlement forced them out of their two-story Colonial into an orange rancher in the projects. Together they weathered their mother's alcoholism that didn't make her mean, just tragic, and finally, just dead, forcing them into foster homes. And though they didn't find any love there, they did manage to stay together for the year and a half till they turned eighteen.

Then he went to Georgia Tech on a scholarship and she, still at a loss for what she wanted to do in life, took odd jobs in the city. The teeny one bedroom apartment they shared seemed like their very own castle. After a couple of years, he convinced her she was going nowhere without a degree, so she started at the University of Georgia. For the first time they were separated. But Athens was only a couple hours away and he visited when he could and still paid for everything financial aid didn't. She'd tried to convince him she could make it on her own, but he never listened, still determined to be the provider their father had never been.

When she graduated, she moved back to Atlanta with her journalism degree under her belt and started out as a copy editor for a local events magazine. Tate got his masters in computer engineering at the same time and snagged a highly competitive job as a software designer for an up-and-coming software development company. It didn't take long for them to recognize Tate's brilliance at anything with code, and the promotions seemed to come one after the other.

Things had been so good then. They were both happy, both making money, though she was only making a little and he, more and more as time went by. The photo in her hands had been taken back then, when the world was his for the taking. Before it all fell apart for him with that one twist of fate that had ruined everything—

Stop, she told herself, shaking off the unpleasant memory. The whole episode had nearly killed Tate, and she didn't like to dwell on it. It had left him practically suicidal until, finally, this Inverse job came along. When it did, she thought that everything would get better, that things would just go back to normal. But they didn't. Instead Tate had just slowly disappeared from her life, consumed by making his career work...

She brushed his frozen smile with her fingers. Affection and pity and a need for the only person who had ever made her feel like she was a part of something special swelled, finally beating out the aggravation she had been indulging. As she set the frame back on the table, her phone rang.

Speak of the devil, she thought, smiling as she reached for her cell.

"Hello?"

A deep, tentative voice that did not belong to her brother answered.

*****

It never ceased to amaze him how death could be so close to a person without them sensing it at all. Four hours had passed and she hadn't noticed a thing. It was dark now, and rain that was turning to sleet ticked steadily on the car, draping him in a curtain of sound as he watched her vague grey shadow float back and forth against the glow of her drawn Roman blinds. He was invisible here, hunkered down across the street behind the tinted windows of his dark Chevy Impala, swathed in the added darkness of the thick oaks lining the neighbor's yard.

Invisible eyes watching. Waiting.

Watch. Wait. Simple enough instructions. But more were coming. Out of habit he felt the Glock cradled in his jacket and fleetingly wondered *why* he was watching her, before quickly realizing he didn't care. He wasn't paid to wonder.

He was just a hired gun. A temporary fix until the big guns arrived. But, even so . . .

He scanned the yard. The dog was gone. She was completely alone. *It would be, oh, so easy.*

But he was being paid to watch. Nothing more.

Her shadow danced incessantly from one end of the room to the other. Apparently the news had her pacing.

What would she do if she knew she was one phone call away from never making a shadow dance again?

ABOUT THE AUTHOR

D.L. Wood is an attorney and best-selling Christian Mystery & Suspense author on Amazon with over two million pages read on Kindle Unlimited. Her books have won multiple awards and offer CleanCaptivatingFiction™ that entertains and uplifts. She loves the art of storytelling, particularly any story involving suspense or the epic struggle of good versus evil. In her novels, Wood tries to give readers the same thing she wants: a "can't-put-it-down-stay-up-till-3am-story" that stays clean without sacrificing an iota of quality, believability or adrenaline.

If she isn't writing, you'll probably catch her curled up with a cup of Earl Grey and her Westies—Frodo and Dobby—bingeing on the latest BBC detective series to show up on Netflix. Speaking of which, if you have one to recommend, please email her immediately, because she's nearly exhausted the ones she knows about. She loves to hear from readers, and you can reach her at dlwood@dlwoodonline.com. D.L. lives in North Alabama with her husband and twin daughters.

BOOKS BY D.L. WOOD

The Unintended Series

Unintended Target

Unintended Witness

BOOK THREE: COMING 2020

The Criminal Collection

A Criminal Game

BOOK TWO: COMING SOON

CPSIA information can be obtained
at www.ICGtesting.com
Printed in the USA
LVHW090010200420
654088LV00001B/24

9 781696 075299